Praise for Stephanie Burgis's *A Most Improper Magick*,
the first instalment of The Unladylike Adventures
of Kat Stephenson:

'A blend of *What Katy Did?* and *Pride and Prejudice*, this book
manages to appeal to a modern reader. Burgis has written a
winning tale.' **ronk**

'The very first sentence of this charming and funny book sets
the tone... this is an excellent book and as it is the first of a
trilogy, there is the promise of more reading pleasure to come.'
thebookbag.co.uk

'Heartwarming, magical and full of adventure.
I loved this book!' **Chicklish**

'Stephanie Burgis's debut novel is a more substantial foray into
the Regency world of Austen and Heyer than that of Meg Cabot;
albeit with elements of J. K. Rowling thrown in for good
measure...' **The School Librarian**

'Regency romance and fantasy adventure all in one,
this is a satisfying read and a promising beginning
to a trilogy that is sure to be popular...'
School Library Journal

A Tangle of Magicks

A TEMPLAR BOOK

First published in the UK in 2011 by Templar Publishing,
an imprint of The Templar Company Limited,
The Granary, North Street, Dorking, Surrey, RH4 1DN, UK
www.templarco.co.uk

ISBN 978-1-84877-470-4

Printed and bound in Great Britain by
CPI Bookmarque, Croydon, Surrey

The ᵁᴺLadylike Adventures of Kat Stephenson

Book Two:

A Tangle of Magicks

Stephanie Burgis

templar

FOR MY GRANDMA, SANDRA BURGIS, WHO HAS ALWAYS
UNDERSTOOD THE IMPORTANCE OF CIRCULATING LIBRARIES
AND EXCITING NOVELS; AND FOR MY SON, WHO TEACHES
ME ABOUT WILD MAGIC EVERY DAY.

CHAPTER ONE

MY BROTHER CHARLES WAS A HOPELESS GAMESTER, A RIDICULOUS over-sleeper and the one sibling too lazy to take part in any family arguments, no matter how exasperating our sisters might have been (and usually were).

But he had one shining virtue as an older brother: he was infinitely persuadable.

"You do know, Kat," he whispered, "Stepmama will murder you for this if she finds out." He was yawning so hard that most people wouldn't have been able to decipher his words, but I had long experience. Ever since Charles had been sent home from Oxford in disgrace, he'd resorted to sleep as his safest escape from family obligations. Even as he yawned and complained, though, he was obediently following me down the creaking wooden stairs to the ground floor of our family's vicarage.

It was simply too much trouble for Charles to hold out against anyone who didn't give up the first time he said "no".

And I – as all three of my siblings could testify – was definitely stubborn enough for the task.

It was still dark outside and the candle in my hand was the only light in the stairwell. I held it up high for Charles's sake and carefully stepped over the spots on the stairs where the ancient wood was beginning to rot.

"Stepmama won't murder me," I whispered back, "because she won't find out. Anyway, she'll be too busy preparing for the wedding to bother with either of us when she wakes up."

"Huh." As usual, he didn't bother to pursue the argument... which was just as well, since nothing could have changed my mind.

In three hours, my oldest sister was going to be married. In four hours – five at the most, if the wedding breakfast took longer than expected – Elissa would be gone, and all our lives would change forever. Even when she came back for visits, from now on, she would always bring her husband with her – and as much as I liked her sweet-tempered fiancé, Mr Collingwood, it could never be the same. They would be sharing a bedroom, for one thing. That meant I wouldn't be free to slip into Elissa's room any time in the day or night to get comfort or advice or help against Stepmama... or even just to let Elissa fuss over me, the way she had ever since I had been born and our mother had died, leaving my two older sisters to raise me.

For all that I'd complained over the years about Elissa's prissiness and high-handedness, her lectures on propriety, and the fact that she never seemed to realise I was twelve years old and not a baby anymore... well, somehow, none of that seemed to matter now.

I'd woken up this morning at four o'clock and lain staring into the darkness of my attic bedroom for a full hour before I'd given up and come down to pull Charles out of bed. What we were about to do would have horrified Elissa to the depths of her ladylike soul – but if I didn't do it, I just might explode.

I stepped off the last stair and breathed a sigh of relief. We hadn't woken anyone else. "Come on," I whispered. "Mrs Watkins won't be in the kitchen yet. No one will hear us there."

Shrugging, Charles padded after me. He was still wearing his dressing gown, nightcap and slippers. His blonde hair, the same buttery shade as Elissa's and (before it greyed) Papa's, stuck out in wild tufts from beneath the cap – he'd been sleeping face down when I'd shaken him awake. I didn't understand how he'd even been able to breathe in that position. Then again, I hadn't understood much at all about Charles ever since Stepmama had first arrived in our lives five years ago and sent him off to Harrow to become a gentleman.

He might have come back from boarding school a different person, but at least one good thing had come of it: he had developed some very useful skills.

The kitchen fire was banked and the big room was chilly. I built up the fire, lit two more tallow candles against the darkness that pressed in from the narrow windows and got Charles to help me push the heavy wooden table to one side.

"Excellent." I stepped into the space we'd cleared and raised my fists in the way he'd taught me over a year ago, the first time he was sent home from Oxford for bad behaviour. Above me, bunches of herbs and meat dangled from the ceiling, waiting to be used in the grand wedding breakfast later this morning, along with the covered dishes already sitting on the kitchen table. I tried not to think about any of them, or what they meant.

Elissa... My throat wanted to choke up. I didn't let it. Instead, I kicked off my slippers and bounced on the pads of my feet on the cold floor. "Come on, then!"

"If I must." Charles rolled out his shoulders and started to raise his own fists into position. Then he dropped them. "You know, it's too early for fisticuffs. And if either of us has a bruise at the wedding service, Stepmama really will pitch a fit."

"Charles..." I fixed him with my most imperious glare. I'd learned it from Angeline, our other sister, who was an expert. "You gave me your word of honour."

"And I'm not backing out," he said hastily. "If you insist on fisticuffs, that's what we'll do. But what about wrestling this time instead?"

"Wrestling?" I lowered my fists, thinking.

Charles had taught me fisticuffs and fencing last year, and Frederick Carlyle – officially Papa's latest Classics student, but unofficially the only man in England who could match and measure up to Angeline – had taught me how to play billiards two weeks ago. Somehow, though, I'd never even considered adding wrestling to my list of useful and illicit skills.

"No bruises," Charles said, "and no arguments."

"Fine." I dropped my arms to my sides. "Show me."

"You'd better be the one to do it, not me." He was frowning. "If anything goes wrong... erm. Look here, I'll tell you what to do. Come at me... yes, like that... grab me, here and here" – he put my hands in place – "and then twist with your hips. No, wait! I mean..." He turned bright red. "Dash it. If Stepmama had heard me say that– "

"I know I have hips, Charles." I rolled my eyes. "Just because ladies aren't supposed to use the word—"

"Ladies aren't even supposed to understand the word,"

Charles muttered. "Not that you'd care about that, obviously."

"Obviously," I agreed. "So I twist, like this—"

"No, no, you aren't doing it right. Like this..." We changed positions, and he showed me, moving slowly. "If you do it with enough force, you can throw your opponent over your hip. See, first you shift them off balance, and then—"

"What on earth is going on here?"

Angeline spoke from the doorway. I slipped as I turned in Charles's arms. And Charles, caught in mid-demonstration, panicked.

He twisted with his hips – and I launched through the air.

"Oh, dash it!"

Sometimes I forgot how strong my hapless older brother really was. I flew across the kitchen, heading straight for the big wooden table. I gritted my teeth, preparing to hit it...

But instead, my body froze in mid-air as Angeline whispered something under her breath and the scent of fresh lilacs filled the room. I hung, unmoving, three feet from the ground and a full ten inches from the table.

Sometimes it was useful to have a practising witch in the family.

"Brilliant," Angeline said. "Simply brilliant, both of you. Just what Elissa would have wanted on her wedding day."

And sometimes it was only irritating.

"Oh, give over." I stuck out my tongue at her. "Elissa wasn't going to find out."

"Not even when Charles threw you straight onto the dough for all of Mrs Watkins's pastries?" She nodded at the covered dishes on the table.

Charles, of course, was already sidling towards the door, trying to avoid eye contact with either of us.

"It wouldn't have happened if you hadn't startled him," I said. "Anyway, Elissa would be just as shocked to see you use magic. Remember how you told her and Stepmama that you wouldn't cast any more spells, in case someone else found out? Witchcraft is much more improper than a bit of wrestling."

"Is that so?" Angeline crossed her arms and raised one eyebrow. "Fine. I won't cast any more spells, then. Not a single one." She looked pointedly at me as I hung, horizontal in mid-air. "After all, I wouldn't want to shock your delicate sensibilities."

"Look here, Angeline, really, you know I couldn't care less about any of that magical nonsense, but..." Looking desperate, Charles edged closer to the doorway that Angeline was blocking. "If a fellow could only be allowed to get some sleep, for once, in this madhouse..."

Angeline didn't spare him so much as a glance as she stepped aside. "Well, Kat?"

I sighed. "Fine. Don't put me down. I don't need your help anyway."

Angeline had been the one to find our real mother's old magic books, with all of Mama's spells inside, the magic that had made Mama such a scandal to Society. The talent for witchcraft might pass to every one of a witch's children, but Elissa was far too proper to ever even consider making use of it, Charles probably didn't even know he had it and Angeline wasn't about to share Mama's magic books with me. A witch without any spells to cast was as powerless as any proper lady; and with Angeline hogging both of Mama's books, I didn't know a single spell that could help me now.

But Mama hadn't only been a witch. She had also been something much rarer, something most people had never even heard of: a secret Guardian, with the natural power and responsibility to protect Society from malevolent magic-users. Only one of a Guardian's children ever inherited their parent's powers. Unfortunately for my sister, that child was me.

And a Guardian didn't need spells to work magic.

I closed my eyes and summoned up the familiar, tingling pressure. It rose through my chest and into my head, until it was all I could feel. Electricity crackled in my ears. With my eyes closed, I *looked* for Angeline's spell and found it.

"NO!" I hissed, using all my Guardian strength.

Angeline's spell snapped.

I fell three feet onto the ground, twisting as I fell, and landed hard on my back.

"Ouch! Ouch, ouch, ouch..." I sat up, massaging my shoulders. "There has to be a better way to do that."

"And I'm sure you'll learn one in time." Angeline sighed and crossed the kitchen to me. Her voice was as acerbic as ever, but she knelt down beside me and rubbed my back exactly where I needed it. "Haven't you started lessons with that Order of yours yet?"

"Not yet." I leaned back into her warmth, luxuriating in the feeling of her strong fingers working out the knots. "Mr Gregson says it should all be sorted out soon. I just need to be initiated first. For some reason it's taking longer than expected."

Well, the truth was, I knew exactly why it was taking so long. But I had never told Angeline the whole story.

Mama had been a Guardian, it was true. But when she had met and fallen in love with Papa, she'd been so desperate that she'd turned to witchcraft to help win him. If there was anyone who disapproved of witchcraft more than the propriety-obsessed leaders of Society, it was the Order of the Guardians, who blamed witches for Society's hatred of all magic. Mama had been expelled from the Order for her spell-casting, and it had nearly broken her heart.

As soon as I was a full member of the Order, I was determined to restore her reputation and knock aside their stupid prejudices... but that meant being initiated into the Order in the first place, which was turning out to be harder than I had expected. Mama had died young, but her enemies within the Order hadn't.

"Oh well." Angeline gave my back one last firm pat and stood up. "Come along, Kat. As long as you're awake, you can help me get the church ready."

"Ugh." All the dread-filled weight I'd been trying to ignore descended straight back onto my shoulders with her reminder. "Do we have to?" I looked around the room for distraction, anything to put off the inevitable. "Couldn't we make some toast first? Or—"

"There's no time for any of that," Angeline said, and brushed off her skirts. She was already wearing a morning dress of rose-coloured muslin, and she looked as cool and collected as if it were any ordinary day, not one of the most important days of our sister's life. "Why do you think I came down so early? You want Elissa's wedding to be perfect, don't you?"

"Of course I do." Sighing, I pushed myself up off the floor. "But if you mean we have to spend hours hanging up ribbons and lace and... Wait." I frowned as I caught sight of the kitchen windows. "It's still dark outside. You hate early mornings. Even Stepmama isn't out of bed yet. It can't be time for wedding preparations."

"And that's exactly why I'm up." Angeline filched a pair of apples from the bushel on one of the sideboards and tossed one to me. "You wouldn't want me casting any spells where other people might see them, would you? Since you're such a slave to propriety?"

"Well, if you put it that way..." I bit a chunk out of my apple and grinned at my older sister. "I suppose I'd better come along and keep an eye on you, after all. Just to keep everything proper."

CHAPTER TWO

I MUST HAVE STEPPED INSIDE OUR LITTLE STONE CHURCH AT LEAST ten thousand times before Elissa's wedding day. All four of us had been baptised there, and I'd spent every Sunday morning I could remember sitting in the front row of hard wooden benches between my older sisters, listening to Papa sermonise while his patron, Squire Briggs, snored gustily in the main pew.

At least, I'd tried to listen. Papa had an unfortunate tendency to lose his way in the middle of his sermons. All too often, he would start out well but end up spending half an hour debating with himself about different possible interpretations of Greek and Latin texts that nobody else had ever heard of. I supposed it might have been interesting to someone who actually understood either of those languages, but my sisters and I had only ever studied French – and only Angeline had ever shown any real talent for it. Luckily, England had been at war with France for so many years that, as far as I was concerned, speaking French was a fairly useless accomplishment.

But I had sat there anyway, trying to look attentive for Papa's sake, because almost no one else ever bothered. While the local farmers and villagers had whispered or slept behind me, I had memorised each and every swirl of colour in the tiny stained-glass window set in the back wall, and I had counted out every one of the ancient dark-grey flagstones laid into the floor under our feet. After all those years, I hadn't thought our church could ever look new to me again.

But I had been wrong.

White roses clustered high in the rafters of the arched roof and twined around the edges of the wooden pews, filling the room with scent. They weren't the same colour as the enchanted roses that Mama used to grow in our garden, but they were every bit as heavenly. Watching Angeline cast the final spell to hold them in place, I remembered all the times Elissa had taken me out to visit Mama's roses, before Stepmama had cut them down, and I had to fight a terrible, humiliating urge to weep.

"Well, Kat?" Angeline finally turned back to me, dusting her hands. "Are you ready for your part?"

"Of course," I said, and swallowed hard to push back the tears. Perfect. Finally, Angeline was going to teach me another spell to cast, after all my months of nagging her. Once I was officially inducted as a Guardian, I would have to give up casting spells entirely, so I was determined to make use of my witchcraft while I still could. "What shall I do?" I looked around the church, which was full of colour and beauty and wonder – just right for Elissa's wedding. "I can't see anything missing..."

"Oh, don't worry." Angeline smiled. "I've thought of the perfect task for you."

I knew that smile. It never signalled good things.

Ten minutes later, I was cursing my luck once again for having been born the youngest sister, as I finished dragging the heavy ladder from our shed behind the vicarage and up the green hill to the church. I shoved it against the outer wall with a grunt of effort and glared at Angeline, who was lounging on the wide, flat stone steps before the doors, finally eating her apple. The closest farmer's cockerels were crowing, and the sun was just beginning to rise over the long line of hills in the distance.

"You are going to regret that," I told her.

She widened her dark eyes at me in a look of perfect innocence. "But Kat, you were the one who reminded me how dangerous it would be for all of us if anyone found out about the magic. You wouldn't want our guests to suspect anything, would you? If Mrs Briggs noticed how high some of those roses were and didn't have any explanation for how we had hung them there – you know she already suspects us all because of Mama.

I narrowed my eyes at her, in an imitation of her own most threatening look. "Just wait," I said. "As soon as Elissa's wedding is over..."

But that moment was coming sooner than I wanted to admit. As soon as we stepped into the vicarage, I could smell food baking in the kitchen. Mrs Watkins was awake and hard at work.

She wasn't the only one. Stepmama's voice sounded in the sitting room, high and anxious. "And if – heaven forbid – you ever see that Mrs Briggs's plate is close to empty, then for all our sakes, and the sake of your pay, don't forget—"

"*The new maids,*" Angeline mouthed. She closed the front door silently behind her.

I peeked through the open doorway into the sitting room.

Stepmama had hired two girls from the village to act as temporary maids for the day, to help with the grand wedding breakfast she was laying out after the ceremony. Both girls looked absolutely petrified as she paced back and forth in front of them. I winced in sympathy. They were right to be afraid.

Ever since Elissa had become engaged to Mr Collingwood – a gentleman so wealthy he'd agreed without a blink to pay off every one of Charles's horrid gaming debts – Stepmama had been wound up as tightly as a new watch, just waiting for something to go wrong. Even the fact that Mr Collingwood was quite obviously besotted with Elissa didn't seem to be enough to soothe her jangled nerves. She seemed to be irrationally convinced that some mysterious catastrophe would descend upon us and change Mr Collingwood's mind – and our family's unprecedented good fortune – if she left even a single detail to chance. Her new wedding mania had made her even harder to live with than she ever had been before – and when it came to Stepmama, that was saying a good deal.

At least we had one thing to be thankful for. Despite the bragging Stepmama had always done about her grand connections in Society, almost none of her wealthy relatives had bothered to reply to the wedding invitations, and not a single one of them cared enough to travel to Yorkshire for the wedding. So at least we were saved the sight of Stepmama going into absolute hysteria trying to impress them as well. Impressing the village gentility – especially Squire Briggs and his horrid new wife – was driving her quite mad enough already.

Her voice rose now, shifting from panic to threat: "If I see a single drop of wine spilled on any of our guests...!"

Angeline and I looked at each other and winced. Then we both tried to speak at once.

I got my words out first. "You have to tell her about the roses. I did the ladder."

"Fine." Angeline sighed. "But you have to promise me, when Frederick and I are ma— I mean...!" She caught herself, blinking rapidly. "If Frederick Carlyle and I are ever married – and of course we aren't actually betrothed – it's not as if he's even proposed, so I certainly don't expect—"

"He will," I said, and rolled my eyes. Angeline worrying about Frederick Carlyle's intentions was every bit as daft as Stepmama thinking anything could stop Elissa's wedding now. Even two months of sharing a room with Charles hadn't been enough to drive the man away. Instead, he'd taught himself to fix leaks in the roof – probably the first time in his life he'd ever had to do any manual labour – so that he could move into our abandoned spare room and stay in easy reach of Angeline all day, every day, for teasing and flirting and hot, longing looks when they thought no one else was looking.

"He's mad about you, in case you hadn't noticed," I said. "He's only waiting until he turns twenty-one so the betrothal will be legal. He explained it all to me during our billiards lesson."

Colour swept across Angeline's cheeks. For once, my confident older sister looked flustered. Any mention of Frederick Carlyle tended to do that to her. It was one of the reasons I approved of him so much.

"Regardless," Angeline said, and fixed me with a look. "If it ever happens, you have to promise me you'll lock Stepmama safely in a cupboard and not let her out until the wedding ceremony is over. Understood?"

"I promise," I said, and escaped up to my bedroom.

✩ ✩

But I couldn't stay there forever. All too soon, Stepmama was berating me for not being dressed yet and I was scrambling into the horrible gown she'd chosen for me – all ruffles and puce muslin, the price I'd had to pay for missing that particular shopping expedition.

And then everything seemed to both speed up and slow down in an almost magical way.

First I was standing in the bedroom my older sisters shared – the bedroom they had shared, all my life until today – and Angeline was pinning the floor-length wedding veil to Elissa's bonnet. Both of them were chattering away somewhere far, far away in the distance, but I couldn't hear a word of it. I was too busy gazing at my beautiful oldest sister, her blue eyes shining with happiness and excitement, looking more like an angel than ever. Elissa's pale blonde hair curled in ringlets around her cheeks, and her white veil fell around her like a cloud. She looked as if she could float right through the air away from me, and I dug my fingernails into my palms and tried to memorise her face for always.

Then Stepmama was bustling in to gather us up, and we were hurrying outside, back up the green hill, while carriages and farmer's gigs rolled up the long road from the village and the cool September breeze blew Elissa's veil up around her, tangling with her legs. Elissa and Angeline were laughing as they beat it back, and Stepmama fussed. For a moment, it all felt safely like a dream.

But then Stepmama was gone, seated inside the church with everybody else, waiting for the ceremony to begin.

Only the three of us were left standing outside on the grass in front of the closed doors. Organ music struck up inside, and suddenly everything felt all too real.

"Elissa," I said. My voice came out as a thin, fragile whisper, caught by the breeze and thrown away.

But Elissa and Angeline both heard me, and they both put their arms out at the same time. Elissa looked as if she could either cry or laugh; Angeline's face was full of warm sympathy with, for once, no irony. We all held each other's hands for one perfect moment that felt like forever.

The doors swung open.

Angeline and Elissa's hands fell away.

Angeline gave me a firm nod. I took a deep breath and nodded back. Together, we started forward, carrying our bouquets.

The church was full of people – Papa's parishioners, Stepmama's friends and, of course, Squire Briggs in his pew, looking pleased and self-important, while his wife looked as pursed-up as a prune. The sight of her suspicious, disapproving face actually helped, for once. It steadied me, giving me the nerve to lift my chin and square my shoulders and pretend to be as cool and collected as Angeline as I walked down the aisle.

This was Elissa's wedding day, and no one was allowed to spoil it.

The whole church looked perfect. Angeline's white roses bloomed around us, buoying up my spirits with their scent. Papa stood at the altar beside Mr Collingwood, looking so tall and distinguished that no one would ever guess how impractical he was in real life. Mr Collingwood himself looked close to swooning with excitement as he stared past us at Elissa.

And standing next to Mr Collingwood...

Frederick Carlyle was Mr Collingwood's best man, but all his attention was focused on Angeline. He gave her a smile so tender and knowing, I actually had to look away. For the first time since we'd entered the church, Angeline lost her cool composure. She flushed darker than I'd ever seen her as she met his gaze. I could almost feel the air crackle between them.

It was utterly embarrassing.

"Careful," I whispered, out of the side of my mouth. "You don't want to trip on your gown in front of him."

"Shh!" Angeline hissed back. But she glanced quickly down at her feet. I grinned.

We each stepped to one side of the altar. Elissa passed Angeline her bouquet. Her eyes were modestly lowered. She was breathing quickly. Mr Collingwood looked positively goggle-eyed as he gazed at her. Papa cleared his throat.

"Dearly beloved..." he began in his rich, rolling voice.

The big wooden doors flew open, slamming against the stone walls of the church. I spun round, almost dropping my bouquet.

A short, round, crimson figure stood in the open doorway, flanked by servants and brandishing a parasol like a weapon.

"Where is he?" she bellowed. "Where is my son? And what has that trollop done to him?"

CHAPTER THREE

THE WHOLE CHURCH ERUPTED INTO WHISPERS. I BARELY FELT the bouquet crumple in my hands as I stared at the woman in the doorway. I had never seen her before in my life.

From her pelisse to her towering bonnet and the thick cluster of dyed ostrich feathers that rose above it, she was dressed in blindingly bright crimson. It would have been hard to take my eyes off her even if she hadn't been so obviously mad. That was the only possible explanation: she must be mad, to come barging in like this to a stranger's wedding. Poor Elissa would have to wait to finish the ceremony until someone had escorted her safely away. People would be talking about it for weeks.

But then I recognised two of the servants clustered behind her: our own temporary maids. They were wringing their hands and looking close to tears. For the first time, real dread began to trickle into my chest. The woman's round, stubborn-looking face was full of rage.

And if, by any horrible chance, she wasn't actually mad...

Then Frederick Carlyle spoke.

"Mama?" he said. He stepped away from his place by the altar. "What are you doing here?"

"Frederick?" Her jaw dropped so wide open she looked like a beached fish. "Oh, dear heaven, please say I am not too late!"

"Too late for what?" he said. "Mama, I don't know what you're thinking of, but—"

"Quiet!" She tucked her head down for speed and hurtled towards us, knocking the roses off the pews with the sharp end of her parasol. "Tell me!" she screeched, and pointed at Papa. "Are they married?"

"Ah..." Papa looked as staggered as I felt. "My dear Madam—"

"Are – they – married?" she repeated, banging her parasol against Squire Briggs's pew for emphasis.

Mrs Briggs stiffened with outrage, and Squire Briggs's face darkened to near purple, but even they didn't dare to protest.

"Well," Papa said, "we've only just begun, so technically—"

"Get away from that altar!" Mrs Carlyle bellowed to Frederick. She drew herself up to her full height – not even quite as tall as me – and laid one small, gloved hand on the crimson-silk chest of her pelisse. "This wedding may not take place! The groom is under-age, and I do NOT consent to the match!"

"Mama," Frederick Carlyle began.

"Madam, really," said Papa.

Stepmama began to shriek wordlessly in the audience.

Mr Collingwood stepped forward, chin up, and looked Mrs Carlyle in the eye with a bravery that impressed me. "I do beg your pardon, Madam," he said, "but I am fully six-and-twenty, and in need of no one's permission to wed."

"Who's talking about you, you fool? Frederick—"

"He's the one being married, Mama," Frederick Carlyle said. "Not me." It was the first time I'd ever seen confident Mr Carlyle flushed with embarrassment.

She turned to stare at him, her mouth working. Only one word came out: "Not..."

"You appear to be suffering from a dreadful mis-apprehension, Madam," said Papa. "You have interrupted the wedding ceremony of my eldest daughter to this gentleman, Mr Collingwood. Mr Carlyle is merely acting as his best man."

"Best—"

"Best man," Frederick Carlyle repeated firmly. "What were you thinking, Mama?"

"But..." Her parasol twitched dangerously. Mr Collingwood leaped back. She swivelled round to aim it directly at Elissa. "Are you trying to claim you haven't ensnared my son with your wicked, unnatural wiles?"

Stepmama's shrieks faded into a single, low moan of despair. Charles slumped deep into his seat on the bench beside her, covering his eyes.

"I beg your pardon!" said Elissa. She drew herself up to her own full height, which was a full six inches taller than Mrs Carlyle.

"My sister has no wiles, unnatural or otherwise," Angeline said in a voice like honed steel. Frederick Carlyle winced and put one hand out to stop her, but it was too late. Angeline continued: "I think it must be me you're thinking of, Madam."

"Ha!" Mrs Carlyle spun round. Her parasol quivered in mid-air as it pointed straight at Angeline's middle, like a sword about to strike. "I knew it!"

"Mama," Mr Carlyle began, "you are completely mistaken. No one has ensnared me. No one is tricking me into anything. No one—"

"No one tricked you into anything?" She let out a harsh laugh. "If only I could believe that! When you've abandoned your studies at Oxford in mid-term—"

"I've been studying Classics with Mr Stephenson—"

"Abandoned all communication with your friends and family, written me letters barely two pages long at most, and only once a week – never even suggested visiting, despite all you know about my poor health—"

"I was going to visit you after the wedding, next week—"

"I knew something suspicious was going on. A mother always knows!"

"Indeed, you must have remarkable powers of perception, Madam," said Angeline. Her face was white with rage, and I wished I could reach across to pinch her before she could make matters even worse. But Frederick Carlyle was standing between us, and Angeline continued. "To intuit wicked, unnatural wiles from weekly letters of two pages apiece? That suggests a truly astonishing imagination."

The look Mrs Carlyle shot back at her was so venomous, the air between them should have sizzled with its force. "I needed no powers of intuition or imagination to know all about what has been going on here. You may be interested to learn, young lady, that I know what happened at Grantham Abbey!"

Mr Collingwood blanched. "I say, if it's about the highwayman—"

Elissa cut him off with a look. "Mrs Carlyle," she began, in a tone of sweet reason, "whatever reports you may have heard—"

"You," Mrs Carlyle said to her son, "came chasing after

the family like a madman, only to be by Miss *Angeline*'s side!" She pronounced my sister's name with as much loathing as if she were referring to a poisonous spider. "You may be interested to know that more than one person took note of it! And one of the most admired personages at Grantham understood it all."

"Mama—"

"Perhaps we could continue this highly enlightening conversation later?" Angeline suggested. "After my sister is finally married? And perhaps..." Her dark gaze swept across the fascinated audience in the church pews and benches, including Squire Briggs, who looked ready to have an apoplectic fit, and Mrs Briggs, who was listening with an expression of gleeful horror. "In private?"

"Ha! I've no doubt you would prefer that." Mrs Carlyle sneered.

"Yes, I would, for my sister's sake," said Angeline. "You may think nothing of interrupting an innocent couple's wedding ceremony, but—"

"What do you know of innocence?" Mrs Carlyle shrieked.

Even Angeline retreated. Her mouth dropped open. "How dare you say such a thing?"

"Madam!" Papa said, more firmly than I had ever heard him speak in my life. "I must beg you to control yourself."

"Mama, that's enough!" Mr Carlyle snatched the parasol out of her hand, glaring at her. "Your behaviour is outrageous. To speak in such a way of any young lady—"

"Ha!" said Mrs Carlyle, and scooped a letter out of her reticule. "Miss Angeline Stephenson is no lady. Miss Angeline" – she waved the letter – "is a witch!"

✧ ✧

Papa staggered back as if he'd been struck a blow. He had to clutch the altar to stay upright; his face had turned sickly pale. Stepmama let out a wail and collapsed in a swoon on her bench. Beside her, Charles scanned the high rafters of the ceiling as if searching for an escape.

Whispers swarmed through the church, growing louder and louder. Mrs Briggs's face was filled with smug delight. Squire Briggs's jaw wobbled up and down in wordless fury. Even Angeline and Mr Carlyle looked transfixed with horror.

It was obvious that no one else knew what to do. So it was time for me to take command of the situation.

"That," I said, pitching my voice to carry through the church, "is the most ridiculous thing I have ever heard."

"Ridiculous, is it? Ridiculous?" Mrs Carlyle thrust the letter in my face, so close I had to blow it away from my nose. I went cross-eyed trying to read the handwriting before she snatched it away again. "I know all! The whole sorry scheme!"

"Someone has been telling you lies," I said.

"Lies? Lies?!" Her face suffused with crimson until it matched her gown. "How dare you – you snip of a girl! – cast aspersions on one of the most respectable women in England!"

I eyed her doubtfully. "I beg your pardon, but you don't actually look terribly respectable just now."

"Ohhh!" She clenched her fist around the letter until it crumpled in her grasp. "I am not speaking of myself, you idiot child. I am speaking of the kind friend who sent me this news, Lady Fotherington herself!"

"What?" I stepped back involuntarily. I had to force the words out around the shock in my chest. "Who did you say? Not—"

"Yes! Lady Fotherington, the noted Society hostess! Lady Fotherington, one of the most admired leaders of London high fashion and an intimate of Prince George himself! Even you have heard of her, I see. You can hardly cast aspersions on her honesty!"

Oh yes, I can, I thought. But the words stuck in my throat.

Lady Fotherington wasn't only a leader of fashion. Lady Fotherington was a Guardian – the Guardian who had discovered Mama's secret experiments in witchcraft. Lady Fotherington was the Guardian who had brought about Mama's expulsion from the Order and done so with malicious glee, as a final victory. More than that, she had tried her best to persuade the rest of the Order into 'pacifying' Mama – a process that would have taken away all of her magical powers and damaged her mind, too.

Three months ago, Lady Fotherington had tried to make me her magical slave and, if I hadn't accepted my own powers as a Guardian, she would have succeeded. I'd thought she'd given up her feud against our family once I became strong enough to withstand her.

Obviously, I'd been wrong.

"But I barely even met Lady Fotherington at Grantham Abbey." Angeline's voice didn't sound like steel anymore; it sounded fragile, as if it might break at any moment. "She didn't even arrive until the day after Frederick – I mean, Mr Carlyle – arrived. Why would she say such things about me?"

"About us," Mr Carlyle corrected her. He stepped up to her side and gave her his arm. As Angeline closed her hand around it, he turned to his mother, his jaw set. "Whatever rumours Lady Fotherington or anyone else passed on to you, Mama, they were mistaken. I am under no enchantments."

"What else could possibly explain your behaviour? Walking all across England to this godforsaken village in the middle of nowhere? Abandoning everyone you knew? Of course you must have been bewitched!"

Mr Carlyle and Angeline exchanged a speaking glance. "I swear to you, Mama, I am not bewitched," Mr Carlyle said firmly, and I admired how well he'd sidestepped the question of what had brought him here in the first place.

He might have forgiven Angeline for the spell she'd cast to bring her true love to her, but I couldn't imagine his mother would be so understanding.

She was sputtering now, almost too angry to talk. "I know about this – this dreadful family! Their mother – the woman who would be your mother-in-law!"

A whimper of horror came from the benches behind me. I recognised the voice.

"Stepmama is perfectly respectable," I said.

"I am not speaking of her, but of your true mother, the disgrace! Everyone knows of her shame. Everyone knows how she ruined your father's career – everyone knows she was a witch!"

I looked to Papa, but he was only staring at the altar, his shoulders sagging. Of course, I might as well expect the altar itself to defend us as expect Papa to stand up to anybody, especially when it came to the question of Mama.

So I took a deep breath and tried again. "Just because Mama was a witch doesn't mean she taught any of us witchcraft. How could she? She died when I was born. Angeline was only five years old."

"I know your mother left her magic books behind her," Mrs Carlyle said, and I sent a silent curse to Lady Fotherington for her thoroughness. "But that hardly matters. Even if the three of you were as pure as snow" – she sniffed

– "as unlikely as that sounds, it would have no effect on me. My son will not be ensnared by a family that has been tainted with witchcraft! My son has all the birth and breeding that you lack. If you think I would allow him to ally himself with a family that has brought only scandal and disgrace—"

"I shall," said Mr Carlyle. He was breathing quickly, but his voice was firm, and his handsome face had hardened into determination. "I am going to marry Miss Angeline Stephenson, Mama. So I would very much appreciate it if you would refrain from slandering her any further."

"You shall not!" Mrs Carlyle snatched the parasol back and held it like a weapon. "I will never allow it!"

"I will be twenty-one in three months," said Mr Carlyle. "And then neither you nor my guardian will have anything to say about the matter."

"No?" She let out a crack of laughter. "You haven't spoken to your guardian about this yet, clearly."

He frowned. "Uncle Henry—"

"You may come of age in three months, but under the terms of your father's will, your uncle has the right to decide when and under what conditions to release your inheritance to you. And he is allowed to wait until you are thirty!"

"What?" He stared at her. "No one ever told me that!"

"It hardly mattered when we trusted you," Mrs Carlyle said. "But the good son I took such pride in is gone. Bewitched! Defiled!"

"Mama, I told you—"

"I consulted your uncle before I came to rescue you," said Mrs Carlyle, "and we came to an agreement. Should you be shameless enough to enter into any clandestine betrothal with Miss Angeline Stephenson, we shall know you are unfit to be trusted with your father's inheritance."

"Mama—"

"You shall remain safely under my eye from now on," she said. "And if you attempt any contact with Miss Angeline or any other member of her wretched family, your allowance will be entirely cut off. You will be penniless!"

Mr Carlyle's face was pale with shock. "Mama, you cannot do this. Please, if you would only listen—"

"I have listened enough!" Mrs Carlyle swept her gaze across all of us. "This family is even more shocking and degraded than I had dreamed possible, and you will have nothing more to do with them. Do you understand?" She gestured to her servants, who were clustered against the back wall of the church, looking nervous. "Jenkins! Prepare the carriage. Harris, fetch my son's belongings from the vicarage. He won't be going back there."

"This is absurd," Mr Carlyle said. "If you would only see reason..."

"She won't," said Angeline. Her voice caught. "She doesn't want to. All she wants is to take you away from me."

"It won't work." Mr Carlyle turned to take her hands. "Listen to me, Angeline. I will be back. I'll find a way around this."

"I'll wait for you," Angeline said. Her lips twisted. "I'm good at waiting."

He bent to kiss her hands. His mother's parasol cracked sharply across his shoulder.

"Ouch!" He turned around, glaring. "That's enough, Mama!"

"Indeed it is," she said. Her cheeks were nearly purple now, but she held her head high. "You will precede me out of this church, Frederick, or your allowance will be withheld for the next six months!"

Mr Carlyle gritted his teeth. "As you say, ma'am." He released Angeline's hands and stepped away. As he turned, I saw Angeline's lips move. A faint but unmistakable flowery smell sprang up around her: the beginnings of a spell.

Exactly what Lady Fotherington would be waiting for.

I gritted my own teeth and focused, until the familiar electricity crackled in my ears.

"NO!" I hissed.

Angeline's spell was extinguished as quickly as it had begun. She fell back, grabbing Elissa's arm for balance... then turned her glare to me.

Later, I mouthed silently.

She shot me a look that said she wouldn't forget.

I felt sick as I watched Mr Carlyle walk down the church aisle away from us, past all the staring, whispering wedding guests. His mother's footmen held the front doors open for him, their faces carefully expressionless. He passed through the doors ahead of his mother, then turned to look back.

Mrs Carlyle's voice cracked through the air. "*Now*, Frederick!"

The footmen slammed the doors in his face, leaving the church echoing behind them.

CHAPTER FOUR

THE REST OF THE WEDDING WENT BY IN A BLUR. PAPA READ OUT his lines in a voice that sounded only half full, as if it – and he – might blow away entirely in the next strong breeze. Elissa and Mr Collingwood stumbled through their responses. Angeline looked ready to shatter into either violence or, worse yet, tears at the slightest provocation. Stepmama wept silently in her seat, while Charles dealt with all the misery around him in his usual manner – by falling snoringly sound asleep to escape it.

The entire audience whispered throughout the ceremony, especially Mrs Briggs, who looked to be haranguing her husband in their pew. Everyone in the village knew that ever since she'd married the squire, six months ago, she'd been trying to persuade him to dismiss Papa from his post, only because of the old scandal about Mama. I had a terrible feeling that Mrs Carlyle might have just supplied the perfect new excuse.

As I watched the ruination of my oldest sister's wedding, and saw the frightened, lost look grow in Angeline's dark eyes, my own rage expanded until I could barely see or think past it. Everything inside me wanted to erupt in a magic-destroying explosion. There were no magic spells here to vanquish, though. Only the power of stupid, selfish Society's prejudice, and neither of the women who wielded it were here to face my anger.

I knew how to find one of them, though.

As soon as the wedding ended, Elissa and Mr Collingwood went straight to their travelling carriage without even waiting to attend the grand wedding breakfast that Mrs Watkins and the maids had laid out so carefully in the vicarage. There was no point in pretence; all the guests had already scattered to bear the delicious gossip back to their own homes. Squire and Mrs Briggs hadn't even bothered to offer any congratulations to the bride and groom on their way out.

At the side of the carriage, Elissa embraced Angeline as carefully as she would a delicate porcelain doll. She tried to whisper something in her ear, but Angeline pulled away and stalked back to the vicarage, leaving Elissa frowning after her.

When I stepped forward for my own hug, Elissa said, "Take care of Angeline. Don't let her..."

"I won't," I said, and we exchanged a look of perfect accord. We both knew what our sister was capable of, in a rage.

I stood at the head of our drive waving to Elissa and Mr Collingwood until the carriage finally disappeared around the winding curve that led away from our house and into their future. Then I picked up my skirts, turned for home, and ran as fast as my legs would carry me. If Elissa had still been here, she would have reproved me for being so unladylike, but my oldest sister was gone and there was no one else who could stop me.

The wedding breakfast was still laid out on the dining room table, looking lonely and unwanted. I heard Angeline's door slam shut as I ran into the house. Stepmama's voice rose and fell in another room, bewailing her misfortunes to Papa, whose defeated tones were nearly inaudible. Charles had disappeared. *Of course.* Well, I didn't need his help this time.

I snatched up a roll from the table, stuffed it in my mouth, and raced up the stairs to the ladder that led to my attic. The puce ruffles of my morning gown tangled in the ladder's steps. I kicked them aside impatiently, listening to them rip with a feeling of distinct relief. At least Stepmama could never make me wear this gown again.

I shoved a heavy case across the attic's trapdoor, just in case. Then – safe at last – I reached into my reticule and drew out Mama's magic mirror. It was my only inheritance from her, and the best one I could imagine.

The round golden case glowed with heat against the palm of my hand. I heard the faint echo of voices coming from inside it. *Good.*

I snapped the clasp open and dived inside.

☆ ☆

I landed in the Guardian's Golden Hall, on my feet and seething. High, rounded walls surrounded me, rising to a shining arch high above. Three people stood together on the smooth, open floor.

"Why, Katherine." It was my tutor, Mr Gregson, small and dapper. He bowed politely, his bald spot shining in the warm, honey light. "Shouldn't you still be celebrating with your family?"

"I would," I said, "except that no one's celebrating anymore." I turned my glare to the tall, black-haired woman who stood behind him: a perfect fashion plate in every detail, even down to the elegantly contemptuous sneer. "Lady Fotherington saw to that."

"I beg your pardon?" Lady Fotherington arched her perfectly plucked eyebrows. "My dear, imaginative child. I have been here with Mr Gregson and" – she nodded to the brightly clad man who stood beside her, peering down at me through his quizzing glass – "Lord Ravenscroft for the past hour or more and, although this may surprise you, we had rather more important matters to discuss than your sister's shameful little country wedding."

"There was nothing shameful about it." I had to grit the words through my teeth. Even the sound of her voice was enough to make my fists and jaw clench. The first time I'd met Lady Fotherington, she'd set a magic-working on me to force magical obedience, and I'd broken her nose. Once I had come into my natural powers and agreed to become a member of the Order, she had abandoned her attempts to control me with magic, and I'd promised Mr Gregson not to hit her again.

Now I was regretting that promise.

"No?" Lady Fotherington said, and her sneer spread into a smirk. "I see that your stepmother dressed you properly for the occasion, at least. One could hardly call you" – she looked pointedly at the multiple rows of puce ruffles on my gown – "less ruffled than the occasion called for?"

Lady Fotherington's gown, of course, had only a single, discreet row of ruffles. Even as I realised that, she nodded. "Yes, last season – or perhaps two seasons ago – that dress might have been considered fashionable enough for such a small, unimportant event. Although perhaps not when ornamented with a rip at the seam and – are those bread crumbs? Really, Katherine. At your own sister's wedding..."

Just one quick blow to her perfect face, the way Charles had taught me...

Mr Gregson coughed and stepped between us as hastily as if he'd read my mind. "What exactly did happen, Katherine? I take it not everything went as planned?"

"It went exactly as Lady Fotherington planned," I said, and fought to keep my voice steady. "Mr Carlyle's mother charged inside the church in the middle of the wedding to kidnap her son and inform all the guests that my sister was a witch who had bewitched him – exactly as her good friend Lady Fotherington had explained to her."

"Lydia?" Mr Gregson frowned and turned to Lady Fotherington. "Surely there has been some mistake or misunderstanding. You could not have meant to—"

"And was it a falsehood?" Lady Fotherington said to me, ignoring him. "Can you genuinely accuse me of anything but telling the truth to an innocent woman?"

"She dragged him away!" I said. "She said if he contacts Angeline again, he'll have his allowance cut off entirely. If he marries her – if he even becomes betrothed to her – he won't receive his inheritance for another ten years!"

"What a pity." Lady Fotherington shrugged. "I rather doubt she can hold his interest through ten years of waiting. She'll have to look for another gullible fool, one without any family to look after his interests."

"He is not gullible. He's—" I began, and then stopped, biting down hard on my lower lip. I didn't want to hear Lady Fotherington's opinion of true love. Instead, I said,

"Squire Briggs was in the church when it happened. He heard everything!"

She laughed. "And you expect me to recognise the name of this, er, squire? Really, Katherine, your imagination..."

"He could take away Papa's living!"

"If your father cannot control his own daughter's witchcraft, then perhaps that would be for the best."

My hands clenched into tighter fists. I started forward.

"Katherine!" Mr Gregson said sharply.

I dropped my fists and forced myself to stand still. I could hear my pulse pounding in my ears.

Lady Fotherington looked pointedly from me to Lord Ravenscroft. "You see? She is quite feral."

"Tho it appearth," Lord Ravenscroft agreed, in a lisp so high pitched and so affected that I had to think twice before I could puzzle out exactly what he had said. He drew a canary-yellow silk handkerchief to his nose, as if protecting himself from some outlandish stench. Judging by his expression, that stench came from me.

It only took one look for me to understand. From the top of his oiled brown hair to his ridiculously tall cravat, his tight-fitting, peacock-blue coat, and the huge emerald and ruby rings he wore on almost all of his pale fingers, Lord Ravenscroft was a fop and a deuced dandy. I'd never met one before, but I had heard plenty about them from Charles. All that any dandy cared about was following fashion and seducing women.

So I ignored him and turned back to Lady Fotherington. "You have to tell Mrs Carlyle that you made a mistake."

"I shall do no such thing." Her voice was suddenly full of poison, bleeding through the pretence of elegant boredom that she'd affected. "Did you really expect me to sit by and watch while another family of birth and breeding is drawn into your family's web? While you and your sisters, just like your mother before you, fool everyone into thinking—"

"Don't you dare insult Mama!" I said.

"I'll say what I like about her."

"Lydia!" Mr Gregson said sharply. "And Katherine. Perhaps we ought to take some time to calm our tempers."

"Don't tell me to calm my temper after what she's done!" I said.

Power was buzzing in my ears, filling my veins with pulsing energy. I didn't know any spells or magic-workings I could use, but Charles had shown me other options, options that felt all too tempting right now.

Ladies of breeding never resort to using their fists, Elissa always said. A proper lady wouldn't dream of punching Lady Fotherington, no matter how much she deserved it. *Ladies of breeding never...* I repeated to myself. But my Guardian power was surging through me, making it hard to think anything at all.

"Miss Katherine's temper is incapable of restraint," said Lady Fotherington. "As was clear to me from the moment we met. Exactly like her mother's, in fact." She walked towards me slowly, glidingly, her emerald silk skirts swishing around her legs, her elegant slippers whispering against the floor. Her green eyes focused on mine until they were all I could see. My skin tingled with discomfort, but I couldn't look away. "Her mother was a traitress and a fool who could not restrain her own wild passions, and her daughters – all three of her daughters – are exactly the same." Her mouth formed the word even before she spat it through her lips: "Shameless."

That did it. I was lunging through the air before she

even finished speaking. There was no thought in me, only fury, only my fist swinging in a perfectly aimed arc through the air...

And then I was flying backwards across the hall as if shot from a cannon. Pain lanced through me as I flew, but it was nothing to the pain that came next as I crashed onto my back and slammed my head against the floor. I tried to moan or turn or lift my arm. I couldn't. My body had turned into jelly.

It had to be a magic-working. Limp on the ground, I couldn't see the other three, but I knew Lady Fotherington had to be behind it. Well, I knew how to defeat Guardian workings and I was certain she couldn't stand against me.

I took a deep breath, forcing myself past the pain. I pulled the energy up through my body, into my head, until it made a pounding pressure even stronger than the throbbing of the headache that was already there. I gathered it all up and, with full force, threw it at the magic that held me down.

NO! I thought, with all my strength.

But absolutely nothing happened. I tried to pull the power back up again. It was gone.

I heard footsteps approach across the smooth golden floor. I couldn't move. My breath came quickly, hurting my chest. Whatever Lady Fotherington had done, whatever she had in mind for me, Mr Gregson was here to see it, and to protect me. He would stop her from doing anything too drastic. He...

It was Lord Ravenscroft, not Lady Fotherington, who stood above me. He raised his quizzing glass and looked down at me with utter contempt in his muddy, green-brown eyes.

"Yeth," he said. "You were quite right about her, Lydia. I can thee that now."

I tried to swallow. I couldn't. The power that emanated from Lord Ravenscroft held me pinned like a piece of meat on a knife. Under his gaze, I couldn't even blink.

"Lord Ravenscroft," Mr Gregson said. I'd never heard him sound so wary or so humble. "I beg of you not to make too much of this one incident. Miss Katherine was greatly distressed by her sister's disappointment, and could hardly be expected—"

"To behave like a rational and civilised member of Society?" Lady Fotherington finished for him. She stepped up to join Lord Ravenscroft, and her lips curved into a smile of pure satisfaction. With the tip of one fashionable slipper, she nudged my waist. Her smile deepened. "And this, Aloysius, is the girl you expect us all to welcome with open arms into our ancient Order? To, heaven help us, aid in protecting Society from misdirected and malicious magic?"

"It doethn't bear thinking of," said Lord Ravenscroft. "You were right, Lydia – she ith pothitively feral."

I tried to speak. Only a wordless gurgle emerged from my throat. It hurt.

Lady Fotherington made an exaggerated gesture of surprise. "But I haven't made the proper introductions yet, have I?" She gestured down at me. "Lord Ravenscroft, may I present to you Miss Katherine Stephenson, youngest daughter of Olivia Amberson, who broke the most vital laws of our Order to make the most unsuitable marriage imaginable, to ruin her husband's life and aspirations and ignore all the obligations of her own calling. And this..." She placed one hand lightly on Lord Ravenscroft's arm, in a gesture of possession. "This, Miss Katherine, is Lord Ravenscroft, Head of the Order of Guardians, and our leader."

I gurgled. Mr Gregson's face appeared in the edge of my line of sight, looking more unhappy than I'd ever seen him.

"Lord Ravenscroft, please—" he began.

"No, Aloysius." Lord Ravenscroft waved Mr Gregson off with a gesture as hard and cutting as his own voice had suddenly become, dropping the fashionable lisp. "I was willing to listen to your arguments earlier, but I have the evidence of my own eyes before me now. Lady Fotherington was absolutely correct. This..." – his upper lip curled into a sneer as he looked down at me – "this wild, unnatural girl must never, ever be allowed to become a Guardian."

CHAPTER FIVE

"BUT I AM A GUARDIAN," I SAID.

Ten minutes had passed since Lord Ravenscroft's pronouncement; two minutes since he and Lady Fotherington had left the Golden Hall together. The magic-working had vanished the moment Lord Ravenscroft disappeared from the hall, but my muscles still felt as weak and shivery as if I'd run twenty miles or been trampled by an elephant. Mr Gregson had to help me to my feet. My legs were shaking too badly to stand on pride alone.

When I spoke, he sighed but didn't answer. The look in his eyes gave me a horrible twinge of fear. It had to be a mistake – it couldn't be anything but a mistake – and yet...

I pulled myself up straighter, ignoring the trembling in my muscles, and lifted my chin high. "I *am* a Guardian!" I repeated. "You know I am. I have Mama's mirror, I have all her powers – you're the one who told me that. So Lord Ravenscroft will just have to admit—"

47

"Shh," Mr Gregson said. "Shh." He frowned down at my hand where it rested on his arm. "Are you quite well enough yet to return home, or do you need to take some rest first?"

I yanked my hand off his arm. "I don't need to rest, and I don't need you to look after me like some... some missish, swooning young lady! I need you to tell me the truth. What just happened? How could he say I can't become a Guardian when I already am one?" Mr Gregson sighed again and looked away, and I nearly screamed with frustration. "Just tell me!"

"Very well, Katherine." Mr Gregson looked into my eyes. His own were filled with an expression that was even worse than the contempt of Lady Fotherington and Lord Ravenscroft.

It was pity.

"You did inherit your mother's powers," he said. "As well as her portal to this hall. But you are not yet able to use the powers you were born with."

"I certainly am!" I almost laughed. It was too absurd. "You've seen me – you know I can. I stopped Sir Neville's spells at Grantham Abbey, and Angeline's – I've even stopped your magic-workings."

"Yes," he said. "But you could do so much more, if you only knew how. Being a Guardian is more than instinct, more than the power to will other people's magic out of existence. A true Guardian can create magic-workings of her own."

I didn't say anything. I knew it was true. And a sick, horrible feeling was twisting inside me.

You'll learn in time... Angeline had said it only this morning. I'd thought it was true. I'd been so confident. Even after Mr Gregson had told me the Order was debating my admission, I'd never really worried that I wouldn't succeed in the end. It had never even occurred to me that Lady Fotherington might outwit me.

"Without further training," Mr Gregson said, his voice as gentle and regretful as ever, "you will remain stunted and weak, like a magical invalid. You can never grow into your full strength without the training our Order supplies."

It would have been too easy to be afraid. So I focused on being angry instead. "You're my tutor, remember? You're the one who came after me and told me I had to join the Order in the first place. You're going to teach me..."

His quiet voice cut across mine. "I cannot teach you a single lesson against the will of Lord Ravenscroft. He is the Head of our Order. You felt his power just now. His decisions are law to all of us."

"But that's absurd!" I said. "He's only just met me. He can't—"

"He can," said Mr Gregson, "and he will. He is a powerful man and a powerful enemy."

"But..." I stumbled to a halt. The sick feeling in my stomach was growing stronger. It felt like... I didn't know what. But if I let myself stop to think about it, I might lose the anger that was the only thing still holding me upright. So instead I said, "I'm not going to accept his word as law, no matter what anyone else thinks. And next time I come back to this hall—"

"You won't," Mr Gregson said.

"I beg your pardon?"

"You won't come back to this hall," he said. "I am truly sorry, Katherine. But you will find that your portal no longer works. Once it has taken you safely home today..." His voice dropped. "It will become no more than an ordinary mirror."

"What?" My voice came out as a croak. "That isn't possible."

"Lord Ravenscroft's father, our former Head, cut off your mother's access to the Hall when she was expelled," said Mr Gregson. "He only reopened her portal when she died, leaving it ready to be discovered by whichever of her children inherited her Guardian powers. But after today, you, too, will be exiled from the Golden Hall, and from our Order."

"But..."

I couldn't finish. I knew what the sick feeling was now: certainty. The certainty of my own stupidity, losing me everything I'd wanted for my future – everything I could have so easily had, if only I'd followed my oldest sister's advice and, for once, acted like a lady.

I looked into my tutor's eyes, pale blue behind his spectacles.

"I am sorry," Mr Gregson said. "I shall miss you, Katherine."

☆ ☆

I landed back on the floor of my attic room and promptly tripped on the torn ruffle of my dress. I fell with a thud and landed face down on the floor. A layer of dust pressed rough into my cheek.

Perhaps I should have taken more care last time I swept the room.

Perhaps I should have done that more recently than a month ago. Or was it two months? I'd told Stepmama that I was going to sweep it only a few days ago, but of course I hadn't.

I'd been making a lot of mistakes lately. But compared to the one that I'd just made...

I pushed myself up fast, before I could think, sneezing dust. It was only when I was standing, brushing off my dust-covered puce skirts, that I realised the golden mirror wasn't in my hand.

I spun around, searching. It wasn't waiting on my bed either.

Mama's mirror always found me. Always.

They couldn't have taken it away from me, could they? Mr Gregson had only said it wouldn't work anymore, not that Lord Ravenscroft would actually confiscate it. If he had – if he and Lady Fotherington had it right now and were laughing over it with each other...

I ground my teeth so hard my jaw hurt and dropped back down to my hands and knees. It took me ten minutes of crawling around the floor before I finally found the mirror, lying still and dusty underneath the bed. When I closed my fingers around it, it felt all wrong. It didn't tingle against my hand. It wasn't warm, or strange, or magical. It was only a cold, dust-covered travel mirror, clasped and boring.

I took a deep breath and pushed myself up to my knees. *Please let him be wrong. Please, Mama....* I undid the clasp.

My own face stared back at me from the round mirror inside. There were dust streaks all along my cheeks. My short hair stuck out around my face in wild tufts, bereft of all the pins Stepmama had jabbed into it earlier.

I had never seen myself in that mirror before. Not once.

I slammed the case shut. Without even thinking, I swung my arm back to throw the mirror across the room and let it smash.

Then my mind caught up with me, and a gasp tore out of my throat. I lowered my arm again, clamping my fingers tightly around the mirror.

It felt like carrying something dead. I couldn't even make myself look at it. But it was the only one of Mama's possessions I had left. When Stepmama had first moved into the vicarage, she'd locked every reminder of Mama and her scandals into a cabinet none of us were allowed to open. The first time I'd travelled to the Golden Hall, I'd accidentally destroyed almost everything in that cabinet with the magical force of my journey. Angeline still had Mama's magic books, because she'd stolen them from the cabinet weeks beforehand. Mama's miniature portrait had survived, but Elissa had taken that with her when she left.

All that I had was Mama's mirror. I couldn't break that, too.

"I'm sorry, Mama," I whispered. Heat prickled behind my eyes. I squeezed them tightly shut. I would not cry. I wouldn't give Lady Fotherington or Lord Ravenscroft that satisfaction. Instead, I said out loud, "I will fix the magic in your mirror. I will make it work again. I promise!"

A scream from downstairs interrupted my vow.

Oh, no. I recognised that scream. It was the sound of Stepmama at her wits' end, taking a terrible stand. Those stands never turned out well for any of us.

"Oh, yes, you will, young lady!" she shrieked. "And I will not hear another word against it!"

Oh Lord. Out of sheer habit, I started to stuff Mama's mirror into my reticule, to carry it with me. Then I realised: I didn't need to anymore. When it was full of magic, the mirror had followed me everywhere. The reticule had been the only way to keep it safely out of other people's sight. Now, though, it would lie quiet and still no matter how far away I went.

It wasn't a relief.

"I'll be back for you," I whispered. I tucked it under my

bedcovers, patting them down as gently as if I were covering an invalid.

Then I shoved the heavy case off the trapdoor and hurtled down the ladder to the second floor, where trouble was definitely brewing.

Stepmama stood in Angeline's bedroom doorway, vibrating with outrage. "You," she shrieked into the room, "will begin your packing! Now!"

"What's happening?" I said.

Stepmama jerked round. "And you...!" Her shriek dropped to a horrified whisper. "What in the world have you done to yourself this time?"

"What do you mean? Oh." I raised one hand to my dirty face. "I— well..."

"This is the first time you've worn that gown. How could you have ruined it already?"

"Um..." I thought quickly. "I tripped?"

"Hmmph." She snorted. "We will discuss that story later... as you work on mending, cleaning and pressing your gown, young lady!"

"Why bother?" I shrugged. "I'll never wear it again. It's too fine for everyday, and I won't be a bridesmaid again for at least another ten years. By then it won't even fit anymore."

"Ohhh!" Stepmama rolled her eyes up to heaven. "Will you two girls stop talking such nonsense? You are not waiting ten years for anything, and neither is your sister!"

Only a steely silence came from Angeline's room in reply. It meant that she was too angry even to speak... which, with my sister, was the most dangerous response of all. Judging by the high spots of colour on Stepmama's cheekbones, she knew that as well as I did.

Stepmama enunciated her words as carefully as if she were speaking to an infant, or an idiot. "We are not going to wait ten years in the hope that one particular thirty-year-old gentleman will choose to remember the promises he made at twenty to a girl he hasn't seen in a decade, whom all his relatives detest. Only a daydreamer or a ninny would have faith in such an event ever taking place."

"Mr Carlyle wouldn't betray Angeline," I said. "He's her true—"

"If anyone utters the words 'true love' to me, I shall have strong hysterics," Stepmama said. "We are leaving tomorrow morning."

"Why?" I said. "Where?"

She darted a look into Angeline's bedroom, then turned back to me with a martyred sigh. "You girls are each lucky enough to have a small dowry now, gifted by your new brother-in-law. It is too early to make use of yours, but if we wait even a month, it may be too late for Angeline. We cannot hope to outrun the gossip for long."

"But why?"

"Your sister," said Stepmama, "is going to find a fiancé."

Angeline's voice cut through the air like a rapier. "I have already found one."

"Any promises Mr Carlyle made to you are legally invalid. He is not of age. In court, his mother and guardian could—"

"You cannot force me to become betrothed to anyone else in the world," said Angeline.

"You think not?"

Oh, no. The whole air rippled with the tension of a disaster about to happen. This was the moment when Elissa was supposed to step in. I glanced at the open door, half-expecting her to come hurrying out. She always did, at this point. She would soothe Stepmama and force Angeline to be quiet and negotiate between them so nothing too desperate could happen, and then...

"I," said Stepmama, "have done my duty by you and your sisters for over five years. Despite every evidence of ingratitude, misbehaviour and the most shocking want of ladylike propriety—"

"Wait," I said, and stepped forward. What would Elissa say now? I'd never paid much attention to how she calmed Stepmama down. I was usually too busy shouting back at Stepmama to notice – and too annoyed by Elissa's interference in our arguments. But now I was beginning to understand just how important that interference had truly been.

"Stepmama," I said, and cleared my throat. "Can I make you some tea?"

"Tea?" Stepmama drew herself up like a ruffled hen. "Don't be absurd. I do not desire tea at a moment like this. What I wish to say is—"

"Eggs!" I said. "There are still hard-boiled eggs and rolls and chicken on the table downstairs. And wedding cake! Why don't you and I go downstairs and finally eat our breakfast, and then we'll all feel better."

"What are you going on about now?" Stepmama blinked at me. "Have you run mad, Kat?"

"No," I said. "I mean, yes. You have to take me downstairs and feed me before I can do anything dreadful."

Angeline's voice spoke again from the bedroom, in a tone as sweet and as lethally cold as a stream deep in the Yorkshire Dales. "What Kat is on about this time, ma'am, is a blatant attempt to distract you. Because she never has been able to tell when something is none of her business."

Quick footsteps sounded across the bedroom floor and Angeline appeared at the door.

I gulped at the sight of her. Her thick, dark-brown hair

was perfectly smooth, still arranged to perfection in its wedding style; her gown, unlike mine, was perfectly clean and unwrinkled. But her face looked as white and stretched as a ghost's, and her dark eyes burned.

"Tell me," said Angeline to Stepmama, "what you were about to say."

"After breakfast!" I said. "We'll all eat first, and then..." My voice trailed off as I looked between them. Neither of them was listening to me.

Stepmama's eyes were on Angeline's, and her voice was just as inflexible as Angeline's own. "I have done my duty for the past five years," she repeated, "but you are a grown woman now, not a girl who can be forgiven for her mis-behaviour. You have done untold damage to our family with your disobedience and your shocking witchcraft. If you choose to thwart me now and throw aside all of my and your father's best efforts and hopes for your own welfare—"

"I really don't think we should—" I began.

"We leave for Bath tomorrow," Stepmama said to Angeline. "While we are there, you will behave like a modest, respectable young lady who has never even heard of magic. You will do your very best to find an eligible new fiancé before the news of your social ruin can be carried across the country."

Angeline's lips curled into a sneer. "And if I do not?"

"If you do not," said Stepmama, "then when we return home afterwards, you will not accompany us."

CHAPTER SIX

WE LEFT FOR BATH THE NEXT MORNING.

The last time we had travelled, Squire Briggs had lent us his second-best travelling carriage. This time, all five of us rode packed like kippers in a crowded public stagecoach: me, Angeline, Stepmama, Papa and Charles, all squashed so tightly against each other and our baggage that I could barely breathe, much less think.

Luckily, no one was speaking to each other by then anyway.

Papa looked too miserable to utter even a single word. Charles, of course, retreated from the boredom of several days' travel by sleeping the entire way. Angeline and Stepmama each radiated a rage so icy it was almost enough to keep the whole packed stagecoach cool. There were four other passengers: a woman and her daughter sitting on the roof above us, carrying geese that honked on and off from their baskets throughout the journey, and two boys of my own age travelling to meet their family. The goose women laughed and chattered all the way, while the geese honked accompaniment. I thought longing thoughts about changing families, and wished I could sit up on the roof.

Mama's mirror stayed quiet and cool inside my reticule. I couldn't help touching it every so often, though, just in case. Anything could be happening in the Golden Hall. Perhaps Mr Gregson had talked Lord Ravenscroft into seeing sense; perhaps Lady Fotherington had felt ashamed and confessed everything. Perhaps... But every time I reached into my reticule and felt the cool, unresponsive – *dead* – gold against my fingers, I felt sick all over again.

Two stops before Bath, Stepmama made us all get out. Charles groaned, blinked awake, and lurched out of the coach on command, still yawning. Papa followed him into the crowded inn yard, head hanging, without question. Angeline followed Stepmama out with a spine so stiff it could have snapped in two.

I said, "But we aren't there yet!"

The inn yard was a crowded, chaotic mess. Besides our stagecoach, there were three others stopping at the same time. Passengers flooded in and out of the inn and the gathered coaches. Ostlers hurried through the yard, shouting at stable boys. Salesmen wandered in and out of the crowd, hawking ribbons and buttons, and the innkeeper shouted instructions at everybody. I could hear what sounded like drunken carousing coming from the open doors of the inn itself, even though it was only mid-afternoon.

Stepmama said, "For heaven's sake, Kat, get down and stop staring. And you!" she snapped at the nearest stable boy. "We'll need our bags, and quickly."

"Yes'm," the boy said, and started forward. He was barely as tall as my shoulder, and terribly skinny.

I reached for the first valise beside me. "I can help you."

Stepmama's gloved hand closed around my shoulder. "No, you may not," she said. "You and your sister will wait in a private room inside the inn, like modest and proper young ladies, until your father and I come for you. Do you understand?"

I twisted away from her. "Fine." Gritting my teeth, I jumped down onto the muck-covered ground.

"Charles!" Stepmama's tone made my brother straighten away from the side of the coach with a start. "You will escort your sisters."

"Yes, ma'am," he said, and yawned so widely I could see all the way to the back of his tongue. It was disgusting.

Stepmama shuddered and looked away.

Angeline and I followed Charles across the crowded courtyard to the inn. It was surprisingly uncomfortable to have to squeeze through the press of men that surrounded us. Most of them didn't pay any attention to me, but Angeline attracted notice from all of them. Colour mounted in her cheeks as the men she passed whispered into her ears, but her lips stayed tightly closed, and she never turned to look at them. Of course, Charles would have responded for her if he'd been a proper sort of gentlemanly escort... but Charles was Charles, for better or worse. He probably didn't even realise what was happening behind him.

Only the thought of Stepmama watching us from the carriage stopped me from responding with my fists at least half a dozen times along the way.

But enough was enough. Just as we reached the doorway, one man lurched forward, grabbing for Angeline.

His eyes were bleary with drink, and I started forward as his big hand closed over her elbow. Angeline's lips moved. Before I could do a thing, the scent of lilacs filled the air. The man lurched back as if he'd been struck a blow straight to his gut. He landed in the muck that covered the yard, groaning.

With a grin, I lowered my fists. Angeline only smiled demurely, her eyelashes lowered like a modest young lady, and followed Charles into the inn. Thank goodness, no one else had been close enough to hear her whisper the spell, and the lout himself was far too intoxicated to understand what had knocked him down.

The taproom of the inn was just as crowded as the yard outside, and full of dense smoke. Charles left me and Angeline in the foyer as he went inside to negotiate with the landlord. We had to flatten ourselves against the striped wallpaper to keep from being trampled by the press of men going in and out.

Still, at least we were out of the carriage and away from Stepmama. I felt better than I had in days.

"This is rather exciting, isn't it?" I said. "Perhaps if we went inside too, for a moment, just to look around—"

"Don't even think of it," said Angeline. "The last thing any of us need right now is for you to provoke a public brawl before we even reach Bath."

"Ha," I said. "I'm not the one who knocked down that man outside."

Angeline only gave me a quelling look as another group of men shoved past us. I peered after them into the packed taproom. Charles had disappeared from sight. There seemed to be a card game going on in the back corner, though, and that was enough to explain everything. By the time he did reappear, he probably would have lost all his clothes and his allowance for the next ten years. Poor Charles was hopeless at gambling, despite all his practice.

I wouldn't have minded playing one round of cards myself, just to see what it was like. After all, anything that helped me understand Charles's recent idiocy was bound to be helpful. When I shot Angeline a speculative glance, though, I found her dark eyes fixed on me in an uncomfortably knowing look.

"No," she said. "Just wait."

"Fine." I slumped against the wall, ignoring all of Stepmama's and Elissa's old strictures about ladylike posture. "I don't know when you became so obedient, though. Why would you care if I outraged Stepmama?"

"I wouldn't," Angeline said. "But I have important things on my mind right now, and I can't be bothered saving you from another of your mad scrapes."

I jerked upright. "That is so unjust! You have never had to save me from anything."

"No?" She cocked one eyebrow, an expression I particularly hated. "Let me think..."

"I'm the one who always saves you!" I said.

"Indeed?" Angeline's eyebrow arched higher. "How fortunate you are to have such an active imagination. Because I can very clearly recall several times when—"

"It is not my imagination," I said. "When you cast that spell..." My mind caught up with my tongue, and I stopped myself with a gulp. I really didn't want her to remind her of Mr Carlyle right now.

"Quite," Angeline said, looking pointedly at the group of men passing us on their way to the taproom. Luckily, they'd been talking too loudly to hear me.

I winced.

She sighed. "And now, if you wouldn't mind trying to be

quiet, for once? I really do have more important things to think about before we arrive in Bath."

Well, that was something I did want to ask her about. "Why aren't we in Bath already? Why did Stepmama insist on all of us getting off the coach so early? It doesn't make any sense."

"Oh, Kat," Angeline said, and my back stiffened. I hated it when she used that tone of voice. It meant: *You are too young to understand anything, but I know it all.* "Don't you understand Stepmama by now? She would never allow us to be seen arriving in Bath in a mere public stagecoach. That would hardly suit her purposes. No, I expect that at this very moment she is hiring a beautiful private carriage, so that we can sail into Bath in the height of style, impressing everyone who sees us with the illusion of our magnificence. Because as we all know..." Her lips twisted. "The only thing that matters in life is what Society thinks of us."

"Bravo," said a deep, unfamiliar voice, only a few feet away. "Magnificent indeed, ma'am, if I may be allowed to say so."

I spun round.

A gentleman stood just inside the taproom, wearing a greatcoat with so many enveloping capes, his bulked-out shoulders filled the entire doorway. He raised his gloved hands to clap mockingly. "A remarkable performance," he said to Angeline. "May I ask when you will be repeating it on the public stage?"

I knew enough about Society to know what an insult he had just paid her. "She is not an actress," I said, and glared at him.

"Indeed?" He smiled. It was not a pleasant smile, though his face was attractive enough. "But with such affecting talents—"

"You are impertinent, sir," said Angeline.

"On the contrary, ma'am, I am in awe." He stepped forward, his greatcoat swishing about his knee-high boots, and reached for her hand. "Beauty matched with style and wit – an irresistible combination. I cannot allow you to remain unprotected in so public a situation."

Angeline pulled her hand out of his grip. "I am neither unprotected nor unescorted."

"No?" He looked around pointedly. "And yet..."

"Our brother is escorting us," I said. "He'll be back in only a moment."

"How fortunate for him." The gentleman's smile deepened in a way I liked even less. "Then I will only stay and lend my escort until this mysterious brother of yours chooses to make his appearance."

There wasn't a mysterious bone in Charles's body... but, not for the first time, I cursed his hopelessness. If he had been lured into a card game, he might not remember us for hours. From the look on Angeline's face, she was sending silent curses in our brother's direction, too.

"Truly, sir," she said through gritted teeth, "you need not trouble yourself."

"Oh, I assure you, it is no trouble. But I haven't yet introduced myself, have I?" He swept a bow, removing his beaver hat and revealing black curls so glossy, he must have doused them in hair oil. "Scarwood – Viscount Scarwood – at your service. And most delighted to be so," he added, looking straight into Angeline's eyes.

Angeline's lips only tightened. I clenched my hands into fists and wished that Angeline could knock him over with magic as easily as she'd dealt with the intoxicated ruffian outside. But this was a gentleman of means, an aristocrat, sober enough to recognise witchcraft when he saw it, and we were inside the inn now, in easy view of the taproom. It was far too public a situation for any use of magic, or of fisticuffs. Either tactic would ruin both our reputations. Even Viscount Scarwood's own report, if he told anyone else what we had done – no matter how ungentlemanly his own behaviour – would be enough to ruin us in Society. But without magic or fisticuffs on our side, we were as helpless against him as any pair of tediously proper young ladies.

I should have been able to do so much more. If I had only received my training... I remembered Mr Gregson's words in the Golden Hall. With the training of a real Guardian, I could have controlled my power and used it independently, not only in reaction to other people's magic. Since Guardians didn't need to cast spoken spells, I might even have been able to use my powers to protect us both from insult without anyone around us even guessing that magic had been involved.

If only I hadn't made that dreadful, stupid mistake – if I had only kept control of my damnable temper...

Viscount Scarwood started talking again, and for a moment, I was actually glad to have a distraction from my thoughts. Then I heard what he was saying to Angeline.

"Come now. Any young lady brave enough to stand in a public inn without any visible escort – and to speak so slightingly of Society – can hardly expect to stand upon convention and wait for proper introductions. You may as well tell me your name yourself, rather than requiring me to hunt it down. I will find it out, you know, in the end – and you wouldn't like me to be irritated by the trouble you've forced upon me."

"I have no interest in forcing you to do anything," Angeline said, "except to leave us in peace."

"Ah, but I'm afraid that isn't possible. You've caught my interest, you see."

"Not intentionally, I assure you."

"Nonetheless." He leaned forward and braced one big hand against the wall beside her head. Angeline stiffened and began to slide away. He trapped her with his other hand, closing her in with scandalous intimacy. "It is far too late now to retreat," he breathed, so quietly I could barely hear the words.

Then he leaned forward to kiss her.

Angeline twisted her head away. "Release me!"

I grabbed his arm. "Let her go!"

He looked down at me and laughed. "A brave protectress indeed," he said. "And yet—"

A wholly unexpected voice spoke behind him.

"I say," said Charles. He was holding a half-empty mug of beer and frowning at us. "Is – that is, is everything perfectly all right here?"

"Aha." Scarwood leaned back, shaking my hand off his arm as easily as he might shake off a fly. "The famous brother, I take it."

"Indeed," said Angeline. Her face was flushed. She glared at him, her chin held high. "You may take your leave, sir, at once."

"As Beauty commands," he said, and bowed mockingly. "But I shall only say *au revoir*, rather than *farewell*. You see, I am on my way to Bath as well. I am certain – I am entirely certain – that we shall see each other there. And when we do meet again, I shall know your name."

He strolled down the passageway and out of the front door at an unhurried pace.

As soon as the door closed behind him, Angeline turned on Charles. "Could you possibly have taken any longer?"

He blinked at us. "The private room's all sorted out," he said. "It's just upstairs. The thing is..." He lowered his voice confidentially. "I'm in a bit of a fix, and I wondered – could I possibly borrow a few shillings from one of you? You see, there's a matter of honour I have to attend to, and I've used up all my own money, so—"

"No!" Angeline said. "Good God, Charles, you really are hopeless. If you hadn't run yourself into debt, I daresay you'd still be in there, wouldn't you? I might have known it."

"Yes, but you see, if I don't pay..."

"Here," I said, and reached into my reticule. Of course it was true that Charles was hopeless, but it was also true that he'd been talked into helping me out of my own troubles a thousand times before. I fixed him with a Serious Look. "You can have three shillings. But you can only use them to pay your debt, all right? If you try to gamble more with them, I will tell Stepmama, and then—"

"I won't," he said hastily. "You're a good sort, Kat. I'll pay you back when I can, I promise."

"Ha," said Angeline. "Where exactly is this private room you've found for us, Charles?"

"Oh, that's upstairs. First door on the left – landlord says you couldn't miss it. But look here..." His brows knitted into an expression of unusual gravity as he looked at Angeline. "That fellow I saw you with – that was Scarwood, wasn't it?"

"Viscount Scarwood, yes." Angeline scowled. "He introduced himself. You were nowhere in sight, much to everyone's surprise, and so—"

"But look here, Angeline, that was *Scarwood*."

"Yes, we've covered that point quite sufficiently, I think."

"But I say..." He shook his head. "Scarwood's a bad sort. I've heard stories you wouldn't like to know about him."

"I'm sure we wouldn't." Angeline took my arm. "Come, Kat."

"Well, if Stepmama had seen you, you would be in even more trouble than you already are," Charles said. "The man's a rake. If she thought you were encouraging him, she'd have one of her spasms. So you'd better stay well away from him from now on, if you know what's good for you."

"You don't say." Angeline's eyes gleamed with sudden interest. The sight filled me with dread. Charles, of course, didn't notice – he was already turning away, with my shillings held firmly in his hand. But I was watching, and I saw the slow, dangerous smile spread across Angeline's face. "Thank you, Charles," she said. "For once, you've been exceedingly helpful."

CHAPTER SEVEN

WE RODE INTO BATH IN A HIRED CARRIAGE THAT WOULD have put Squire Briggs's best travelling carriage to shame. The dark blue paint was so glossy, it positively glowed in the bright September sunlight; the four chestnut horses pranced in perfect time. I had no idea how Stepmama had found such an elegant equipage in so short a time, in an unfamiliar town – or how on earth she and Papa had managed to afford it – but Stepmama in the grip of an icy rage was a force that could move mountains, to say nothing of carriages. The poor owner of the carriage-hire was probably still quaking in his boots a full hour later as the spires of Bath rose before us.

If Stepmama had let me, I would have pressed my hands and face to the window to soak it all in. Charles might say all he liked about Bath being a mere spa town and nothing to compare with London itself (where he'd spent all of two days, three years ago), but I'd never seen so large a city in my life. Tall buildings of light-coloured stone loomed around us as we drove through the clustered streets. The wide pavements swarmed with promenading ladies and gentlemen wearing fashions I'd never even seen before. Even through the glass windows of the carriage, the overpowering stench of the city itself nearly choked me.

Our carriage finally came to a halt in the middle of a circle of massive pale stone town houses, each lined with its own set of imposing pillars, like dozens of Greek temples from one of Papa's books, all smashed together into four long, curving buildings. The whole circle of town houses looped smoothly around a patch of parkland scarcely larger than our own back garden at home.

"The Circus," Stepmama announced to the carriage at large. I noticed fresh spots of colour high on her cheeks. She spoke more rapidly than usual. "Not the Royal Crescent itself, unfortunately, but still one of the very most fashionable addresses in Bath. Very few people could ever afford to live here."

I looked out of the window at the sweeping curve of town houses. "Then how can we afford to?"

"You may consider yourselves extremely fortunate in my family connections," Stepmama said, and sailed out of the carriage with a martial look in her eye.

I stifled a groan. "We're staying with Stepmama's best relatives?" I whispered to Angeline. "But we've never even met them. They can't have invited us. They didn't even care enough to send congratulations for Elissa's wedding!"

"Think about this," Angeline murmured back. "Even if Stepmama bothered to ask for an invitation before we left, how could she have received any response?"

"You mean – they might not even know yet that we're coming?"

"Even if they do know by now, they certainly weren't given any choice in the matter, were they?"

"Oh Lord!" I said, and looked at Papa. The melancholy look on his face was even more pronounced than usual. "Papa, is that true? We weren't even invited?"

He only winced in response.

"Oh, jolly good," Charles drawled. "Wake me when it's all over, will you?" He closed his eyes, crossed his arms and settled himself more firmly into the cushions of the carriage. A thick hank of blonde hair fell over his eyes, shielding him even more.

"Girls!" Stepmama snapped, through the carriage doorway. "Hurry!"

Angeline smoothed down her gown, adjusted the tilt of her bonnet, and stepped out onto the pavement with the air of a rather bored visiting princess. I scrambled after her, clutching my reticule.

Even for Stepmama, this sounded like a challenge.

Bright sunshine bounced off all the windows in the closest town house so I couldn't see inside. "Let's hope they're not out of town right now," I said.

"Let's hope they didn't leave town when they heard we were coming," Angeline added.

"That is quite enough from both of you," said Stepmama.

The pavement was crowded with ladies carrying parasols and gentlemen carrying elaborate quizzing glasses – a reminder of Lord Ravenscroft that I didn't need, especially not as we prepared to meet Stepmama's most snobbish relations. All the promenaders watched with undisguised curiosity as Charles and Papa followed us out of the carriage, Charles wearing his most particularly blank expression – retreating, as usual, from any scene of potential conflict. Of course, none of our observers could speak to us without a proper introduction, but I heard the whispers of speculation rise around us as we approached the front door.

No wonder Stepmama had wanted us to arrive in an impressive conveyance... but with our clothes cut in such different fashions to those of the ladies around us, no one could possibly miss the fact that we were country cousins. If Stepmama's relations turned us away at the door, we would certainly provide a good day's gossip for the crowd outside.

Stepmama nodded to Papa, and he stepped forward with sagging shoulders to rap the great brass knocker on the town house's front door. I felt the eyes of the whole crowd fixed upon us as a black-clad butler opened the door. He looked like a relic from the last century with his powdered white wig, but his shoulders were impressively bulky under his uniform, and he stepped forward to block the door as if he were protecting the king himself. I thought that unless Stepmama had taken secret wrestling lessons of her own, we might have difficulty getting past him.

Papa coughed apologetically and held out a calling card. "The, ah, Reverend George Stephenson, Mrs Stephenson, Mr Stephenson, Miss Stephenson and Miss Katherine Stephenson..." As the butler's thick, reddish-brown eyebrows rose higher and higher, Papa's voice ran down into an embarrassed mumble, "... here to present their compliments to Mrs Wingate and her family."

"They are expecting us," Stepmama added, in a much louder voice.

The butler looked down his large nose at both of them. "I'm afraid Mrs Wingate is not at home to visitors."

"I told you they might not be in town," I said.

Angeline's elbow jabbed into my ribs.

Stepmama said, "Nonsense. We are not visitors; we are

family. Come, girls." She took Papa's arm and dragged him with her as she plunged straight ahead.

"Madam!" the butler began.

But it was too late. Stepmama might look slender beside him, but she was powered by sheer, undiluted determination. She shouldered against him, and the tall, feathered plumes from her bonnet poked him directly in the eye. He stumbled back, and she swept triumphantly into the foyer of the town house.

She hadn't needed wrestling lessons after all.

It was obvious, though, that the butler needed lessons in dealing with her. For all his height and bulk, he stood gaping at her like a ninny as she pulled Papa past him. "Madam—!"

"I said come, girls," Stepmama snapped to me and Angeline. Only then did she turn back to the glaring butler. "I have already explained to you that we are expected. Why have you not yet gone to inform your mistress that we've arrived?"

"Why, indeed?" Angeline murmured softly. Behind us, Charles let out a humourless bark of laughter, quickly stifled.

Angeline and I stepped together into the wide foyer. It was wallpapered in a rich, garnet red, and both the floor and the staircase beyond were made of marble, making it feel more like a palace than a house. Charles followed us inside, sighing, and closed the door behind him, shutting out the watching crowd.

The butler's entire face turned as red as an apple beneath his white wig. "As I told you, Madam, Mrs Wingate is not expecting any visitors!"

"And I told you that we are family." Stepmama drew herself up to her full height. "Mrs Wingate will not be pleased when I report your insolence."

He glared at her. "I know of no Stephensons in Mrs Wingate's family."

"That," Stepmama said, "shows how shamefully little you know of your employer. Now, will you announce us to her or must we announce ourselves?"

His mouth opened and closed twice without uttering a word. Then he swung on his heel and stalked towards the staircase, his shoes echoing on the marble floor. "Wait here," he snapped. As he walked up the stairs, every inch of his back and neck vibrated with outrage.

At the top of the staircase, he disappeared behind a closed door, and the five of us were left alone in the grand foyer. Charles shook his head and propped his shoulders against the garnet wallpaper, closing his eyes. Papa shrank in on himself even more.

Stepmama said, "Well! I shall have to speak with my cousin about the quality of her servants."

Angeline didn't say a word, but the expression on her face spoke for her.

I swung my reticule from my arm and turned in a circle to properly take in the foyer around me. After all, it was the grandest place I'd ever been – and this would probably be my last chance to see it.

The door at the top of the staircase opened. The butler strode out, looking as sour as if he'd just bitten into a lemon.

"Mrs Wingate will see you," he announced.

Stepmama raised her eyebrows at him. "Are you not going to take our coats and bonnets first?"

Even Angeline winced. I wouldn't have been surprised if the butler had let out a snarl. Instead, after one frozen moment, he set his jaw and walked back down the stairs, his bearing rigidly correct.

I unbuttoned my pelisse and untied the strings of my

bonnet as hastily as I could. There was no point asking for trouble.

Once the butler had finally disposed of all three pelisses, three bonnets and two greatcoats – handling them with obvious distaste, as if he were instead being forced to carry ladies' undergarments – Stepmama gave him a grim smile.

"Now," she said, "we are ready."

But I recognised that glittering look in her eyes as sheer bravado. It was one thing to overawe a butler, and quite another to over-awe the sort of person who owned a house like this – the sort of person Stepmama herself had always longed to be.

I wondered how long, exactly, it would be before we were packed together in the stagecoach once again, heading back to Yorkshire. I hoped it would be long enough to eat a proper meal first.

We followed the butler up the staircase, Charles and Papa trailing last in line. As the butler opened the door to a large, bright sitting room, his face smoothed back into its original expression of aloof dignity.

"The Reverend George Stephenson," he intoned. "Mrs Stephenson..." His upper lip lifted in a sneer. "And family."

Well, that was us. I curtseyed as deeply as I could without falling over. In my first, quick glance around the room, I'd seen a middle-aged lady on a sofa, two girls at a round table and a footman standing at rigid attention by the tall windows across the room. Now, with my head lowered, all I could see were splashes of sunlight across the luxuriant Persian carpet, exotic Egyptian-styled wooden sofa legs and the middle-aged lady's slippered feet, poking out from beneath her skirts. Her slippers were made of olive-coloured silk and looked as if they'd never been worn before.

"Mrs Stephenson," Mrs Wingate said, in a tone that rivalled even her butler's for haughtiness. "I received your surprising letter this morning."

"Cousin Caroline..." Stepmama started across the Persian carpet, hands outstretched. "How lovely it is to see you again after so many years!"

From the expression on Mrs Wingate's long, heavy-jowelled face, Stepmama might as well have been a rat scurrying across the expensive carpet towards her.

A slow burn started in my stomach, working upwards. Stepmama might be... well, herself... but she didn't deserve to be looked at the way her cousin was looking at her now. No one did.

I looked past the sofa to the round table where the two girls sat. The younger one looked no older than me and she was watching us with open curiosity. I didn't mind that. But the older girl wore a smile that made me want to punch her.

It took Stepmama a moment to realise that Mrs Wingate was not going to take her outstretched hands. Her smile sagged. Her arms lowered. And I made a decision.

I had disliked Stepmama's snobbish relations ever since she'd first opened her mouth to brag about them, approximately two hours after she'd arrived in our vicarage, five years ago. I had certainly never wanted to stay with them.

But I would be dashed if I'd allow them to crush her without a fight.

So before Stepmama could say a word, I said in my sweetest and most innocent voice, "What a very lovely room this is."

It was as if a piece of furniture had spoken out loud. Mrs Wingate's eyebrows rose in surprise, but she didn't even bother to look at me. "Have you encouraged your stepdaughter to be so forward, at her age?" she asked Stepmama.

Stepmama said, "Katherine—"

"Why, this is a much finer house than Lady Fotherington claimed," I said. "I wonder what she could have been thinking to say such rude things about it?"

"I beg your pardon?" Mrs Wingate's head snapped around with the speed of a striking snake. "What did you say?"

"Pardon me," I said, and curtseyed again. "Stepmama always tells me I am much too forward. I shan't say another word, I promise."

Angeline made a choking sound and turned away. Stepmama looked as if she'd seen a ghost.

"Please forgive my youngest stepdaughter, Cousin," she said. "It has been a long journey for a girl her age, and—"

Mrs Wingate waved her to silence without a glance. "What exactly did Lady Fotherington say to you about my house?" she demanded.

I peeked up from beneath demurely lowered eyelashes. "May I speak?" I asked Stepmama.

She raised one hand to her head. "Oh—"

"It's only that I was so surprised," I said to Mrs Wingate. "I don't know how Lady Fotherington came to be so mistaken about your house and your good taste. Why, when I told her we would be staying here, she said... well, I don't think it would be polite to say exactly what she said." I shot a pointed glance at the butler behind us. "Not in front of the servants."

Mrs Wingate's heavy jaw worked up and down. "Why—"

"I am so glad to see that she was wrong," I said. "She had been quite concerned that your house wouldn't be an appropriate place for us to stay, you see, if we wanted to meet really good company in Bath. Why, she even said we might be better off in a hotel if we wished to make a good impression on Society."

Mrs Wingate stared at me. "How could you possibly have had such a conversation? What relation is Lady Fotherington to you?"

I opened my mouth to answer. But Angeline spoke before me. "Why, Madam," she said, with limpid sincerity. "Do you not know who my sister's godmother is?"

Stepmama made a strangled noise in the back of her throat. Papa let out a desperate series of coughs. Charles put one hand to his mouth as if to stifle a yawn... but I could have sworn I saw a grin pulling at the edges of his mouth.

The two girls at the round table began to whisper heatedly.

I smiled sweetly at Mrs Wingate.

It wasn't surprising at all that she didn't know who my godmother was. After all, as far as I knew, I was the only member of my family who didn't have one.

"Well," she said. "Well. Well, really. I don't know..."

I said, "If now is a poor time for you to receive visitors, pray don't distress yourself. Lady Fotherington did so want us to have a good introduction to Bath, and if you don't think you would be able to—"

"Nonsense!" said Mrs Wingate. She was breathing heavily. "Nonsense. We are more than capable of hosting visitors. And you are not guests; you are family. Lady Fotherington – your godmama will soon realise her error, I am sure, when she sees what a successful visit you two girls have had."

"Thank you, ma'am," I said, and curtseyed. "I am sure she will be pleased to hear it."

And truly, if I had had a godmother, I was sure she would have been pleased.

Stepmama's voice came out as a croak. "Cousin – Mrs Wingate – I must apologise and explain—"

"Never mind any of that," Mrs Wingate said. "You have all had a long journey, I daresay, and you'll want rest and refreshment before anything else. Jonathan!" The footman stepped forward. "Show Reverend and Mrs Stephenson and their son to their rooms, and tell Cook to send up food for them as quickly as possible. And perhaps... yes." She glanced over to the round table. "My own daughters will be pleased to show Miss Stephenson and Miss Katherine to their room."

The younger girl smiled and bounced up from her seat, abandoning her sewing. The older one scowled and took as long as she could to neatly fold and put away her work before she rose.

"Well, Kat," Angeline breathed into my ear. "Now you've done it."

CHAPTER EIGHT

I WOKE EARLY THE NEXT MORNING TO THE SOUND OF wheels rattling down the cobblestoned street outside. Men's voices called back and forth to each other, and a high-pitched boy's voice cried out the same word over and over again.

"Mi-ilk! Mi-ilk! Mi-i-ilk!..."

Footsteps sounded in the servants' attic just above our room, and doors opened and closed. I jumped out of bed and hurried to the window seat. Angeline groaned and buried her face in her pillow.

In the dim grey light before dawn, the street outside was filled with people – not the promenading crowd of fashion this time, but men driving heavy carts full of goods, women haggling with them over prices and a boy swinging buckets of milk from both arms. I could have curled up in the window seat and watched the passing crowd all morning long. But I had more important matters to sort out first.

I tucked my knees under my chin, wrapped my arms around my legs for warmth and courage, and took a deep breath. I was about to do something almost no one in my family ever dared to do: wake Angeline from her sleep.

"Angeline!" I said.

She snarled something unintelligible into her pillow and didn't move.

"Angeline," I repeated. "Wake up!"

Growling, she flung herself onto her back and regarded me through slitted dark eyes. "What?" she said. "Tell me, Kat. What could be so earth-shatteringly important that you have to wake me before it's even light outside?"

"It's the only chance we'll have to talk alone today," I said. "Unless you want to do it in front of the Wingate sisters?"

"Heaven forbid. Maria Wingate would sneer and save up all the juicy details to tattle to her mother, and Lucy would probably giggle herself to death from sheer vapidity." Angeline dragged herself up to her elbows and glared at me. "So. Have we talked long enough? Can I go back to sleep now?"

I gritted my teeth. "No. We have to come up with a plan. What are we going to do?"

"About the Wingates? Sigh and bear them, I expect, since you had to jump in and trick them into inviting us."

"Not about them," I said. "About Stepmama. If you don't find a fiancé before we leave Bath—"

Angeline's voice turned ice-cold. "Don't even consider it."

"Well, obviously you're not going to betray Mr Carlyle that way," I said. "I'm not stupid, you know."

"Hmm," said Angeline, and lay back against her pillow. "Well, now that we've made that important decision, I'm going to—"

"Listen to me!" I said. "When you don't find a fiancé, Stepmama is going to think she has to carry through on that ridiculous threat to expel you from the family."

"'Has to carry through'?" Angeline repeated, one eyebrow arching. "She doesn't have to do anything. Are you actually taking her side in this?"

"No," I said. "Of course not. But she would never have made any such threat if you hadn't worked her up into too much of a rage to think clearly."

"Ah. So it's all my fault. How strange that I never thought of asking you for advice on how to handle Stepmama. Silly me. Somehow, I'd completely failed to notice you handling her any better."

"That's not what matters now," I said. "We have to come up with a plan. I was thinking—"

"*We* don't have to do any such thing," Angeline said. "I have never asked you for advice in my life, and I certainly don't plan to start now. I'll handle this by myself."

I glared at her. "So what exactly are you planning to do? Let yourself be thrown out, just to prove you have more pride than she does?"

"If you actually think that's likely, you don't know me well at all." Angeline stretched and settled herself more comfortably in the bed. "I have my own plans, which you needn't concern yourself with."

"Your own plans?" I said. "Oh, well, those will end well, then. Just like the last ones you made. No need for me to worry, then, is there?"

Colour flared in Angeline's cheeks. She pushed herself back up to glare at me. "Just because you've been chosen as some sort of magical Guardian and think yourself so terribly important and high above the rest of us now—"

"I don't," I said, "but—"

"No? What was all that at Elissa's wedding, then? When I tried to cast a spell on Mrs Carlyle, you had to step in and stop me as if—"

"You don't understand!" I said. "Mrs Carlyle had her information from Lady Fotherington. She's friends with Lady Fotherington."

"So?"

"So, didn't you wonder how Lady Fotherington knew all about your earlier spells?" I said. "She's not just a Society leader. She's a Guardian!"

Angeline stared at me. Her flushed cheeks turned pale. "You stopped me from casting that spell because Lady Fotherington is another Guardian? Because she's a member of your stupid little Order?"

"That's not it," I said. "But if she saw—"

"You took her side against me," Angeline said. "I can't believe it. Ever since they chose you instead of me as a Guardian—"

"They didn't choose me," I said. "I inherited the powers from Mama. Lady Fotherington didn't like it, but they all had to accept..." I stumbled to a halt.

They hadn't accepted it in the end, had they? But I couldn't force the words out. To admit to Angeline how stupid I'd been – how I'd ruined my chances there, too...

"So you don't want to make them angry now," she said. "Oh, well done, Kat. Very loyal indeed. No wonder you've been acting so concerned about my situation. You think you can make up for betraying me at the church by solving all my problems yourself now, do you?"

"That isn't—"

"Enough!" she said. "We are not going to talk about this anymore. Even if I'd ever considered letting you help me with my scheme, I certainly wouldn't now. And you can tell that to your whole precious Order, if you like!"

She pulled the covers up over her head and flipped herself away from me.

⋆✦ ✦⋆

Four hours later, Angeline still wasn't speaking to me. Luckily, neither of us was expected to make conversation. We had both been bundled out of the house by Stepmama at barely eight o'clock, carrying umbrellas against the lightly falling rain. Squeezing around other walkers on the crowded pavement, we followed Mrs Wingate, Stepmama, Papa, a desperately yawning Charles and both Wingate sisters down the curving street towards something called the Pump Room. Despite the grey skies and early hour, Stall Street was already packed with other ladies and gentlemen in their finest clothing, all heading in the same direction.

"You may well stare, Miss Katherine," Maria Wingate said loudly. "I can imagine that to country eyes such as your own, the sight of so much high fashion must be dazzling indeed."

I snorted. Luckily, Stepmama was too far ahead of us to hear me. "I was only surprised that they were all awake," I said. "I thought fashionable people always slept until noon." I narrowed my eyes at her through the grey veil of rain that fell between our umbrellas. "Or perhaps that's only in cities like London – really fashionable places."

Maria's thin cheeks flushed with angry colour. But before she could reply, her younger sister broke in.

"London!" Lucy Wingate breathed. "Oh, how I long to go back to London! It is the only place in the world where life is worth living. Do you not agree, Miss Katherine?"

I blinked. "Well..."

"I would be surprised if Miss Katherine has ever been to London, Lucy." Maria's lips pursed into a smirk. "You mustn't embarrass her by asking such revealing questions."

"I am not embarrassed," I said. "But you never answered my question. Why is everyone awake and dressed already? What could be so important?"

Lucy was the one who answered me, her big blue eyes wide and shocked. "But don't you know? It's the Pump Room. Everyone goes to the Pump Room in the mornings."

"Why?"

"Well..." She looked as helpless as if I'd asked her to explain why the rain clouds were grey or the grass green. "It's the Pump Room!"

"Perhaps you are not aware, Miss Katherine," Maria said, "but the waters of Bath are renowned for their healing powers. At the Pump Room, one takes a restorative glass of water every morning for one's health."

I looked at the well-dressed, chattering stream of people all around us, exchanging nods and bows with acquaintances across the street. "None of them look ill."

"You will soon adapt to the ways of fashionable society, I am sure," said Maria. "In the meantime, you will simply have to take my word for it that no one of any consequence would ever allow themselves to sleep late in Bath."

"No one?" Angeline said. It was a shock to hear her speak; she'd held herself rigidly apart for the entire walk until now. If she was willing to start talking again, she couldn't be too enraged anymore... could she?

"No one," Maria repeated.

"Hmm," said Angeline. Her lips curved into a smile. "How very interesting."

Oh Lord. I knew that look, and I wasn't relieved after all.

Streams of people from all directions converged on a broad, cobbled square marked off from Stall Street by a colonnade of tall stone pillars. A great stone church – Bath Abbey – stood at the far end of the square, surrounded by little wooden shops that leaned against its strong walls. Mrs Wingate led us between the broad pillars of the colonnade to a massive building just inside the square, with Grecian laurels carved in stone above its doors.

The cobblestones before it seethed with people heading for the front doors in a positive sea of fashion. Red uniforms stood out like points of flame. Back in our Yorkshire village, the war against France had seemed very far away, but here there were military officers sprinkled all throughout the crowd, with plumed bicorn hats and swords by their sides. The tall peacock feather in Mrs Wingate's hat bobbed like a flag for us to follow as she forged her way through the mass of people.

As we squeezed through the crowd in the foyer to give our umbrellas to the waiting attendants, Lucy Wingate leaned over to whisper in my ear. "Miss Katherine – I am afraid you will think me terribly forward – might I dare to ask you a perfectly shocking question?"

I darted a glance at the others, but none of them had noticed. "Of course," I whispered back.

"I must ask – oh, dear..." Lucy blurted out the words in a sudden rush: "Is your brother Charles betrothed to any young lady yet?"

I stared at her. "Charles?"

My voice came out at normal volume and Lucy leaped backwards, squeaking. Charles glanced back at me in sleepy curiosity. I shook my head at him and he turned away, shrugging.

"No," I whispered. "Of course he isn't. But—"

"Oh, Miss Katherine, you are an angel of kindness to tell me so!" Lucy said. "But I can scarcely believe it to be true. When a young man is so, so handsome and charming and so—"

"*Charles?!*" I repeated. But at least I managed to whisper it, this time.

"Girls!" Mrs Wingate called, and gestured commandingly.

Lucy squeezed my hand. "We must talk later!" she hissed. Then she hurried ahead to join her mother.

I followed her into the big, open main room, my head whirling.

Tall windows lined the opposite wall, flanked by elegant white pillars and benches, but they might as well have been miles away; the press of the crowd was far too intense for me to possibly reach them. Bonnet feathers bobbed madly in the air as a group of middle-aged matrons congregated around Mrs Wingate. Papa hung back, looking pained. Charles had already disappeared.

"Of course, you all already know my own daughters," Mrs Wingate said to the group of ladies. "But may I present my cousin's daughters to you? Miss Stephenson" – Angeline curtseyed, her eyes demurely lowered – "and Miss Katherine Stephenson."

I bobbed a curtsey and wondered whether she would bother to introduce any of the ladies to us. But Mrs Wingate was already leaning forward and dropping her voice to confidential tones.

"You must know, Miss Katherine is the goddaughter of Lady Fotherington herself. She particularly desired Miss Katherine and her sister to have the finest introduction to Bath society."

"Lady Fotherington!"

"Oh, my!"

"My goodness!"

"What a charming girl, indeed," said the fourth lady, and they all beamed at me.

Stepmama looked ready to swoon from sheer anguish.

"And how is dear Lady Fotherington, Mrs Stephenson?" the tallest lady asked her.

"Well..." Stepmama swallowed visibly. "Last time I saw her, she was quite well..."

I had to bite my lip to hold back laughter. I didn't want to incite Stepmama into a Spasm right in the middle of the Pump Room.

The ladies were all looking at me again. "Miss Katherine must be too young to be presented to Society yet...?"

"Oh, yes," Stepmama said hastily. "She is still only twelve. She has at least five years to wait for her début."

Thank goodness, she might as well have added, judging by her tone. I restrained myself from rolling my eyes. Stepmama couldn't dread my début any more than I did.

"Her sister, however" – Stepmama directed a penetrating glare at Angeline – "will be making her Society début here in Bath."

Instead of arguing, Angeline smiled. I could see that Stepmama wasn't relieved by that smile, either.

Luckily, none of the ladies around us knew Angeline's smiles the way Stepmama and I did. "How exciting it must all seem to her," said the oldest lady. "And with such a pretty face and figure – brunettes are quite the rage this year, you know, and if her dowry...?" Her voice trailed off suggestively.

Stepmama lowered her own voice and leaned forward. "Her brother-in-law, Mr Peregrine Collingwood, has been kind enough to settle quite substantial dowries upon both girls," she murmured.

"Ah." All four of the ladies rustled with pleasure. "Well, then..."

'Substantial' wasn't the word Stepmama had used before, when she'd told us about the dowries. I slid a glance at Angeline, but she wasn't looking at me – or at anyone else in our group, for that matter. Her eyelids were lowered discreetly, but I could have sworn she was searching the crowd around us for someone in particular. I frowned.

"If you would excuse us," Angeline said, "Kat has been suffering from a headache this morning, and I am told the water of Bath..."

"Of course, my dear." Mrs Wingate smiled upon us both. "You will find the water being sold by the pump, over there. Meanwhile, I must take your stepmama and papa to sign the guestbook so that the Master of Ceremonies will know you've all arrived."

"Thank you so much," Angeline murmured in her sweetest tone. She closed her fingers around my arm in a grip of steel. "Come, Kat. I'm sure your head will feel much better soon."

I let her lead me away, but as soon as we were out of hearing range, I said, "Why couldn't you be the one with the headache? Stepmama knows I wouldn't be so missish."

Angeline was openly scanning the crowd now, in a way that both Stepmama and Elissa would have condemned as horribly improper and unladylike. She didn't bother to look at me as she replied. "Yes, but Stepmama would have been far more suspicious if I'd tried to leave on my own. That's why I couldn't leave you behind, much as I might like to."

"Hmm," I said. "I can tell you're scheming something,

but if you don't explain it to me, I won't be able to help you with Stepmama."

Angeline's voice chilled. "Have you already forgotten what you admitted to me this morning? Trust me, Kat, I wouldn't accept your help in a thousand years, even if you went down on your knees to beg forgiveness."

I yanked my arm away. "That is never going to happen."

"Well, then." Angeline led me to the pump where glasses of water were being sold. "Drink your water and leave me alone." She slammed a glass into my hand.

I sniffed the cloudy water and wrinkled my nose. Healing properties, indeed! It smelled like rotten eggs, and bubbles popped across its surface. I forced myself to take a dainty sip, though, and didn't let myself gag on the rancid, sulphur-flavoured heat of it. Instead, I smiled as sweetly as Angeline herself could have done, and offered her the glass.

"Mmm," I said. "Delicious. You should really try some. It might do wonders for your temper."

The crowd was shifting behind and around us, suffocatingly close on all sides. The Wingates hadn't been exaggerating after all – everyone in Bath Society must have been in attendance. It was a struggle to stay next to Angeline as we moved away from the water fountain, but I was determined not to let her leave me behind – especially when I saw her eyes light up in triumph. She started forward. I pressed after her.

A gentleman's elbow knocked straight into my arm, tipping the water glass askew.

Warm water splashed across my gown and soaked through the reticule that hung from my wrist.

"I do beg your pardon," said a familiar voice. "I – Good God! Miss Katherine!"

I turned. My mouth fell open. I was facing my erstwhile tutor, Mr Gregson...

And a familiar, magical heat was suddenly emanating from my reticule.

Mama's magic mirror had reawakened.

CHAPTER NINE

"WHAT ARE YOU DOING HERE?" I BLURTED. THE RETICULE was radiating heat against my arm, and I was caught between joy and terror. If Mr Gregson realised what had just happened...

"I might ask the same of you." He adjusted his spectacles and looked around. "Your sisters – your stepmother—"

"Elissa is on her wedding trip, touring the Lake District. Angeline..." I bit my lip. Angeline had disappeared into the crowd. I couldn't spot even a glimpse of her dark head anymore.

Worse yet, at any moment the golden glow of the newly awakened mirror might shine through the thin, beaded reticule. Feeling its heat was the best thing that had happened to me since Elissa's wedding, but it was also the worst timed. If Mr Gregson realised it had returned to its former power, would he feel required to report it to Lord Ravenscroft?

I tucked the reticule into my side, holding my arms tight against it, and gestured with my empty water glass to distract him. "Angeline is here, too. And Stepmama. *And* Papa and Charles."

"Indeed." My former tutor looked perturbed. "You dragged all of them here with you?"

"I didn't drag them. They dragged me. After Mrs Carlyle ruined Elissa's wedding, Stepmama decided—"

"My dear girl," Mr Gregson said, "I do hope you think too highly of me to try fobbing me off with one of your usual wild stories. They may deceive everyone else of your acquaintance, but—"

"What wild stories?" I said. Then I thought of a few he'd heard me tell since we'd met and the one I'd told Mrs Wingate just yesterday. "Oh. Well, I know the kind of stories you mean, but—"

"Can you truly expect me to believe it mere coincidence that you should appear now, just after Lord Ravenscroft's arrival in Bath?"

"Lord Ravenscroft!" I cursed the shifting crowd of people around me. Anyone could be lurking in this packed room, hidden from view until it was too late. My arm tightened around my reticule, despite its heat. "Where—?"

"You should not have come, Katherine." Mr Gregson shook his head. "I understand your reasoning, but you are too impetuous. You will only alienate him further by pursuing him in such an immodest fashion, and just when he is in the middle of managing a crisis."

I snorted and raised myself up on tiptoe to peer through the crowd. "Trust me, I have no intention of pursuing him."

"If you wish to have any hope of someday being restored to membership in the Order—"

"I do!" I snapped my full attention back to Mr Gregson, and landed back on the flats of my feet with a thud. "Can I? Is it even possible?"

"Probably not," Mr Gregson said. "I said nothing before because I did not wish to raise your hopes in vain. I can only hope to eventually persuade Lord Ravenscroft to relent – in two or three years, at the very earliest – if he can be convinced that you have become truly subdued, grown into ladylike propriety and self-control, and sincerely regretful of your immoderate temper. Or in other words, if you can refrain from irritating him any further in the meantime." He gave me a stern look. "If he sees you here now, having followed him to argue your case even though his decision was already declared to be final..."

And pretending to be Lady Fotherington's goddaughter, I added silently. I winced. "What can I do?"

"Go home," he said. "Today, if possible. Before any more harm can be done."

"I can't do that." I slumped, hugging the reticule to my side. "Stepmama would never allow it."

Mr Gregson coughed meaningfully. "Your sudden sense of filial obedience, while admirable, is hardly well timed."

"You don't understand. It's different this time. She's in a rage, and if Angeline doesn't – oh Lord!"

The crowd had shifted yet again, and through the gossiping groups, one couple was left directly in my line of sight: Angeline... and the person she must have been looking for ever since we'd arrived.

Viscount Scarwood.

"I have to go," I said, and hurried forward without waiting for Mr Gregson's reply.

The crowd continued to shift around me as I moved and I lost sight of my quarry. But I knew their direction now and pushed my way through the groups, using my elbows when I needed to and ignoring the gasps and imprecations in my wake. All my worst fears had been confirmed by that one glimpse: Angeline listening to Viscount Scarwood with her eyelashes lowered, her hands modestly clasped... and a smile tugging at her lips.

I was almost certain I knew what her scheme was, now. It was the worst one she had thought up yet.

As I came up behind them, I heard Viscount Scarwood drawl, "Did you really expect not to see me here? After such an unforgettable encounter?"

"Unforgettable?" Angeline said. "But, my lord, I am afraid I had already forgotten it."

"Then I shall have to remind you." His big hand reached out. In defiance of every law of propriety, I could see he was about to touch her cheek.

She did not step away from him.

I pushed myself between them before his fingers could reach her skin. "Angeline," I said, "Stepmama wants you."

"Ah. The ferocious younger sister." I didn't have to look at Viscount Scarwood to know that he was smirking.

I ignored him. "Stepmama—"

"I heard you the first time," Angeline said. "And it is pure nonsense. Stepmama is busy gossiping with a dozen of Mrs Wingate's closest friends, and the last thing she wants is for me to interrupt them."

"How foolish of her. But her loss shall be my gain." Viscount Scarwood offered Angeline his arm. "Will you have pity on me and grant me a promenade around the room, so I may attempt to make a more lasting impression upon you, now that I finally know your name? *Angeline?*"

"'Miss Stephenson' would be a more proper way to address me," Angeline murmured.

"Ah, but we all know what you think of propriety and Society, don't we?"

"Angeline!" I said. "Stepmama wants—"

Angeline took Viscount Scarwood's arm and smiled dazzlingly. "Then you may tell her exactly where I am. Goodbye, Kat."

They sailed forward together and were swallowed by the crowd. Maddeningly, my glare didn't burn even the smallest hole in either of their backs.

Charles's voice spoke over my head a moment later. "I say, Kat. I'm moving on from here – dashed dull place, this. You'll tell Stepmama I made my apologies, won't you?"

"You've found somewhere to gamble," I said flatly. I didn't bother to look up at him. I was still glaring in the direction Angeline and Scarwood had gone. Some of the people in my line of sight were starting to look askance at me, but I didn't care.

"No! I say. Nothing of the sort." Charles sounded positively lively with indignation. "I'm off to look at a couple of horses, that's all. There are some fellows here from Oxford, and they're offering—"

"Never mind," I said. I knew for a fact that Charles couldn't afford even a single horse of his own, but I wasn't in the mood to debate it with him. I had watched my older brother walk around in a daze for the last three months, ever since he'd been sent home from Oxford, and nothing I had tried had helped him. Now he'd finally woken up... but only because he'd met the same friends who'd got him into trouble in the first place! Well, if he honestly preferred the idiots who'd taught him to drink and gamble to his own family... I took a deep, steadying breath. "If Stepmama asks me, I'll tell her what you said."

"You're a good sort, Kat." He started to turn away, then

stopped. "Oh, by the way, I thought I ought to mention – I saw that fellow Scarwood making up to Angeline again, and she didn't seem to be discouraging him, exactly. I'd have a word with her, if I were you. If Stepmama sees them together..."

"I know," I said, through gritted teeth. "Thank you, Charles."

"Oh, well. Just thought I'd mention it." He disappeared into the crowd, leaving me alone and seething.

I had never missed Elissa so badly. If she were here, I could have let her be the one to worry about Angeline and lecture Charles and find a way to placate Stepmama. If she were here, she could be the tiresomely responsible one, while I did whatever I liked and laughed at her for being so proper and prissy. If she were here, Angeline would at least try to be discreet with her mad schemes, and even Charles would show some restraint, if only to avoid her scolds.

But Elissa wasn't here, and I couldn't take her place. I was making a mess of that just like I'd made a mess of my Guardianship. And I had had enough.

By now, the heat from my reticule had died down to mere warmth. I would be dashed if I'd waste any more of my time carrying messages to Stepmama from either of my siblings, or trying to turn the tide by stopping them from getting into even more trouble. If they could be irresponsible, then so could I. I turned around and pushed my way straight through the crowd, out of the Pump Room, and into the privacy of the ladies' retiring room.

The reticule was still damp, and the warmth of the retiring room only magnified the odour of rotten eggs from the spilled water, mingling with the disgusting stench of the cramped room itself. The 'convenience' inside wasn't a mere chamberpot, thank goodness – it was one of the fashionable newer models, where the waste was left in a covered copper pan afterwards – but with dozens of ladies passing through each morning, the smell rising from that pan into the tiny room was unutterably horrid. I reached into my reticule anyway, holding my breath. There were more important things than comfort right now.

Mama's golden mirror was covered in transparent pearls of water, and it was glowing for the first time in days. I closed my eyes for a moment in sheer relief. Then I had to take a breath, and the stench forced my eyes back open. The sooner I was in the Golden Hall, the sooner I'd be free from the smells around me. And if Stepmama wondered where I was... well, then, Angeline could be the one to scramble to make excuses for her sister, this time.

I rubbed the mirror on my dress to dry it off. I didn't think gold could be damaged by water, but water that smelled this bad was capable of anything. The glow had faded by the time the mirror was completely dry, but that didn't matter – the mirror glowed only when it was excited, and I wasn't surprised that its sudden reawakening when I'd bumped into Mr Gregson had overexcited it. I actually preferred it when the mirror was calm and efficient like this, working without attracting anyone else's attention. My own secret magic and my sole connection to Mama.

I cupped the rounded mirror in both my hands and took a deep breath. "I fixed it, Mama," I whispered. "I promised I would, and I did."

I pressed the clasp on the mirror's case. The lid flipped open.

Absolutely nothing happened.

CHAPTER TEN

I ALMOST DROPPED THE MIRROR ONTO THE DIRTY FLOOR of the retiring room. I remembered where I was only just in time to save it. In the mirror's reflection, my face looked flushed and dangerous. I could feel a scream of pure fury working its way up from my chest. Wouldn't it shock every one of Bath's fashionable residents if I let it out?

Instead, I glared at my reflection. *What had gone wrong?*

The mirror really had been awake. I knew it had, for all of Lord Ravenscroft's oaths and prohibitions. But something had put it to sleep again. I took a deep, calming breath and nearly gagged on the odours that filled my throat and nose. Before anything else, I had to get out of this room.

I tucked the mirror back into my reticule and marched out, head held high, past the line of fidgeting ladies in fashionable dress. The Pump Room was just as busy now as when I'd left. I slipped into the moving crowd, hoping to stay out of sight of Stepmama. I needed to think. The mirror had awakened when I'd bumped into Mr Gregson. So it was Mr Gregson who must have...

No. I came to a standstill at the realisation, and the couple behind me bumped into my back. I ignored them and they stepped around me, muttering to each other.

The mirror hadn't awakened when I'd bumped into Mr Gregson. It had awakened when he'd bumped into me and spilled my glass of stinky, restorative Bath water across my reticule. Then the glow of the mirror had faded when I'd wiped off the last drops.

I was on the wrong side of the room to buy more water and it would take me a good ten minutes to push my way back across the crowded floor. But I didn't have to wait that long to make my experiment... not if I was really committed to it.

I turned, narrowing my eyes, and surveyed the crowd around me. I saw a group of dowagers, promenading in a clump with their feathered hats nodding at each other; I saw three giggling girls, a little younger than Angeline, being escorted by three gentlemen with impossibly high, stiff cravats pushing their chins up to awkward angles; and I saw... oh, *perfect*.

I aimed myself like an arrow straight towards them: a couple of pinched-looking women with perfectly enormous, brightly coloured turbans and jewelled necklaces, holding full glasses of Bath water in their hands as they strolled side by side, sneering at the crowd around them. I caught fragments of their conversation on my way:

"She's worn that same gown at least four times in the last two weeks, poor thing, and it looked perfectly wretched on her the first time."

"Well, you can hardly expect a sense of fashion from

someone with her dreadful family origins. Her great-grandfather was in trade, you know, even if they don't want anyone else to remember that – ohhhh!"

I collided with both of them at once, my head turned in the opposite direction, as if I weren't looking where I was going. But I hit exactly where I meant to, and my gasp of pretended shock was easily drowned out by theirs.

"Oh! Outrageous!"

"Such unbearable clumsiness!"

The lady with the crimson turban cried, "It's all over my new gown!"

Well, that simply wasn't true. A few drops of water had spilled onto her gown, perhaps, but I'd taken careful aim, and both of their glasses of water had spilled all over me... and especially onto my reticule, which was perfectly sopping – and beginning to feel wonderfully warm.

I'd been right. The Bath water might taste worse than anything I'd ever drunk, and it might or might not be as curative as everybody seemed to think... but it was certainly magical nonetheless. This time I wasn't wiping off a single drop.

"So sorry," I said, and smiled brilliantly at both of the gabbling ladies as I turned to sail back to the retiring room.

A thin hand clamped around my shoulder with the force of iron. "Where do you think you're going, young lady?"

"Ah..." I met the furious gaze of the woman in the purple turban. "It's all over my dress," I said, and held out my arms to show her the evidence. "I have to find somewhere to dry it off."

"Not before I find your mother and tell her exactly what you've done!"

"It was an accident," I said. "I am terribly sorry."

"I am not interested in your excuses. A girl your age has

no right to be allowed out in public until she has proven herself capable of good behaviour. I have every intention of giving your mother a piece of my mind."

"And so shall I," the other lady added. Her giant crimson turban bobbled with the vigour of her nod.

I gritted my teeth. I didn't have time for this! "Couldn't I just buy you fresh glasses of water to replace the ones I spilled?"

"Enough!" Purple Turban snapped. "Lead us to your mother. Now!"

I sighed. "Very well," I said, as meekly as I could. I slumped my shoulders, letting resignation sag every line of my body. "This way," I said. "But please don't be too unkind. My mama has very weak nerves."

"Ha. I'm not surprised, with such a horrid child." Purple Turban's fingers loosened as I turned. "She must certainly be informed – what are you doing?"

I wrenched myself free and shot through the crowd.

"Come back here!" Purple Turban screeched.

I barrelled through the crush of people, ignoring the cries and sounds of outrage behind me. I aimed myself straight at the door. Two feet shy of it, a hand grasped my arm. I spun around.

It was Lucy Wingate, staring at me. "Why, Miss Katherine. Whatever is the matter? You look so – so—"

"The press of the crowd," I said. "Too much for me." I turned back to look, breathing hard. I couldn't see Purple or Crimson Turban, but the crowd was shifting restlessly and I didn't trust either of them to give up easily. "I'm afraid your sister was right. It was all a bit too much after country life."

"Oh, you poor thing." Lucy's eyes lit up. "But I have it! I've been wanting so badly to go back to the circulating library, but Maria has never been in the right mood. Would you care to accompany me there now, Miss Katherine?"

"To the what? Never mind." I swallowed as I caught sight of the top of a purple turban, only fifteen feet away and moving in my direction. "That sounds marvellous," I said. "Let's go. Now."

"I must tell Mama, first. And of course your stepmama."

"Fine," I said. "Thank you. I'll wait for you outside on Stall Street, while you tell them." I dived out of the door before she could answer. I didn't have my umbrella anymore, but I didn't care. I'd much rather risk the rain than Purple Turban's fury.

The rain was still falling in a cold, steady shower, harder now than earlier, but it didn't stop the streams of people who poured in and out of the cobbled courtyard, filling the drizzly air with their voices. I darted through them and took shelter behind one of the wide stone pillars of the colonnade, facing onto Stall Street. If those two harridans in turbans came flying out demanding blood, the last thing I wanted was to be standing in full view, waiting for them.

If Stepmama ever discovered what I'd done in the most fashionable meeting-place in Bath, she'd have at least ten separate Spasms and might never let me out of the house again. But the reticule hummed with heat against my arm, and happiness thrummed through my veins, even as I shivered from the cold rain that blew under the shelter of the colonnade and soaked through my hair and my thin morning dress. I'd reawakened Mama's mirror, intentionally and knowingly, and I knew how to do it again. All I had to do now was stock up on Bath water, and if that meant I would spend the rest of my life smelling of rotten eggs, then so be it.

I leaned back against the pillar, relaxing and looking out over Stall Street.

Carriages and horses already filled the cobbled street nearly to overflowing, making it almost impossible to cross, but the lure of the Pump Room seemed too strong for anyone to resist. More and more people darted across the street in the gaps between carriages. Nearly all of them followed the same path between the pillars to the Pump Room. But as I waited for Lucy, I noticed a few people who didn't.

They were mostly elderly, and they were the first people I'd seen in Bath who looked as if they might actually need to try the famous water for their health. Some of them were carried down Stall Street in sedan chairs; others hobbled down the pavement, leaning on the strong arms of manservants. There was even one girl much younger than me, whose thin face looked lined and weary, being carried in her father's arms. Every one of them went straight past the line of pillars, ignoring the busy courtyard behind me, to disappear into a smaller stone building to my left, pressed up against the Pump Room but facing onto the busy main street.

One invalid after another passed inside, but no one ever came out. Until...

My stomach gave a sickly lurch as I recognised the tall, elegant figure who emerged from the shelter of the building, dressed in bright blue, canary yellow and white. Tucking his walking stick under his arm, he unfurled a Chinese-style umbrella and lifted his quizzing glass on its velvet ribbon to scan the street around him. With a gasp, I lunged behind my pillar. Hugging my reticule tight to my chest, I pressed my cheek against the cold stone and peeked around the edge. *Can't see me, can't see me, can't see me,* I thought with all my strength. I only hoped it would be true.

Lord Ravenscroft dropped his quizzing glass. He turned towards the line of pillars, his face intent. His black-and-gold walking stick was purely for decoration, unlike the sticks and crutches of the other people who'd gone into the building. He lifted it as he looked around and he swung it gently back and forth, back and forth. It was a strangely hypnotic gesture. I found myself watching it instead of him. Back and forth...

Instead of making plans, schemes for escape or excuses to offer, or even ways to keep the mirror hidden from him, all I could do was watch the black-and-gold walking stick as it swung. Back and forth, back and forth – and then the walking stick stilled.

He headed straight towards my pillar.

A group of girls surged out through the pillars around me, giggling and teasing each other. At the sight of them, Lord Ravenscroft stopped walking. His shoulders lifted in a shrug. He took one last look, then turned and strolled away down Stall Street, tapping his walking stick on the cobblestones all the way.

I let out my held breath and nearly collapsed. Mama's mirror was safe and so was I. But what on earth had foppish Lord Ravenscroft been doing inside a building full of invalids? And what else was in there anyway?

As soon as he was safely out of sight, I darted out for a better look at the building, ignoring the rain. I couldn't get any wetter now, anyway, so there was no point worrying about it.

Wide stone steps led up to a doorway set far back from the main street. 'King's and Queen's Bath', read the words above the door. The building itself was smaller and much less impressive than the massive Pump Room to its left, but the carvings above the doorway were far more elaborate and exotic: two sphinxes, staring intently at a man and a snake. There had to be some symbolism there, but I had never paid enough attention to Papa's Classics to work it out. Greek fashions might be popular, but these carvings looked positively pagan to me – mystical, too – and strange for a building so close to a church. I frowned, trying to guess what they might mean. If only Papa were here to interpret...

"There you are!" Lucy's voice made me jump. She giggled, handing me my umbrella. Her own was already unfurled and her pink dress and blonde curls looked perfectly dry. "Goodness, I did startle you, didn't I? If you could see the look on your face – oh!" She stepped back. If I'd been a rude person, I could have told her something about the look on her own face, as it crinkled up with horror. "What is that smell?"

"It's only the famous Bath water," I said. "Someone spilled it all over me."

"How terrible for you! Oh, and you've been soaked by the rain, too, you poor thing. But no wonder you were in such a hurry to leave – you must have been so humiliated. I would have wanted to lie down and die, if it were me! Would you like to go home first, so you can change your gown before we go to the library?"

"Never mind that," I said. "What is this building?"

"That? Oh, that's only the Baths. They're filled with the same water we all have to drink in the Pump Room, you know, so it's supposed to be terribly healthy to bathe in them. They've been around forever, since before there were even any real people here."

I looked hard at her as I unfurled my umbrella. "Surely

there must have been some people, or else..."

"Oh, I don't know all that dusty history! It was a long time ago, that's all I know, and I'm sure whoever built them wasn't at all civilised. Anyway, it used to be very fashionable to go into the Baths, but of course it isn't anymore, although some people still do it. Can you imagine it, ladies and gentlemen all going in together, with the water right up to their necks! Can you even bear the very thought of anything so indecent?"

"Oh," I said. "Oh. You're right, actually. That is rather shocking. Taking baths together naked—"

"Naked? Oh, you are an absurd creature. As if they wouldn't wear clothing when they went into the Baths! The things you say! Really, if Mama or Maria heard you..." Lucy tucked her hand into my arm. "Come, I'll take you to the circulating library, and we can forget about all of this nonsense. Only the most unfashionable people go into the Baths these days – well, and people who are really ill, I suppose, but they couldn't be fashionable at all, could they? So there's no point looking to them for an example."

"Hmm." I frowned. "Do you think they'll have any books about the Baths in the circulating library?"

"Ohh!" Lucy shook her head at me. "What have I just been telling you, silly? No one would dream of looking for any such thing there. The circulating library is for novels, not tedious history books! And they have some of the most delicious new novels available, straight from London. I've already read the first two volumes of *The Witch's Revenge*, and it is so horrid, you would not believe – it has the most wickedly shocking witches you can imagine! I could scarcely sleep a wink after I finished the second volume. I must find the third volume today or I'll simply perish with anxiety!"

I sighed and let Lucy's chatter wash over me as she led

me down Stall Street, past clothing shops and stationers and delicious-looking pastry cooks. But I shot one last look back at the Baths before they disappeared from view behind us.

I didn't know why Lord Ravenscroft had visited them. But I knew that I – and Mama's mirror – would be coming back soon to find out.

CHAPTER ELEVEN

WHEN WE RETURNED FROM THE LIBRARY, I SAT DOWN TO a task that was far more difficult than I'd originally anticipated. I had promised to write to Elissa every day, but it had already been a week since her wedding and I hadn't had a chance until now. Lucy and I were the only ones in the Wingates' drawing room, as none of the others had returned yet. Lucy sprawled across the chaise longue, reading the third volume of her novel and periodically letting out squeaks of horror and excitement.

I could have told her something about truly shocking witchly behaviour, using Angeline's latest mad scheme as my example... but even if I'd trusted her that much, she was far too involved in her book to ask what I thought of it, or even – for once – to chatter at me.

That meant I had no excuses left. I set out a quarto of letter paper on the round work-table, dipped my pen in a bottle of ink, and began.

Dear Elissa...

Ink spots dripped onto the paper as my hand hovered in mid-air. I rubbed them out with my finger, groaning. Luckily, Lucy was too engrossed in her faux-magical horrors to notice.

What could I say? If I told Elissa the truth, she would cancel her wedding trip and come flying down to Bath to take control of the situation. As much as I wished she could...

I paused, gnawing my lip. Actually, I wasn't so certain I did want that, anymore. It would certainly be useful to have her here to keep a firm eye on Angeline and Charles, but when it came to my own schemes... well, I had to admit, it did make things easier not to have my oldest sister playing propriety mistress to us all. Perhaps I should sort out my own magical worries first, and only then drop Elissa a hint of the troubles we were having.

But not until after her wedding trip was finished. Elissa had played martyr to the family far too many times, and besides, Mr Collingwood really deserved a holiday after the mess Mrs Carlyle had made of his wedding.

All is well, I wrote, and winced at the blatant untruth. *Stepmama has taken us to Bath to stay with her best connections as a* – more ink-spots, as I considered a rationale – *as a distraction for Angeline. Angeline is not happy, but is less distressed than you might expect.*

No, wait. That would alarm Elissa more than anything else I could say, short of the truth. She knew Angeline just as well as I did – and if such a thing were true, it could only mean that our sister was preparing a truly nightmarish scheme. I picked up a pair of the scissors from the work-table and cut out that line from the letter. *Angeline is furious*, I wrote truthfully, next to the telltale hole in the paper, *but she is not without hope, and she is controlling her temper.*

The drawing room door burst open.

"We will speak more of this later!" Stepmama hissed, and Angeline laughed derisively.

"What more is there to speak of, ma'am?" she asked, without bothering to lower her voice. "Am I not following your explicit orders to try to attract an eligible suitor?"

Lucy's head shot up from her novel. She looked agog with fascination.

"Eligible—!" Stepmama's voice cut off. She took a deep breath, and assumed an unconvincing smile. "Dear Cousin Caroline," she said, as Mrs Wingate entered the drawing room.

Lucy scrambled up to a sitting position just in time. Mrs Wingate's haughty gaze passed over the two of us without interest. Maria stepped up behind her, her face pursed with self-satisfaction.

I hope all is well and you are both enjoying the Lakes, I wrote hastily. Yrs, affec.^{tly}, *Kat.* Then I folded up the letter as quickly as I could, before anything else could happen that I'd be lying not to mention. It was a terrible waste of money for Elissa to pay sixpence to receive such a short letter, but then, as Mrs Collingwood, she had plenty of money to waste... and it was far better for all of us than filling up a whole double-sided sheet with the truth would have been.

Angeline's eyes narrowed as I sealed the letter. But Mrs Wingate spoke first.

"Lucy... Katherine... I believe the two of you had better make your excuses."

I blinked. "But—"

"Yes, Mama," Lucy said meekly, and stood to curtsey.

I repressed a groan. How typical, that I would be sent away just when something interesting was about to be discussed. "Actually—" I began.

"*Katherine.*" Stepmama's glare could have pierced armour.

I gritted my teeth, stood, and curtseyed. The others remained maddeningly silent as Lucy and I walked out of the room. Maria Wingate's smug smile felt like thorns against my skin. When I passed Angeline, she only shook her head at me. With an effort, I restrained myself from sticking out my tongue at her. It would have given Maria far too much satisfaction.

I would have stayed and listened at the door, but the footman who closed it for us took up guard outside, his stance rigidly correct. I gave him one considering look, then abandoned the idea of persuading him into anything. As Charles would have said: *Dash it.*

Giving in, I held out my letter to Lucy. "Where should I put this?"

"Shh!" she whispered, and grabbed my hand. "Come, quickly!"

We ran up the stairs to the next floor. She pushed open the second door on the right and pulled me inside a small room filled with bookcases. In the far corner of the room, I saw a huge globe, beautifully painted, standing next to a large, comfortable-looking armchair. Light from the windows shone on an Oriental carpet in the centre of the room.

"The library," Lucy said. "Mama thinks it very proper that I like to sit in here to do my sewing when I'm alone. That's because she and Maria don't realise how useful it is." She took two glasses from the sideboard. "Look!"

She lay down, pulled aside the carpet, and set one of

the glasses down on the wooden floor. I followed suit with the other.

Mrs Wingate's voice sounded in my ear almost as clearly as if I'd been inside the drawing room itself.

"The shocking impropriety of his lifestyle, alone—"

"Whose?" Lucy whispered. "Who do you think they're talking about?"

"Viscount Scarwood," I whispered back.

"Oh!" Her blue eyes widened. "Oh, my goodness. I've heard of him!"

"So has Angeline, now," I muttered. *Unfortunately.* Didn't they have any idea how to manage her?

Apparently not. Maria Wingate's voice was filled with spiteful glee as she spoke. "His reputation is absolutely scandalous. Why, last year he ran away with the Tilburys' oldest daughter and spent three nights with her, away from either of their families – and he did not even marry her afterwards!"

"Maria." Mrs Wingate's voice was repressive. "An unmarried young lady should know nothing of such matters."

Maria's titter sounded through the floorboards. "One would prefer to know nothing of them, Mama, but when such a scandal breaks across Society, one is forced to take a lesson from it. The girl was ruined, of course. Completely ruined. Her family was forced to repudiate her entirely."

"Were they indeed?" Angeline said, in her most lethally innocent tone. "And was Viscount Scarwood ruined, too?"

"Of course not," Maria said. "Oh, her brother called him out, of course, but Scarwood shot him in the arm and his honour was satisfied."

"It is a lesson to all young ladies," Mrs Wingate said.

"Hmm," said Angeline.

I winced.

Lucy's squeak of alarm was the first sign of danger. I'd been so intent on listening, I hadn't even heard the door open behind us. Lucy dropped her glass onto the carpet, her face the very picture of guilt. I shoved my own glass behind my back, scrambled to my knees to face the door... and relaxed.

It was Papa, blinking down at both of us. "Pardon me," he said. "I... er... that is, I beg your pardon. Was I interrupting something, Kat?"

Lucy let out a wordless bleat of panic.

I said, "Don't worry, Papa, we don't mind being interrupted. Was there something you needed?"

"No, no. I only thought I might take the opportunity to investigate the library while... er..." He looked pained. But he didn't need to explain himself any further.

Papa's first instinct, whenever trouble brewed between Stepmama and one of us, was to take instant refuge amidst the safety of his books. He was probably missing his own study terribly right now.

I said, "You can come in as long as you're quiet. You don't have to worry about disturbing us."

"If you're quite sure...?"

"Of course," I said. "Only, be sure to close the door firmly, won't you?"

"Yes, my dear."

He closed the door and stepped around us to peer at the rows of books shelved behind glass in the tall bookcase behind me. I lay back down and set my listening glass against the wooden floor. After a moment, Lucy retrieved her own glass, darting a nervous look back at Papa. He didn't even see it. He was too intent on his perusal.

A moment later, he pulled out a book and retreated to

the armchair by the window with an audible sigh of relief. I pressed my ear back against my glass.

"So what you mean me to understand," Angeline said, "is that although Miss Tilbury has been ruined and left by her family to starve in the streets, Viscount Scarwood's own place in Society is left undamaged?"

"Such is the way of the world," Mrs Wingate said.

"And Miss Tilbury should have known it," Maria added. "One must hold her fully to blame for succumbing to him. A young lady cannot be too careful of her reputation."

"Indeed," Stepmama said, her voice sharp with meaning beyond what any of the Wingates could have understood.

But she might have known better than to expect Angeline to be cowed by the unspoken reference to her witchcraft. Angeline's voice sounded like rich cream as she replied: "So in other words, Viscount Scarwood, as a wealthy and well-bred gentleman of unscathed position in the world, is still an eligible suitor."

"Ohhh!" Stepmama let out a muffled shriek. "That is not–!"

"Should he ever choose to marry, that will undoubtedly be the case," said Mrs Wingate. "However, we cannot hope for him to make such a choice."

"And particularly not—" Maria Wingate's voice cut off abruptly. Perhaps her mother had stopped her from finishing. But it was clear as light that she'd meant to say: *Not for a country nobody like you.*

My fingers curled into fists. I couldn't blame Angeline for the poison-laced sugar in her voice. "Thank you all for explaining matters to me so clearly," she said. "I understand perfectly now."

Stepmama didn't speak. I wished I could have seen her

face as she battled to hold back her temper. She knew that tone of Angeline's voice as well as I did, and she must have known what Angeline's words meant, too... but she could hardly let herself explode in front of Mrs Wingate.

Mrs Wingate herself was clearly taken in. "I am glad to hear it, my dear," she said. "No one could blame you for your ignorance, after such a sheltered upbringing."

Sheltered, my foot, I thought, and snorted. I would have wagered anything that Mrs Wingate's own daughters had never fought any magical battles. But no one spoke up to disagree, and Mrs Wingate sailed on uncontested.

"Tonight, when we visit the Assembly Rooms for your first Society ball, you will meet a number of truly eligible prospects. I am certain we shall soon find..."

I sighed and sat up, pushing my glass aside. There was no point in listening any longer.

Lucy sat up beside me, her cheeks flushed and her eyes glowing. "How utterly thrilling!" she whispered. "Why – Viscount Scarwood! They say he is as handsome as a Greek god but as dangerous as the Devil himself, and no woman can resist him, no matter how hard she tries."

"Ha," I said, and didn't bother to whisper it. "I managed to resist him perfectly well."

"Yes, well..." She shook the objection away. "Do you think your sister is truly in love with him?"

"No," I said. "She most certainly is not." I saw Papa's shoulders hunch in his armchair. He pulled his book closer to his face, and I took pity on him. "We should talk about this in private," I whispered to Lucy, and she gasped and nodded.

"Forgive me!" she mouthed. The look she shot at Papa was filled with dread.

That dread was completely unfounded, as I could have

told her. There was nothing poor Papa wanted less than to overhear shocking secrets – especially any that would have outraged Stepmama and forced him into unpleasant scenes. The only secrets he was interested in were hundreds of years old, and most of them were related to ancient Greece and Rome.

But not all of them.

I paused halfway to the door. The circulating library had been no help at all to me, just as Lucy had predicted. But there was another source of historical information close at hand, one that hadn't even occurred to me until now.

"Papa," I said. "Do you know anything about the Baths?"

He lowered his book, but only a few inches. "Baths, my dear? Yes, I'm sure Mrs Wingate must have bathing facilities available." The book was already creeping back up towards his face. "Perhaps if you ask a footman, or—"

"No, not that kind of bath. The King's and Queen's Baths. You know!" I spoke loudly and slowly, to cut through the book haze that surrounded him. "The Baths on Stall Street, near the Pump Room. There are sphinxes above the entrance, and—"

"Ah, the Roman Baths, you mean!" His face lit up. He set the book down on the brass leopard's head at the end of his chair arm, one finger marking his place. "A fascinating phenomenon, indeed. You know, of course, that they are built upon a natural hot spring?"

"Umm..."

"The Romans thought the spring sacred – a shrine to the goddess Sulis Minerva, who was goddess of wisdom, as – of course – you must already know."

"Mmm..." Actually, I'd never even heard of the goddess Sulis Minerva, but didn't want to distress him by admitting to that.

"Yes, it was over seventeen hundred years ago that the Romans built the first baths there, beneath the medieval baths which we still use now. They considered the steam that rises from the baths, and from the hot spring itself, to be truly mystical, a sign of the goddess's divine presence. Not only did they bathe in the baths, as we do, but they also brought offerings and requests for the goddess on their visits. I'm sure you know the sort, my dear: advancement in their careers, curses against their enemies... Of course, it all came about because of the health-giving properties of the water. It was attributed then to Sulis Minerva's sacred grace, whereas now we understand it has a natural explanation."

I thought of Mama's mirror waking up at the water's touch. "Mmm..." I repeated, even more doubtfully.

Lucy was fidgeting beside me. Her eyes were modestly lowered and her hands clasped in a ladylike manner – Mrs Wingate had obviously trained her half to death in propriety – but she kept sliding me sidelong glances, and I could see the toe of her closest slipper tapping against the ground. Papa could have gone on for another hour, easily, now that I'd started him off, but I knew his lecture wouldn't stay useful for long. Inevitably, it would go the way of all his historical lectures and end in a perishing half-hour description of all the tangled debates over unimportant side matters that were being carried on by German scholars with too much time on their hands.

His next words proved my point exactly. "Of course, Sulis Minerva was hardly the first goddess to be associated with that spring," he said. "Most scholars agree that the goddess the Celts worshipped at that shrine, long before the Romans' arrival—"

"Thank you!" I said hastily. "That's very useful, Papa.

Thank you. We have to go now."

"Very well, my dear, very well. Do have a good time doing... ah, whatever it is you are doing. You needn't tell me." He reopened his book. His gaze fell back down to its pages even as he continued, his voice drifting into near-inaudibility. "If you do have any other questions, though... the issue of the original *genius loci* has certainly never been entirely pinned down, although some scholars argue..."

I gestured to Lucy, and we hurried out of the room.

CHAPTER TWELVE

THE OBVIOUS NEXT STEP WAS TO VISIT THE BATHS MYSELF. But with Lucy filling my ears with speculation about Viscount Scarwood, and pestering me with questions about Charles's every tedious habit, there was no chance of leaving the house undetected that afternoon.

Luckily, the perfect opportunity was only a few hours away.

As I helped Angeline arrange her hair that evening, she watched me in the mirror of our dressing table.

"You look very pleased with yourself," she said. "What are you planning?"

"Planning?" I said, and tried to look innocent.

"Planning," Angeline repeated. "As in 'looking smug and scheming to do something foolish'."

"Ha," I said. "You would know all about that."

"Is this about the letter you wrote this afternoon? If you've summoned Elissa back from her wedding trip—"

"No!" I said. "Of course not. I wouldn't do that."

Her eyebrows rose. I scowled at her reflection.

Well, I hadn't done that. Although I had considered it.

"I'm glad to hear it," Angeline said. "But if that isn't it—"

"You're the one who said we shouldn't concern ourselves with each other's plans," I reminded her, and yanked her hair as I pinned it into place.

She set her teeth and glared at me. "The fact that you paid attention is what worries me."

I smiled dazzlingly. It was Angeline's own most dangerous smile; I'd practised until I could imitate it perfectly. "I would never interfere with your brilliant schemes," I said. "Not when they always succeed so perfectly on their own. Why, I can hardly wait for you to marry Viscount Scarwood. Such a charming brother-in-law to have – and so much more appealing than boring old Mr Carlyle, who's never ravished anyone in his life. Should I start referring to you as Lady Scarwood in all my correspondence from now on?"

Angeline hissed between her teeth. My smile widened.

She left for the Assembly Rooms an hour later with Stepmama, Charles, Papa, Mrs Wingate and Maria. Lucy and I waved them off.

As soon as they were gone, Lucy let out a squeal of excitement and grabbed both my hands. "Isn't it heavenly to have the house all to ourselves? Maria quarrelled with my governess a week ago and Mama hasn't hired a new one yet, so we are free to do anything we like! Shall we listen to the barrel organ in the parlour? It plays some of the most delightful new tunes. Or I could read to you from *The Witch's Revenge* – it's so thrilling! Or we could arrange each other's hair – I know yours is awfully short, but I've learned a marvellous new style that—"

"Maybe tomorrow," I said, and tried not to sound as horrified as I felt. I disengaged my hands as gently as possible. "Tonight I'm too tired for any of that."

"Oh." She drooped. "Perhaps we could just read together in the drawing room, then, or—"

I forced a yawn, patting my mouth with one hand. "The exhaustion of travel, and so much excitement today – it's all been much too much for me. I'd better just retire to bed."

"But..." Lucy's lower lip pouched out. She sighed. "Have a good night's rest, then."

"You, too." I watched her turn away, her shoulders sagging, and I felt a moment of guilt. But no matter how good-hearted and lonely Lucy Wingate might be, I would never select her as a companion for tonight's expedition.

I hurried up the stairs to the bedroom I was sharing with Angeline and waited there for half an hour, just in case. To while away the time, I searched through Angeline's valises, but with no luck – I couldn't find Mama's magic books anywhere, and even when I concentrated with all my might, I couldn't sense any spells in the room to hide them.

I might have been the only one to inherit Mama's powers as a Guardian, but Angeline was bound and determined not to let me share Mama's other magical inheritance. There was only one spell from Mama's books of witchcraft that I had ever had the chance to learn: the spell to disguise oneself as someone else. Tonight was definitely the night to use it.

I'd already brought my pelisse up to the bedroom and slipped Mama's mirror into its secret inner pocket – the only thing I'd ever sewn voluntarily in my life. Now I wrapped the pelisse around me and whispered the words of Mama's spell as I closed my eyes and concentrated with all my might. The smell of fresh, juicy raspberries filled the air. I had to become someone indisputably proper, someone nobody would think to question, even if they saw me leaving the house...

I opened my eyes, looked at myself in the bedroom mirror, and grinned. Maria Wingate grinned back at me with a friendlier smile than I'd ever seen on her pursed-up face. That would have to change. I fixed my features into a haughty scowl.

There. Much more convincing. My pelisse had even turned into Maria's fashionable black gauze cloak, which I fingered with satisfaction. According to both Stepmama and Elissa, no lady would ever walk out in public without a companion, or at least a maid, for propriety's sake – and no lady would ever walk out at night at all, no matter what the circumstances – but I couldn't imagine any of the Wingates' servants daring to question their employer's older daughter, especially after she'd already seen one servant dismissed for quarrelling with her. And it would give me infinite satisfaction to break the social rules while wearing Maria's face, after what she'd said to Angeline that afternoon.

I pulled the hood over my head and crept down the stairs as quietly as I could.

It wasn't quietly enough. The drawing room door popped open. "Maria?" Lucy blinked out at me. "What are you doing back here? Are you ill? Or—"

"I only forgot something," I said. "It's nothing to worry about."

She frowned and started forward. "Are you sure you're all right? Your voice sounds—"

"I'm fine," I snapped, and tried to make my voice as impatient and haughty as Maria's own. "Now I have to go."

"Oh. I'm sorry. I just..." She bit her lip. She looked as if she wanted to say more, or move towards me, but she hung back as if she were actually nervous.

No, it wasn't *as if* she were nervous. She *was* nervous, of her own sister! I could hardly believe it – but of course I could, with such a prune as Maria for an older sister. I felt a flash of thankfulness for Angeline, as annoying as she could be. *Tomorrow*, I promised myself. Tomorrow I would be kind to Lucy: I would listen to her gossip for hours and hours on end, and I would even let her play with my hair if she insisted. But for now I only said, "Have a good evening, Lucy. Perhaps I'll see you tonight when we come back."

"There is something wrong," she said. "I knew it! You never talk like this. Tell me what's—"

Oh, curse it. "Goodbye!" I said, and almost ran down the grand staircase, away from her.

The footman at the front door looked surprised, but he opened the door for me without a word, and I sailed through with my newly thin nose held high in the air.

I'd only performed this spell once before. That time, I'd turned into Lady Fotherington, and I'd had the devil of a time managing her bosoms. This time, I didn't have that problem to contend with, but Maria's body felt awkwardly thin and angled, with far less strength than I was used to in my legs and arms. If I were a gamester like Charles, I would wager any sum that Maria Wingate had never walked further than half a mile in her entire life. The sensible thing, now that I was out of the house, would be to transform back into my own self, if I could only find a quiet spot to make the change.

But there didn't seem to be any quiet spots in the city of Bath, even at night. The darkened streets were full of carriages and sedan chairs rattling up and down the cobblestones, with boys running ahead to light their way with flaming torches. The streetlamps themselves cast only a dim glow, but that was enough to show that the pavements were full of men: men on their own and red-uniformed soldiers in loud, swaggering groups. Rather too many men, in fact. My skin prickled with discomfort as I realised that all of them were taking a great deal of notice of me, despite my enveloping black cloak. I was the only lady walking on the pavement instead of riding in a carriage. The others were all following the rules of Society which I'd so cavalierly dismissed.

Curse it! Why hadn't I thought to transform myself into Charles instead of Maria? He wouldn't draw attention walking out on his own at night. And even if he did, he was strong enough for a proper bout of fisticuffs with any rascal who accosted him. I clenched my fists experimentally and felt how puny they were in Maria's form. There was barely any muscle in the arms I flexed. *Useless.* If only I'd thought more carefully before performing Mama's spell...

But I'd never been to a real city before and the danger hadn't even occurred to me. There was nothing to do now but get through it as quickly as I could, and change to a safer shape as soon as I was alone in the Baths. I quickened my steps, weaving through the groups of men on the pavement before me.

A feminine shriek stopped me in my tracks. I turned round, dread weighting my feet like lead. I knew that voice.

In her bright white pelisse, Lucy Wingate shone like a star in the torchlight from the passing carriages. "Let me go!" she shrieked. She struggled against the two soldiers who held her arms, but she stood barely as tall as their chests and they held her easily.

"Thought we were too foxed to notice you trying to

pick our pockets, did you? Little sneak-thief!" Both soldiers were officers, with dress-swords strapped to their sides. The bigger one's voice was rough with drink. Unfortunately, drunkenness didn't seem to be weakening him. He yanked her back by her hair and spat on the cobblestones in front of her. "I'll see you transported to Australia for that. *If* you're not hung outright for thievery."

"I wasn't— I swear— my name is Lucy Wingate, I was only trying to find my sister—"

"And that's why you squeezed between us in such a rush?" The shorter officer laughed, and my spirits sank. He was foxed, too. "Come off it. There's only one reason why street rats like you are out at night. You picked the wrong victims this time, and you'll have to pay the price."

Other men were stopping to watch now, and carriages slowed so that their passengers could watch the confrontation. Two finely dressed ladies pressed their faces to the windows of the closest carriage in gleeful horror. They even opened the door an inch, to catch all the words.

None of them, it was clear, was going to be any help at all.

I clenched Maria Wingate's useless, puny fists and marched forward. "Let her go!"

The men on the outskirts of the circle stumbled back as I shoved through them.

"Maria!" Lucy said. She was breathing fast, and I could see tears shining in her eyes. If I met her gaze, I might start to feel afraid, too. So I didn't. I just grabbed her shoulder and yanked her towards me.

The officer on her right was so surprised, he let go. But the bigger officer only laughed.

"The 'sister', I see."

"Of course this is my sister," I lied, and looked him

straight in the eye. "Check your pockets – she hasn't stolen anything. Neither of us are thieves. Now let her go!"

At a look from the bigger one, the shorter officer grabbed my shoulder. I wrenched against him, but his grip was too strong. Panic clenched my chest. I said, "Would you let your own sisters be marched off to the magistrate just because they were out at night and walked too close to some drunken idiot?"

"Our sisters," the bigger officer snarled, "would never go out at night without a suitable escort. No lady would." He turned to the watching men. "We've been out defending the likes of you and yours from invasion by the French, living in dirt and hardship so you can stay safe and secure in your own homes. Now we come home to our own country for just two weeks and this pair of trollops want to get away with trying to steal our purses! Do you intend to stand for it?"

A low rumble of agreement rippled through the crowd. Behind me, someone yelled, "They deserve a good whipping!"

Flares from the torches illuminated the avid faces watching from the carriages and made the greedy looks of the men around us all too frighteningly clear.

"If you would all just listen to me—!" I began.

"We've heard enough." The shorter officer clapped his hand hard over my mouth. His skin was rough and stank of cigar smoke. He looked at his companion, ignoring my struggles. "What d'you think? Should we take 'em straight to the magistrate or give 'em a sound whipping first for their insolence?"

Lucy's plump shoulders shook with her soundless sobs. I tried to bite my captor. His hand was clamped too tightly around my mouth. I couldn't even move my lips.

Panic overwhelmed me for a sickly, horrible moment.

It was hopeless – *I* was hopeless – but all I could think, over and over, with every bit of strength left in me, was exactly what I'd thought to myself that morning as Lord Ravenscroft had stepped out from the Baths.

You can't see me, you can't see me, you can't see me...

"Hey!" My captor let go of me. I was so surprised, I stumbled right into Lucy and had to grab her shoulder for balance. "What happened? What—?"

The officer on Lucy's left swore and dropped his hand from her arm. "Where the hell did they go?"

Lucy and I stared at each other. The circle of men broke apart as they all exploded into arguments.

"They couldn't have vanished. They must have—"

"Witches! They were witches, they—"

"Don't be ridiculous." It was the bigger officer, his voice hoarsening with anger. "Witchcraft's nothing but a fairy story. No one—"

"I saw them disappear! One moment they were there, the next—"

Lucy's eyes were very wide. She opened her mouth to speak.

I put my hand across her mouth and shook my head.

We were free, at least for a moment. I didn't understand what had just happened... but nothing was going to stop me from taking advantage of it.

I'd made enough mistakes tonight already.

We slipped together through a newly opened gap in the crowd, my hand still firmly clasped around Lucy's shoulder. I was afraid to let go. My hand was shaking, and I couldn't seem to breathe right. I kept thinking about the looks in the men's eyes, and how close we'd both come to something horrible, because of me.

I'd thought it would be funny to break Society's rules as Maria Wingate. *Funny.*

I felt sick.

We were two full streets away when it finally felt safe enough to stop walking. I pulled Lucy into the sheltered doorway of a closed pastry-cook shop. She was panting with exertion and staring at me with huge eyes.

"Maria, you— you—"

I said, "I'm not Maria."

"What?" She shook her head so hard that her blonde hair fell out of its topknot, scattering pins. "What are you talking about? First you act so strange I have to follow you to find out what's wrong – I thought you had a romantic assignation! Or a dangerous meeting with a blackmailer, or—"

"A what?" I stared at her. "Why on earth would you think—?"

"And then those horrible men!" She had fresh tears in her eyes, sparkling in the dim glow from the streetlamps. "And then you did magic! Maria! How could you never have told me you were a witch?!"

"I told you," I said. "I'm not Maria. I'm Kat. Kat Stephenson."

Her mouth fell open. She stared at me. A wordless bleat of disbelief came from her open lips.

I sighed. At least my pulse was starting to settle again, finally, and just in time. This part would take true control.

I closed my eyes, keeping one hand on Lucy's shoulder. Focusing with all my might, I reached out with my mind and tested the magic in the air. There was Mama's spell of disguise, still giving off the faint scent of raspberries that attended all my spells; and there... *that* was a buzzing sensation in the air that didn't feel like a witch's spell. It was a magic-working – and a strong one.

I'd made us invisible with my Guardian powers. *Take that, Lord Ravenscroft!* I had learned something new on my own, after all.

Carefully, gritting my teeth with concentration, I reached out to the witch spell, brought up the familiar electric pressure through my body, and released it. The spell snapped. Lucy gasped. I opened my eyes.

"You— you—"

Walking just a few feet away, a pair of men turned at the sound of her voice. But their eyes passed straight over us. We were still invisible.

"Shh," I whispered, as soon as they were safely past. "I told you it was me. But we can't stay here. I have to get you safely home, and then—"

"What about you?" she whispered. "Where are you going?"

"Out," I said. "I have a mission." It was true – and no matter how shaken I might feel right now, it was more necessary than ever. "But you needn't worry about any of that. Just—"

"Oh no, you don't," Lucy Wingate said. She narrowed her big, blue eyes at me. "You're not sending me back home without so much as an explanation while you go off on a mysterious, romantic adventure."

"It is not romantic!" I almost snarled with impatience. "I'll explain it to you later, I promise. But I don't have much time. I have to be back by the time everyone else returns from the Assembly Ball, so—"

"Fine," said Lucy. "Then take me with you."

I stared at her. She stared back, her chin stuck out in a mulish expression.

There was obviously no moving her.

I gritted my teeth as I looked at her silly, good-natured,

stubborn face. "You have to promise not to tell anyone else about this," I said. "And I warn you: I'm going to be practising magic. Scandalous magic. Totally shocking, just like in your novels. If your mother or Maria ever found out you'd been involved—"

"Perfect," Lucy said, and beamed at me. "I can't wait."

CHAPTER THIRTEEN

IT HAD NEVER TAKEN ME SO LONG TO WALK A HUNDRED yards in my life. With Lucy clinging to my hand and both of us walking in an awkward shuffle-step to keep the connection for our invisibility, we moved at approximately the speed of an exhausted snail. It didn't help that Lucy kept letting out perfectly audible giggles that surprised everyone we passed. As soon as we got back to her house that night, I was going to give her a stern talking-to about exactly what was and was not stealthy and subtle behaviour in a dangerous situation.

It was probably my aggravation that made me take so long to notice: the closer we came to the Baths, the more the air prickled against my skin. Mama's mirror tingled through my reticule, not quite awake, but *noticing*. There was magic in the air.

I came to a stop at the end of the colonnade, just before the Baths.

"What?" Lucy hissed. She pushed my hand away from her mouth. "What is it?"

I shook my head at her for silence. The shops on Stall Street were closed and dark. Only the inn across the street was still alight and busy with guests streaming in and out. The stone building that held the Baths loomed in the darkness ahead of us, as silent and as apparently empty as the Pump Room to our left. But still, the prickling against my skin was so intense, I could barely stand it.

It wasn't witch magic, but it wasn't Guardian magic, either. It was something wild and strange. I'd never felt anything like it, but I knew one thing for sure: it was coming from inside the Baths.

Of course, Lucy hadn't noticed the magic. She was too busy peering through the pillars of the colonnade towards the darkened windows of the Pump Room.

"What do you think it's like at night when everyone is gone?" she asked. "Do you think it's full of ghosts from long ago in great hoop skirts, still taking the waters and gossiping in the darkness?"

I snorted. "If they're still forcing down that disgusting water even after they're safely dead..."

Lucy pressed her free hand to her heart like a stage heroine. "Perhaps there are great romances occurring there even now. Lovers who were forced to part in life by their cruel parents—"

"Hmm," I said. I tried to imagine Angeline and Mr Carlyle as ghosts. I couldn't imagine either of them being so impractical as to stay cooped up in the Pump Room after they were dead, much less choosing to drink the water there. "Unlikely," I decided. "Anyway, it's time to go."

"Go? Where?" Lucy swung round. "We've only just arrived!"

"Yes, but..." I took one last look at the Baths. If I'd been a ninny like Lucy, I might have pressed my own hand to my heart in longing. There was nothing I wanted to do more than to get inside and investigate properly. The wild magic itched at my skin, tempting me even now. But I wasn't a ninny, and I did have some sense of responsibility, no matter what Stepmama might think.

"It's more dangerous than I'd thought," I said. "So I need to take you home." As her mouth dropped open in indignation, I added, "I'm coming, too, don't worry. I won't investigate without you." *Not tonight, anyway*, I added silently to myself.

"But—"

I clapped my free hand back over her mouth. Her outraged squeak was muffled by my fingers. Then she saw what I'd just seen and went blessedly silent.

There were three shadows at the far end of the courtyard on our left, slipping past Bath Abbey on their way towards the Pump Room. The one in front carried a lantern, but from our distance, the light was only enough to outline three male figures. They paused as we watched them and their voices drifted towards us through the darkness.

"I say, did you hear something?"

"Don't worry, old man. Bath's not a quiet city at the best of times, eh? It's probably just some ladybirds having a bit of fun."

"If someone saw us—"

"No one's going to see us. Who would be looking? This area ain't exactly the height of fashion at night. That's what makes it so brilliant. I told you, he's got it all worked out."

I started to shuffle slowly backwards. Lucy shuffled with me. Then third shadow spoke, and we both froze.

"Well, then," said a horribly familiar, jovial voice.

"We ought to hurry, eh? If I'm going to make it back to the Assembly Rooms before m'stepmother notices and flies into one of her fits..."

Lucy and I stared at each other. The other men laughed.

"Poor man," said the first shadow. "Come on, then, Stephenson. You deserve at least a taste of what you've been missing out on since they sent you home to rusticate in the wilds."

There was a door tucked into the end of the colonnade behind the final pillar. The shadows opened it and slipped through. I took my hand off Lucy's mouth.

"But— but—" she said. "But that was—"

"Charles," I finished for her, in a growl. "I know."

Typical Charles. He could never turn down any game or wager, especially when it was offered by one of his friends. And he had just walked straight into the source of all that prickling, wild magic.

I looked at Lucy and felt my responsibilities twist into an impossible coil. Taking her home was the only right thing to do. Everyone would agree with that. But that would mean leaving my feckless, impossible older brother in danger, unprotected.

I couldn't do it.

"You'll have to be absolutely silent," I hissed. "Do you understand? There are people using magic in there, and if they hear either of us..."

She was breathing quickly. "Dangerous magic?" she asked.

"I don't know," I said. "But I think so."

She lifted her chin. "In that case, we must go inside. What if poor Charles needs our help?"

Poor Charles indeed, I thought, as sourly as Angeline herself could have done. But I only nodded.

Sticking close together, we shuffled past the row of pillars to the hidden door the men had used. Its handle turned easily in my hand. I opened the door, and we stepped into a small, dark foyer. To our left, one door led towards the Pump Room. Straight ahead was another door, leading towards the Baths... and the magic.

I knew exactly which one to take. I took a deep breath and stepped through.

The floor fell away beneath my feet. I stumbled, and Lucy yanked my arm to keep me from falling down the sudden flight of stairs, into utter darkness.

"Thank you," I whispered. I was breathing hard.

She only squeezed my hand in answer. Her own hand was damp with sweat.

We fumbled down the steps in the darkness, holding each other steady. I put out my free hand for balance. The wall of the narrow stairwell was covered with roughly textured tiles that tingled against my palm. In the distance, I heard the muted echoes of men's voices, calling back and forth.

We both stumbled as we hit the bottom of the stairwell. A foot further, and we ran into what felt like another wall. It took a minute of desperate fumbling before I found a door handle.

Cautiously, I opened the door. Light flickered near the end of the long, narrow corridor that stretched out before us. The sound of men's voices wasn't muted anymore; they were singing and talking loudly, and there were too many of them for me to make out any individual words or voices. I'd been wrong, though, when I thought they were calling back and forth to each other. It was only that the sound was bouncing back and forth, creating an eerie set of echoes that travelled down the corridor towards us like warnings.

I heard something else, too: the unmistakable sound of splashing water. I closed my eyes to test the air. The buzz of Guardian magic was still there; we were still invisible. Thank goodness.

We shuffled down the corridor. We didn't have to worry about making noise anymore. The men's voices grew louder and louder as we approached, covering up any scuffling sounds we might have made. The bouncing echoes grew more and more overwhelming as the corridor turned left. Torchlight flickered through an open doorway and the corridor beyond split into two.

I could hear more voices coming from our right, but straight ahead of us a row of narrow wooden doors tugged at my attention. The closest one stood ajar and steam leaked through the opening. It spread across the floor, lapping at our shoes, hot and prickling with wild magic. As Lucy and I shuffled towards the open doorway, I found myself holding my breath, bracing myself against the tingle of magic, afraid of what I might see beyond.

Shallow steps led from the doorway down into dark, swirling water. As I pulled the door further open, more steam billowed through, filling my lungs and my eyes and veiling the Bath beyond. The smell and the heat were so intense and overwhelming, I had to force my gaze upwards and take slow, deep breaths to clear my head.

There was no roof above the water, only the open night sky, its black expanse studded with bright stars. A few torches set about the Bath sent shadows flickering through the darkened alcoves and doorways that surrounded the water on three sides. The flickering light reflected off glass windows set high above in a darkened building that overlooked the Bath.

And inside the bath itself... *Oh Lord.* As I looked back

down, through the thick cloud of mist, it took all my willpower not to drop my magical focus. Lucy's mouth dropped open. I had my free hand ready to clap over her mouth, but she didn't say a word. Not even a squeak escaped her mouth. Shock had finally silenced her.

The Bath was full of young men, none of them older than Charles, all frolicking in the steaming water and singing rude drinking songs. And they weren't wearing any clothing.

I yanked my attention back to the star-studded night sky. *Focus!* I ordered myself. But when a pink form flashed in the corner of my eye, scrambling out of the water, I couldn't help it. I looked.

Oh. They were wearing underclothes. Well. Thank goodness.

I forced my attention to the Bath itself, trying to ignore the young men inside it. With the amount of noise they were making, we should have heard them from outside, no matter how many buildings stood around the water, but I hadn't heard a peep... and that had to be related to the magic. Of course, the veil of mist that rose from the water could just be ordinary steam from the natural hot spring that Papa said fed the Baths. But I didn't believe that for an instant.

I narrowed my eyes, concentrating my attention. There was definitely something more to it. The whole area smelled faintly of rotten eggs, just like the disgusting water I'd drunk at the Pump Room that morning, but that wasn't all. When I half-closed my eyes the mist sparkled with strange, flashing colours. The prickly, chaotic magic that I'd sensed outside clouded the air here like a second layer of mist. Something was setting it off. But what?

"Honestly, Kat!" Lucy hissed, and poked me in the side.

Even at a whisper, her voice trembled with repressed giggles. "You mustn't look!"

I glared at her. "I was not looking," I hissed back. "I'm just trying to figure out—"

"Some of them are quite handsome, though, don't you think?" She put her free hand over her mouth. Her blue eyes sparkled. "And I think... Yes, there's your brother!"

Oh Lord. I really didn't want to see that. But I followed her gaze. Straight across from us, three young men crowded into an arched doorway, each of them wearing large white underclothes. Charles looked positively blue with cold, but he was grinning with excitement. Lucy let out a soft sigh beside me. I gritted my teeth and wished I could wring my brother's neck.

All the men in the Bath stopped singing and splashing and jammed together into a semicircle, waiting for the three newcomers to join them.

"Come on – the water's hot!"

"Hurry up!"

"Come on, Stephenson!"

The red-haired man on Charles's right lifted his arms, and all the men shouted together: "Hail, Sulis Minerva!"

Wild magic rocketed through the air, flashing through me like an electric shock. I staggered. If Lucy hadn't held me, I would have fallen.

"What is it?" she whispered. "What happened?"

I only shook my head. I couldn't look away. The man behind Charles pushed him forward to the edge of the water, and Charles, grinning stupidly, yelled:

"Grant me good luck at the gaming tables, goddess!"

He opened one hand over the steaming water. Something too small for me to identify fell into the mist.

"Hail, Sulis Minerva!" the men in the water chorused.

Wild magic exploded through the air again.

That time I did fall over. There was a moment when I couldn't see anything around me – only sparks of colour flying before my closed eyes. When I opened them again, I was lying flat on my back with my legs hanging over the wet stone steps and my feet submerged in water, and Lucy was kneeling beside me, trying to pull me up.

"Wake up, Kat," she whispered. "Please, please, please..."

I struggled up onto my elbows and looked out over the Bath. Charles had disappeared – he must have dived in after making his offering. Yes, there he was now, shaking water out of his eyes and sputtering as he surfaced surrounded by a circle of laughing, back-thumping men. But his two companions still stood in the open doorway across from us.

Both of them were staring straight at me and Lucy.

CHAPTER FOURTEEN

CURSE IT! I'D DROPPED THE MAGIC-WORKING.

Can't see us, can't see us, can't us! I thought. But my brain still felt scalded by the wild magic that had passed through us, and I couldn't summon any Guardian power. Even as I took a deep breath, trying to focus, the red-haired man raised his right arm and pointed at us.

"Intruders on Sulis Minerva's sacred mysteries!" he bellowed.

Damnation. I leaped to my feet, tugging Lucy with me, and slammed our wooden door shut against him.

I spun round to race back the same way we'd come – then stopped as I heard new, cheerfully intoxicated male voices coming from the entrance we'd used. *Curses.* More Minerva-worshippers! The last thing I wanted was to be trapped between two groups of drunken lunatics, especially when one group was dripping wet and already outraged. So I pulled Lucy round and ran further down the corridor, past the line of closed doors and windows that all faced onto the Bath, skidding across the damp, tiled floor and plunging deeper into the building.

We raced through an open archway and into a small, pitch-black room filled with the sound of dripping pumps – most of which I managed to slam into in the darkness. From Lucy's whimper, I guessed she'd tripped into one, as well. The tiles were soaked and slippery. As I slid and caught myself for the third time, I comforted myself with the thought that at least they'd slow down our pursuers, too. Male bellows followed close after us, though, echoing off the walls like the sound of enraged bulls.

Lucy ran slower and slower, panting with exertion. "What— how— I thought we were invisible!"

"We were," I said grimly. "We're not anymore. And until I find a safe spot for a moment of peace and quiet..."

But every door we passed was locked, and there were no stairs in sight. Lucy dragged me to a halt at the turn in the corridor, gasping for breath. "Honestly. It can't be that hard, can it?" She shook her head at me like a disapproving older sister. "Just use your witchcraft!"

"That's not as easy as it sounds," I snarled, and dragged her with me around the turn, into another room annoyingly full of pumps.

If only Angeline hadn't been so stingy with Mama's magic books, Lucy might have been right. But disguising ourselves as different people wouldn't make our pursuers any more likely to let us off, even if there had been time for me to stand still and recite the only spell I knew. I could hear pounding footsteps behind us. I hurtled with Lucy out of the door straight ahead of us – and almost fell into the Bath.

More men yelled and shouted, splashing towards us.

I could have screamed, or wept with frustration. Instead, I spun around and pulled Lucy back into the room full of pumps, looking for something... anything...

Lucy said, "Look!"

There was another door, five feet away, almost hidden behind one of the pumps. I'd been running too quickly to notice it before. There was a sign on the door that I couldn't read in the darkness, but the meaning was easy enough to guess: *No Visitors Allowed*. It had to be a workman's entrance. If it was locked, like all the other doors we'd passed...

I didn't have any choice but to try.

I tugged on the handle. It opened with a telltale squeak. Lucy and I barrelled through the doorway together, and I closed the door behind us as quietly as I could.

Maybe the men wouldn't notice the door. Maybe they would assume it was locked like all the rest of them. Maybe...

There was no light to guide us, but this time I was ready for the flight of stairs before my feet. We stumbled down them as fast as we could. The prickling pressure of wild magic grew stronger with every step, and I had to cling to Lucy to keep my balance. When we hit the bottom, Lucy yanked her hand out of mine and collapsed on the final step.

Wild magic filled the air like a cloud of pure electricity, distracting me with every prick against my skin, every spark that flashed against my inner eye. The thought of summoning the power I needed for our invisibility felt as impossible as asking Lucy to run two miles across the hills of Yorkshire. Still, I took a deep breath, summoned up all my flagging energy, narrowed my gaze, and—

A flash of light suddenly sparked behind me. A familiar voice spoke into my ear.

"I might have expected it," said Mr Gregson. "Katherine, what have you done this time?"

˟ ˟ ˟

Luckily, Lucy's shriek covered up my gasp, so I was able to look perfectly collected as I turned to face my former tutor. He stood in front of a pool of steaming, dark-green water. It bubbled up from the ground in a rush before flowing away down a stone-lined culvert and disappearing beneath the remains of an ancient wall that looked distinctly Roman. Mist wreathed Mr Gregson's small, neat figure. Behind him, blocks of old stone lay in uneven piles, some of them glinting with faded colour – broken murals, from the looks of them. The light he had summoned gave tantalising glimpses of strange carvings peeking out from the walls around us.

"Mr Gregson," I said. "How nice to see you. I'm afraid we don't have time to chat. There are some people chasing us right now, so..."

"Not exactly unusual circumstances for you." Mr Gregson sighed and closed his eyes. Through the cloud of wild magic, I felt a new sensation in the air. It vibrated like the gong of a deep-throated bell, echoing through my bones. He opened his eyes and looked at us mildly through his spectacles. "I believe they will not think to look for you here," he said. "And now, if you would care to explain?"

"Well." I sank down onto the bottom step, letting out my pent-up breath in a whoosh. "It was really only a case of bad timing, but—"

Lucy grabbed my arm. "Ka-at?" Her voice turned into a squeak as she looked between us. "What's happening?"

"Oh." I stood back up, belatedly remembering the

143

proprieties. "Lucy, may I present Mr Gregson? He used to be my... er... that is..." I darted a *help-me!* glance at Mr Gregson, but he only looked back at me with bland interest. "We met him at Lady Graves's house party," I said. "Mr Gregson, this is Miss Lucy Wingate. Her mother is a cousin of my stepmama. We're staying at their house while we're in Bath."

"Miss Wingate..." As Lucy dropped into a curtsey, Mr Gregson bowed politely. He spoiled the effect, though, with the disapproving look he gave me as he straightened. "You thought it wise to bring her along on this adventure? Some might question the practicality of—"

"She brought herself," I snapped, and scowled at him. "I didn't have a choice about it."

"Really!" Lucy rose from her curtsey with more speed than grace. "How rude!"

I ground my teeth and shot a considering look back at the stairs. I was almost ready to run back up to the Bath and the crazed Minerva-men.

But not quite. So I said, "I didn't mean to be rude. I was only explaining that I hadn't been irresponsible."

Lucy frowned at me. Mr Gregson only coughed... but it was an infuriatingly sceptical sound. I took a deep, steadying breath and kept my expression as placid as a cow's. Before either of my companions could utter another word to make me lose my temper, I said, "We have more important things to talk about. What's causing all this magic? And what kind is it, anyway? I've never felt anything like it."

Mr Gregson said, "Perhaps you had better begin by telling me where you first sensed this unusual magic, and anything you may have observed about it so far."

"Why?" I looked at him suspiciously. He had a closed-up expression that gave nothing away. "You know something about it that you don't want to tell me, don't you?"

"Katherine..."

"Fine." I sighed. "But after I tell you what I know, you have to tell me what you know." I crossed my arms in a pose that would have sent Stepmama into a fit of strong hysterics. "I sensed the magic this morning in that disgusting water at the Pump Room, but it wasn't nearly this strong. I came back here to see what the Baths were like—"

"So that's why you were asking me all those bizarre questions!" Lucy said.

I ignored her interruption. "But when we came here tonight, I could feel the magic even from the street outside. It got stronger and stronger as we came towards the water. Then we saw the men at the main Bath acting like idiots, and the magic exploded, and now..." I frowned, looking around the large, shadowy room, filled with rubble and carved stone. "Now it's the strongest yet," I said. "Have you been doing it?"

"No," Mr Gregson said. "I have not. I have been observing the magic levels here since first dark, however, and they have been steadily increasing. I would very much like to know what has been causing it."

"Why here?" I said, and gave a dubious look at the puny pool of water. "It doesn't look terribly important."

"It is the primary outlet of the Source," Mr Gregson said.

I frowned at him. "The source of what?"

He looked at me over the top of his spectacles, dropping into his tutorial voice. "The natural hot spring from which all the Baths are filled."

"The spring sacred to Sulis Minerva," I said, remembering Papa's lecture. Then I remembered the rest of that lecture and felt my mouth drop open. "And they were giving it offerings. Oh Lord..."

"Offerings?" Mr Gregson said sharply. "What sort—"

But he was interrupted by Lucy. Her face was bright red and streaming with perspiration. "What do you mean – you *felt* the magic?" she asked.

I shrugged impatiently. "It's just a sense I have, now that I've been practising magic for a while. You wouldn't be able to—"

"Is it an itching feeling?" Lucy said. She swayed as she spoke and her voice grew faint. "A sort of scratching, burning—"

"Lucy?" I said. I took her arm. "Are you..."

Mr Gregson started forward, frowning. "Miss Wingate, could you describe exactly—?"

But before either of us could finish our sentences, Lucy's eyes closed and she pitched forward in a faint.

Mr Gregson caught her before she could hit the ground. Her eyelashes didn't so much as flutter in reaction. She had genuinely swooned, just like all the nitwitted heroines of her favourite books. As much as I hated gothic novels, I couldn't bring myself to feel anything but worry as I looked at Lucy's slack face, helpless in unconsciousness.

"What's wrong with her?" I said.

"I don't know." There was a pinched line of worry between Mr Gregson's eyebrows. "Perhaps..."

He shook his head, frowning harder, and lowered her carefully to the floor, propping her back against the steps. Lucy looked horribly vulnerable with her blonde head lolling against her shoulder.

"She was clearly sensitive to the uncontrolled magic in the air," said Mr Gregson. "Does her family have any history of magical practice to explain it?"

"The Wingates?" I stared at him. Despite my worry, I had

to fight back a laugh. "If you had ever met Mrs Wingate or Lucy's older sister..."

"Hmm," Mr Gregson said. "So, not recently – or, at least, not on her mother's side of the family."

"No," I said. "Definitely not."

"In that case, I'm afraid something far more dangerous may have occurred." He drew a deep breath. "Shall we take a look?"

He knelt down and gently lifted Lucy's left eyelid.

"Ahh!" I jumped back before I could stop myself.

Sparks of golden light filled Lucy's eye, dancing across the eyeball. Mr Gregson sighed heavily.

"Uncontrolled magic," he said. "It will always seek a host eventually." He let go of Lucy's eyelid and it dropped back into place. Looking as grim as I'd ever seen him, Mr Gregson turned to me. "Now," he said. "Tell me exactly what was going on in the Baths above us. You said there were offerings?"

"Yes," I said. I knelt down beside him and took Lucy's limp hand. The tingling of wild magic in the air around us had disappeared, but it wasn't a relief, not now that I knew where it had gone. I tried to speak as steadily as I could. "There was a group of men in the main Bath. Young men. They were intoxicated and they weren't taking any of it seriously. They thought it was all a game, throwing offerings to Sulis Minerva and asking her for favours. They didn't even notice when the wild magic got stronger after every offering." I thought of Charles, grinning and foolish, asking the goddess for luck at gambling. "They didn't know what they were doing," I said. "Someone else must have come up with the idea and talked them into it. When I heard some of them talking outside, they said that 'he' had figured it all out."

"Hmm." Mr Gregson didn't look away from Lucy's slack face. "To come up with such a scheme for this particular spot certainly argues more knowledge of history than the average young man would possess."

"Well..." I hesitated, torn between loyalties. "I think... I think some of them may be students at Oxford right now. So I suppose they might be studying history there. But I'm certain they didn't know what they were doing!"

Mr Gregson's eyes flicked to my face. "You sound very fervent," he said. "Do you know these young men, by any chance?"

I met my former tutor's gaze and shook my head. "No," I said, keeping my voice clear and confident. "I've never seen them before in my life."

"Hmm," Mr Gregson repeated. He did not look away from me.

I said quickly, "Is this the magical crisis you were called to Bath to investigate?"

"That is Guardian business, Katherine."

"I saw Lord Ravenscroft coming out of the Baths earlier today, so—"

"Katherine!" Mr Gregson stiffened. "I am not averse to occasional wild stories from you. I understand you are a creative child and lack interest in your daily life. However—"

"I beg your pardon!" I glared at him. "I do not—"

"However," Mr Gregson continued, speaking over me, "I will beg you not to tell wild stories about the head of my Order, if you please, no matter how much his recent decisions may have irritated you. Such an act is wholly unacceptable under any circumstances, and if you ever wish to be readmitted—"

"I am not telling wild stories," I said. "Why should I?

I saw Lord Ravenscroft not half an hour after I met you in the Pump Room this morning."

"Then I am sorry to say I have caught you in an outright lie, which is something I did not expect from you at such a grave moment. I am extremely disappointed in you, Katherine." Mr Gregson looked at me reproachfully. "You may be interested to learn that Lord Ravenscroft spent today in Clifton, some miles from Bath, on personal business. It was the first day in the past week that he has spent outside this city, and it is the only day on which your fabrication could not possibly be believed. Now, perhaps, you would care to adjust your story?"

"No," I said. "It's the truth. Why would Lord Ravenscroft tell you he was going to Clifton when he was really staying in Bath? If he wasn't—"

"Enough!" Mr Gregson snapped. "I will not continue this conversation. However, I hope you will consider your behaviour carefully tonight, after we have parted. I can understand disappointment and even anger at Lord Ravenscroft after your expulsion, but I certainly expected better from you than such childish and malicious libels." He glared at me. "Perhaps I have been deceived in my estimation of your character."

"Not by me," I said, and glared right back at him. "I'm not the one who's lying to you."

His face tightened. He looked pointedly away. "We have a more important matter to see to," he said, and gestured at Lucy. "Where is this young lady's house?"

"We can't just take her home." I said. "She's full of wild magic!"

"And what do you propose to do about that?"

"Make it go away!" I stared at him. "You're the Guardian. Do something about it!"

He sighed. "Fine. Try to break the magic's spell. You've always been good at that."

"Fine," I said. I closed my eyes, summoned up the power inside me, focused on the sparking, prickling energy that radiated from Lucy, and let the power explode.

It knocked me a foot back along the tiled floor, shaking my hand loose from Lucy's. I skidded and almost fell. My palm stung as if the magic had burned me. "What—what—?"

"No one has cast a spell for you to break," Mr Gregson said. "This magic has not been merely filtered into the world through a witch's spell or a Guardian's working. It is uncontrolled and operating entirely of its own volition. That is an extraordinarily rare and dangerous phenomenon."

Massaging my sore palm, I looked down at Lucy. "But what can we do about it?"

"Absolutely nothing, at the moment." Mr Gregson rose to his feet. "I shall research the matter in the Order's library and see if any similar situations have ever been successfully reversed. In the meantime, we must see her back to a safe place."

I scrambled up to my feet. "But what am I going to tell everybody? Her mother and sister won't understand."

"I'm sure you'll think of something," Mr Gregson said, and looked at me, for once, without a hint of sympathy. "You've always been good at wild stories."

CHAPTER FIFTEEN

IT WAS No EASY TASK To CARRY LUCY ALL THE WAY ACROSS Bath to the Wingates' town house, even with Mr Gregson bearing most of the weight and maintaining our invisibility. Of course, he didn't know that I could have done that part myself, but I didn't see any reason to volunteer the information – not after everything he'd said to me that night. Still, between the strain on my protesting arm muscles, the exertion of keeping our unwieldy procession out of the way of all the groups we passed on the city pavements, and, worst of all, the sheer, unmitigated aggravation of Mr Gregson's cold silence, I was ready to collapse by the time we finally arrived at the town house.

First, though, I had to find Lucy's bedroom, tuck her into bed, see Mr Gregson out of the side door with cold civility and make my way back, undetected by the servants, to the room I shared with Angeline. I was so exhausted by the end of it, I fell straight into bed without even bothering to change into my nightgown.

I was just in time.

The others arrived home from the Assembly Rooms less than five minutes later. For once, I was too tired to even try to eavesdrop on the hissing, under-voiced lecture Stepmama delivered to Angeline just outside our closed bedroom door. I had already blown the bedside candle out. As Angeline stepped inside, I pulled the covers over my head to keep out any light from the corridor. I was asleep before she'd even climbed into bed.

But when I woke up the next morning, I knew my troubles had only just begun.

Lucy. Before I even opened my eyes, it all came back to me. The wild magic filling Lucy's eyes with sparks of golden light... I scrambled out of bed, heading straight for the door.

Angeline's voice stopped me halfway across the room. "What on earth have you been up to?"

I turned. She was sitting up in bed, her arms propped on her pillows, watching me with an expression that looked anything but tired. *Curses*.

"Everything's fine," I said, and reached for the door handle. "I'm just—"

"You are wearing your pelisse," said Angeline.

"Oh." I glanced down at the crumpled pelisse, half unbuttoned over my even-more-crumpled gown from last night. Automatically, I tried to smooth them both down. It didn't work. "Ah, that's only—"

"You went to sleep in it," Angeline said, and narrowed her eyes at me like an Indian cobra preparing for the kill.

I swallowed, frozen in her cobra glare. "Um... I was cold?"

She arched one eyebrow. "Indeed. So you went all the way downstairs to find your pelisse instead of using the spare blanket in the cupboard beside the bed."

"Well..." I bounced on my toes. I didn't have time for this! "The truth is, I went out for a walk last night, after all of you left. I wasn't tired and I wanted some exercise."

"You went for a walk," Angeline said evenly. "In the middle of Bath. At night."

"I told you so, didn't I?" I turned and reached for the door handle once more. "I know, I know, it was a stupid thing to do, but I didn't get hurt, and I have to go now, so—"

"Give it up, Kat," Angeline said. "I know exactly what you did last night."

"You do?" I turned back around to stare at her. "How?"

"Because it is painfully obvious." She sighed. "You followed us to the Assembly Rooms to spy on me. That's why you didn't have time to change into your nightgown – you must have left the moment you saw us call for our cloaks, and then you ran all the way home to get here before me." She shook her head. "You are completely ridiculous, do you know that? Were you at least satisfied by what you saw?"

"Uh..." My mind raced. I said, "Yes...?"

"Ha." Angeline crossed her arms. "Well, then, you'll be happy to know that today you aren't going to have to resort to any such tricks in order to spy on me. Today, I'm going to let you come with me."

"Fine," I said. "Later. I'll go anywhere you like, but first..."

"We're going to the Baths."

My jaw dropped. I couldn't speak.

"Well, don't just stare at me!" Angeline said. "I'm sure you noticed the Baths. They're just around the corner from the Pump Room."

"Why are we going to the Baths?" My voice came out as an agonised squeak. Had she been involved last night, too? Was my entire family going to turn into a band of crazed Minerva-worshippers? "If Charles talked you into this—"

"Charles?" She blinked. "What does Charles have to do with anything?"

I had to be certain. "He didn't suggest that you go to the Baths? Last night—"

"Charles disappeared partway through the evening and only came back just in time to leave with the rest of us," Angeline said, "by which point he was far too foxed to speak a word of sense to me or anybody else. He has nothing to do with this. You do."

"How?"

She smiled like a cat who had just seen a whole bowl full of delicious cream belonging to someone else... and was getting ready to lick up every last drop of it. "You, darling Kat, have been feeling most unwell. Remember? That's why you had to leave the Pump Room with such immoderate speed yesterday morning. That's why you drank the Bath water in the first place."

"Ah..."

"So I am going to be a good, kind sister and take you to the Baths for your health. For which no one could possibly blame me."

I narrowed my eyes at her. "Why would you want to?"

"I just do," Angeline said, and shrugged. "Call it a whim."

Call it a wild story, I thought, and snorted. I didn't have time to pursue it any further, though. So I only said, "Can you swear to me that this has nothing to do with Sulis Minerva?"

Angeline looked at me as if I were mad. "With whom?"

"Never mind," I said, and fled through the bedroom door, into the corridor outside.

I was heading for Lucy's bedroom, on the other side of the staircase, but a shriek from downstairs brought me to a halt. It sounded like Maria's voice, and it was followed by a bellow so massive and so undignified, I would never have imagined it coming from Mrs Wingate:

"Lu-*ceee*!!!"

Oh Lord. I turned and ran for the stairs.

Stepmama caught me partway down. Even as her lace cap bobbed into view below me, she had already started her lecture. "Katherine," she said in her most long-suffering tone, "how many times must I be forced to tell you that running is not ladylike – ohh!" We came into full view of each other, and she gasped. "What on earth have you been doing?"

"Nothing," I said, and hurried the rest of the way down to where she blocked the staircase. "Sleeping. But I'm very hungry now, so I thought I would find breakfast, and then—"

"Your gown; your pelisse!" I thought Stepmama might swoon with horror. She took the crumpled sleeve of my pelisse in her hand and gazed at it as soulfully as if it were an injured puppy. "How could you have ruined your clothing this early in the morning?"

I shrugged off her arm. I could hear Maria's voice gabbling incomprehensibly from the direction of the breakfast room, on the floor just below us.

"Please," I said. "I am very hungry, so if I could just—"

"Not until you've marched back up to your room and changed into something appropriate!" Stepmama drew herself to her full height and pointed up the staircase like an avenging angel. "I don't want to see you down here again until you are wearing a clean and neatly pressed morning gown and—"

"Oh, for—"

"No, Katherine!" She lifted her chin and glared at me. "Firstly, the Wingates are having a private family discussion at the moment" – there was a crash from the breakfast room – "and do not require any company. And secondly" – she looked me up and down and shuddered – "you will *not* embarrass our entire family by appearing in such a state in the Wingates' breakfast room today or any other day. Did you even brush your hair this morning?"

I ground my teeth. A second crash, even louder than the first, sounded in the breakfast room, accompanied by more shrieks from Maria. I looked longingly past Stepmama's rigid figure. "Please! If I absolutely swear to change my clothing directly afterwards..."

The door to the library cracked open, just beside the breakfast room. The noise from the Wingates' argument must have driven Papa out of his refuge. His expression, as he poked his head out from the library, looked distinctly hunted. But when he saw us on the steps just above him, and took in Stepmama's threatening position, he looked positively horrified. He hastily drew back, like a tortoise retreating into his shell.

"Ah, I do beg your pardon, my dears. I'll just—"

"George!" Stepmama said, and swivelled so that her accusing finger pointed straight at him. "Do you see what your daughter has done this time?"

Her distraction was exactly what I needed. I leaped forward, sliding between her and the wall and ignoring her gasp of outrage. Papa only closed his eyes with an expression of pain as I whisked straight past him.

"Katherine Ann Stephenson, get back here NOW!" Stepmama hissed.

But it was too late. I was already pushing open the door to the breakfast room and the chaos inside.

Shattered china covered the ornate Chinese carpet. The heavy, polished wooden table lay toppled on its side, spilling toast and jam and coffee everywhere. Maria stood flattened against one wall, eyes wild; Mrs Wingate was puce with outrage against another... and Lucy stood in the middle of the chaos, blinking out at us all with innocent confusion.

Wild magic filled the room, sparking off my skin. I sidled in as carefully as if I were approaching a bull in his own field.

The Wingates didn't even seem to notice me, or Stepmama, who arrived behind me a moment later and stopped dead in the open doorway. Needless to say, Papa did not accompany her.

"Good heavens," Stepmama said weakly. "What has happened here?"

Lucy's lip quivered. She opened her mouth as if to speak, but Maria got there first.

"It was Lucy!" she said, and pointed.

Lucy's eyes filled with tears. She let out a sob, but didn't speak.

Stepmama looked doubtfully at the toppled table. "But— surely Miss Lucy isn't strong enough to—"

"You think that because you don't know the worst!" Maria said. Her hair was dishevelled, straggling from its pins and brushed with specks of broken china, but her face was pinched with righteous fury. "Not only is she wicked and shameless, she's a—"

"Maria!" Mrs Wingate said sharply.

Even as she spoke, three silver candlesticks flew off the sideboard and slammed straight into the wall by Maria's

head. I saw Lucy's face crumple with horror, but her moan
was buried by Maria's shriek of shock and fury.

"That is quite enough, young lady!" Mrs Wingate
gathered herself up and glowered at Lucy. "Bad enough to
have disgraced yourself in front of your own family. Bad
enough to frighten your own sister and behave like a hoyden
who can never, ever be allowed in public. But to disgrace
us all with your shame in front of our guests—"

"I didn't mean to!" Lucy said. "Mama, please! Truly,
I didn't—"

"Silence!" Mrs Wingate thundered. "There is nothing
you could say that would excuse your behaviour. Never has
such a scandal been known in our family! That I should
live to see my own daughter reveal herself to be" – her face
quivered with disgust, as if she could barely bring herself
to even form the words – "a *witch*!"

Stepmama fell back against the door. "Ohhh," she
moaned softly. "Oh..."

"You see?" Maria added. "You've shocked Mrs Stephenson,
too. Everyone will be shocked when they find out the truth
about you!"

But I met Stepmama's gaze, and I knew what she was
really thinking. Seen only by me, Stepmama's lips formed
the unmistakable question: *Kat, what have you done?*

I sighed. It was time to take charge of the situation.

"No one will find out the truth," Mrs Wingate was
saying heavily. "Because Lucy will be sent away."

"Lucy," I said, and crossed the room quickly to take her
hands. I was just in time, too – one of the fallen chairs was
just beginning to rise from the floor, its jerky, spinning
motion matching Lucy's agitation. I bit back a gasp as our
skin touched. The wild magic burned my hands. When our
eyes met, though, the chair slowly lowered itself to the

ground. Lucy clung to my hands. Her blue eyes brimmed with tears. Speaking loudly and clearly for everyone around us to hear, I said, "You look so unwell!"

"I..." She blinked at me, and I narrowed my eyes at her purposefully. "I feel fi—" she began, but I squeezed her hands hard and glared at her, and she gasped. "Oh!" she said. "I mean, I do feel unwell. Actually." She slid a frightened glance at her mother.

"Very unwell," I said firmly, and was careful not to look at anyone else, even though I could feel them all watching me. "Let me support you before you faint."

"Um – thank you?" Lucy leaned tentatively against me.

I tucked her head into my shoulder. Under the cover of her hair, I hissed, "Faint! Quickly!"

"Ohhh!" Lucy sighed, and fell fully into my arms with all the gusto of a fully fledged romantic heroine.

I staggered. "Oh, do help me – someone, please!"

The Wingates only stared at me from their different sides of the room, but Stepmama hurried across the room to join us. Colour rose high in her cheeks and I knew I would hear more about this later, but for now, she took Lucy's other arm and half her weight.

"She needs to be laid down on a couch," said Stepmama. "Does anyone have any smelling salts?"

Lucy twitched at the suggestion. I kicked her ankle, and she subsided.

"Shall we take her to the drawing room?" Stepmama suggested. "Or—"

"She is not going into the drawing room!" Maria said. "Only imagine, Mama, if anyone should come to call—"

"It isn't to be thought of," Mrs Wingate said. "No, you may put the girl in her own room, where she belongs. And then lock the door!"

Stepmama frowned and opened her mouth as if to argue. Then she shut it tightly. When she spoke again, after a moment's pause, her voice was mild but her cheeks were even more flushed. "Very well," she said submissively. "But perhaps a doctor...?"

"No doctors," said Mrs Wingate. "We shall not discuss our family's shame with—"

"No doctors?" said Angeline. She was standing in the doorway. We all swung around at the sound of her voice. She stood there looking as innocent as snow – but I hadn't heard the door open and I wondered how long she had stood there watching us before she had decided it was time to speak.

She stepped into the room now, looking kindly at Lucy's limp figure. "Poor Cousin Lucy," she said. "No, of course you don't want to call a doctor. I have a much better idea. Kat and I were already planning a healthful trip to the Baths this morning, weren't we, Kat?"

"Well..." I said.

"There, now." She smiled sunnily at Mrs Wingate's puce face. "What a delightful notion. The Baths are so unfashionable nowadays, you know, that no one of any consequence will be there, and this distressing little illness will be sorted out immediately. I promise you, ma'am, we shall take very good care of Lucy. It will be just the thing for her."

CHAPTER SIXTEEN

THE BATH-HOUSE IN THE MORNING WAS VERY DIFFERENT from the dark, echoey place it became at night. The Baths might not be popular or fashionable anymore, but there was still a steady trickle of invalids flowing into the building along with us, and there was a whole flotilla of officious attendants lying in wait for visitors, whether we wanted their help or not. Three cloth-women led us into a changing room on the ground floor and took our measurements for special bathing gowns made of bilious yellow linen. There was no sign of any rowdy young men or other Minerva-worshippers in the warm, fire-lit changing room, and the Baths' own wild magic was so muted I could scarcely feel it.

Lucy's skin still sparked with wild magic, though, and the closer we came to the Baths themselves, the stronger and sharper the sparks became, until it hurt to hold her hand. I gritted my teeth and kept a firm grip anyway.

Beneath the brim of her fashionable bonnet, her eyes looked like a frightened doe's, and the last thing I needed was her agitation getting the better of her. If the wild magic took over again in a public place, Mrs Wingate would probably have her locked up forever.

I only let go of Lucy's hand so that my cloth-woman could pull the hideous linen bathing gown over my arms. As soon as I could see again, the first thing I did was look for Lucy. She was having her own gown put on, and, so far, nothing in the room seemed to be spinning or lifting of its own volition. I let out a very small sigh, but didn't let myself relax. We still had to see what would happen in the Baths.

Angeline, of course, looked like a queen being served by her attendant – serene and untroubled by any worries – as her own bathing gown was buttoned up. Of course, Angeline thought she'd done a marvellously good deed by helping Lucy escape the house for a few hours – but then, Angeline hadn't seen the wild magic in action. She assumed that Lucy was just another witch who'd foolishly lost control of her temper. Her only response to the chaos in the breakfast room, as we'd bundled Lucy out of the house, had been a softly spoken comment in Lucy's ear that had left Lucy looking even more lost and bewildered than ever. There had been no way to explain the truth to my aggravating older sister on our way through the crowded streets of Bath, so I hadn't yet been able to knock the smug look off her face.

Taking Lucy back to the Baths, just hours after the wild magic had possessed her, was one of the worst ideas Angeline had ever had. So it was even more annoying than usual to see her brimming with self-satisfaction.

As the last button was buttoned, Angeline's cloth-woman

asked, "And which Bath will you three ladies wish to enjoy, Miss? The Queen's Bath is most—"

"We shall be bathing in the King's Bath," Angeline said firmly.

Lucy gasped, and her hand flew to her mouth. The cloth-woman only nodded and led the way out of the changing room, into the corridor where a guide waited for us; Angeline followed directly afterwards, head held high, and Lucy and I trailed behind.

"What is it?" I hissed. "What's wrong?"

Lucy's eyes were wide with shock but not, I was relieved to see, with unhappiness or fear. We were in no danger from the wild magic... at least not yet. "The Queen's Bath is for ladies, only," she whispered. "The King's Bath... well!" She squeezed my arm, her cheeks as pink as the ribbons on her bonnet. "It allows gentlemen as well!"

"Oh!" I blinked. Then I said, "Well, at least it can't be any worse than what we saw last night."

Lucy burst into irrepressible giggles. Angeline looked back at us with a quelling frown and Lucy pressed her lips together, but the giggles leaked out anyway. For once, I didn't actually mind. They made her seem more herself than she had all day.

The guide led us down a set of steps and across depressingly familiar, damp tiles to a wooden doorway that opened onto the same bath where the Minerva-worshippers had frolicked last night. Nine or ten invalids were already bathing in the steaming water, accompanied by their guides. Two of them sat together on a covered platform in the centre of the Bath, with the water up to their shoulders, while their guides chatted nearby. Others sat with their eyes closed, resting on underwater benches inside the dark stone alcoves that surrounded the pool. Beyond the terraced wall, I could hear more splashing and female voices – the Queen's Bath, I assumed. The *proper* Bath, Elissa would have said. I sighed.

The fresh air was cool but not cold and bright sunlight streamed down from the open sky above us, blending into the thick veil of mist that rose from the Bath. In the full morning light, the water was a deep, mysterious green, and little copper bowls floated on its surface.

A flash of light against one of the copper bowls caught my eye, and I looked up. *Oh, no.*

The large windows that looked down onto the Bath had been dark and empty last night, and I had been too busy to even wonder what building they might be part of. This morning, I could see flickers of colour moving back and forth through the glass, and I realised I had made a bad mistake.

"What's behind those windows?" I said to Lucy, and pointed. But I was afraid I already knew.

"Why, the Pump Room, of course," she said. "Didn't you look out the windows yesterday to see the bathers?"

I shook my head. In the press of the crowd yesterday morning, I'd never even neared the windows, much less looked out of them. But I had the beginnings of a horrible suspicion.

Angeline had manoeuvred us out to the Baths early in the morning, just as the fashionable elite were all assembling next door in the Pump Room. She had chosen this particular Bath, just underneath the Pump Room windows. That meant she had wanted us to be seen. And *that* meant...

"So you did dare, after all," said a deep, horribly familiar voice just behind us. "Brave girl indeed."

I groaned as Angeline turned round. "Lord Scarwood,"

she said, and smiled as she curtseyed. Her eyelashes flickered down to cover her eyes. "Did you doubt my courage?"

Lucy let out a squeak of sheer excitement. I ground my teeth. Lord Scarwood was wearing a bilious yellow bathing outfit of his own, which looked particularly bizarre beneath his fashionable beaver hat, but he looked as oiled and polished as ever – and enormously pleased with himself. The guides stood watching us like a prime theatrical entertainment.

"Lord Scarwood," I said, and did not curtsey. "You don't look ill."

"No?" He raised one eyebrow and looked at me with a gaze I didn't like at all. It looked half-contemptuous and half... something I didn't even want to interpret. "And yet, I must tell you you are mistaken, for I have been mortally wounded by the arrow of love."

Lucy sighed audibly. I fought the urge to be physically sick.

"Come," Angeline said. "Shouldn't we all bathe, as that's what we came for?"

I shot a look at the big windows overlooking the Bath. From this distance, I couldn't make out any individual faces. They couldn't see us yet, either, as we stood in the shadows of the doorway.

"I'm not in the mood anymore," I said. "I'd rather—"

"But Kat, we aren't here for you," Angeline said. "We are here for poor Cousin Lucy, who was so agitated by her nerves this morning. Come, Lucy." She reached out and took Lucy's hand.

I started forward. "Wait!"

But it was too late. Together, they ran down the steps into the mist-covered water, and headed for the centre of the Bath.

"Brave indeed," Lord Scarwood murmured, and strode into the water with a predatory grin. Steaming water rose halfway up the back of his yellow coat, and his black hat shone in the bright sunlight as he struck out through the hot water, after Angeline.

I groaned, took one last, desperate glance at the overlooking windows, and splashed in after them.

Water closed around my body like a warm embrace, almost intoxicating in its sensation of comfort. As I sank neck-deep into the Bath, mist swirled around my head, blinding me. For one brief, intense moment, I couldn't see or move or even think – only *feel*, with every inch of my skin. Sparks sizzled along the length of my body. Instead of feeling painful, they felt invigorating. They fizzed inside my head like tiny bubbles exploding.

I understood for the first time why people thought the water of Bath must be health-giving. It was certainly filled with magic.

Magic. I forced myself to focus. Shapes bobbed around in front of me, hard to make out in the mist that swirled around my head and neck. I pushed myself forward through the water until I could reach out and touch Lucy's arm.

It burned against my skin. I jumped back, gasping.

"Lucy? Are you all right?"

She turned her face to me. Even through the mist, I could see her exalted expression. "Oh, Kat. I feel... I feel..." She opened her eyes. Sparks danced inside them. "I feel so strange," she whispered.

"We have to get you out of here." I took hold of her shoulder, wincing at the shock of pain, and pushed her gently. "Go! Get out of the Bath, now. I'll be with you in a moment. I just have to make sure Angeline isn't doing anything stupid." *Much hope of that*, I added silently.

Lucy nodded, but she didn't move. "I feel so..."

"Go!" I said, and pushed her harder. She started to move in the right direction, and I splashed through the hot water, blinking sulphur-scented steam out of my eyes.

The water felt thick with heat and magic, forcing me into slow, heavy steps. With every movement, I had to fight my body's urge to stop and stand still to luxuriate in the heat that surrounded me and the wild sparks of magic that raced up and down my skin.

I gritted my teeth and pushed onwards. The Bath hadn't looked so large when I'd seen it from the doorway – I'd been able to look across it in one glance and take in every bather. Now, though, with my head veiled by mist, all I could see were dark shapes around me, and the Bath felt as wide as a river, and almost as impassable.

Magic, I thought, with loathing.

I tipped my head back, blinking and focusing on the bright blue sky above me to clear my head. Colours flashed in the corner of my vision. I turned and saw a trio of people framed inside one of the large windows in the Pump Room.

Oh, no. Stepmama, Maria and Mrs Wingate were all standing together, looking down at us. And what else might they be seeing?

I lowered my head and plunged forward with new determination. Even if Angeline wanted to throw away the rest of her reputation on the stupidest scheme I'd ever heard of, I was not about to let her do it unchallenged. If Elissa had been here, she would have kept Angeline from stepping into the Bath in the first place. All I could do was keep our sister from damaging her chances even further.

I heard their voices before I saw them.

"Don't tell me you're afraid now, after such a display of courage." That was Viscount Scarwood, of course, his voice damnably self-satisfied, like warm toffee swirling in heavy cream.

"I didn't say I was afraid..." Angeline sounded meek and breathy and nothing like herself. She was definitely up to something. As I finally glimpsed her through the steam, she held her head shyly lowered, looking to one side instead of meeting Scarwood's eyes. She looked every inch the innocent young lady, quivering with nerves. "But my lord, how can I tell if you are sincere? When I have heard such tales of your... adventures..." She let the word trail modestly off, wrapping the euphemism in the mist that swirled around them.

I thought: *If Viscount Scarwood can't tell that she's acting, he is a fool.*

But perhaps he'd had too many successful seductions to even think of questioning a new victory.

"Rumours," he said, and chuckled. "People have been trying to frighten you with rumours and tall tales, because they are jealous. Jealous of your beauty and jealous of your luck in catching my eye when no other woman has before."

I snorted. But I was still too far away for them to hear me.

"I shall tell you what is the truth," said Viscount Scarwood, his voice lowering to an even deeper, throbbing baritone. "The moment I first saw you, Cupid's arrow struck me."

I gagged. Sulphurous mist entered my throat and made me choke. I clung to my neck, trying to cough the mist out. I almost didn't catch his next line until it was too late.

"Ever since I first saw you," Viscount Scarwood continued,

his voice dropping so low I could barely make it out, "I have wanted to do... *this*."

"No!" I yelled. I threw myself forward, splashing through the hot water. But I was too slow. Even as I watched, Viscount Scarwood's head tipped towards my sister. He closed his hand around her shoulders. She leaned into him, yielding pliantly to his embrace...

An unexpected voice spoke, breaking the spell.

"Angeline?"

Angeline broke out of the embrace, gasping. I spun round, blinking through the mist.

I forgot all about Stepmama in the window above us. I forgot about Mrs Wingate's disapproval and Maria's vicious, gossiping tongue.

Frederick Carlyle stood in the closest doorway, holding his mother's arm and staring at Angeline, his face pale with shock and betrayal.

CHAPTER SEVENTEEN

AT FIRST I COULDN'T EVEN BELIEVE IT. FREDERICK CARLYLE was halfway across the country. He couldn't be here. It simply wasn't possible.

Then I saw the smug look on his mother's face and I knew I wasn't imagining anything.

"You see?" Mrs Carlyle said. "I told you she was a trollop. I *told* you—!"

"No!" Angeline broke away from Viscount Scarwood. "Frederick!" she said. "Wait. It's not—"

"'Frederick'?" Scarwood sounded richly amused. I didn't turn to look at him; I was too hypnotised by the look of pain and shock frozen onto Frederick Carlyle's face. "I take it I have a rival," Scarwood drawled. "But perhaps—"

"No." Mr Carlyle broke out of his trance. His face hardened. He gave a short, jerky bow. "I assure you, sir, you are entirely mistaken." He shot one last, burning look at Angeline. "As was I. Obviously."

"Frederick!" Angeline struck through the water towards him, splashing through mist.

"No," he said. "No. We have nothing to say to one another anymore."

"But—"

He turned his back on her and strode away.

"Frederick!" his mother squawked. Her smug look disappeared. She turned to scurry after him, holding up her heavy yellow bathing skirts. "You may not leave until you have finished escorting me through the Baths. *You may not...*"

They disappeared into the shadows beyond the doorway, her hectoring voice trailing behind them.

Angeline stood like a statue of horror, staring after them.

Viscount Scarwood reached for her arm. "Now, my delectable angel, you mustn't let one priggish old suitor from the country discompose you."

"Ohhh!" She struck his arm away with a sound of pure frustration and lunged across the Bath to the opposite doorway. In a moment, she was up the stairs and running, but – I could hardly believe it – she was heading in the direction of the changing rooms. She wasn't even trying to go after Frederick Carlyle like a sensible person.

I shook my head, sighing. Yet again, it was up to me to manage things.

Rather than looking offended or displeased, Viscount Scarwood looked disturbingly self-satisfied as I splashed past him. He was whistling between his teeth, a tune I didn't recognise. I doubted I would want to know the words.

"You may tell your angelic sister," he called out, "that I look forward to seeing her again very soon."

I scowled and hurried up the wide steps that led out of

the Bath, through the doorway that the Carlyles had used. I could hear Scarwood splashing up the steps behind me, still whistling, but I ignored him. My mind was already working on possible tactics to get Mr Carlyle away from his mother – or, failing that, the best way to force the truth into him without his mother's interruption.

I was so absorbed in my plans, I didn't even notice the wild magic growing stronger behind me until it was too late.

"HAIL SULIS MINERVA!!!!"

I spun round.

The water of the Bath wasn't just steaming anymore. It looked like it was boiling. People were screaming and scrambling for the steps. The closest doorway was full of invalids and guides pushing and shoving against each other. I raced to a window and pressed my face against it. Sparks of wild magic formed a spiralling tunnel above the bubbling water swirling around a single person: *Lucy*.

She hadn't left the Bath when I'd told her to, after all. She stood in the centre, surrounded by boiling water and wild magic, and tipped her head back to face the open sky. Her bonnet had come off and her hair, freed from its pins, whirled in a blonde mass around her face and shoulders. Her arms swept out to each side as if they were holding up the sky itself. And her face...

Her face was utterly unrecognisable.

"HAIL SULIS MINERVA!" her voice said again, with the force of a million buzzing sparks of magic, and the great stone walls around the Bath trembled.

For the first time in my life, I had to fight against the impulse to swoon.

Instead, I headed for the doorway, forcing my way past the increasing crowd in the corridor. Moving towards the

Bath felt like running through sludge; the pressure of the wild magic pushing against me was so intense, I had to fight my way forward with every step.

"Lucy!" I screamed.

People were screaming all around me as they fled for safety – not just the invalids who'd been in the King's Bath with us, but more bathers running down the corridor from the Queen's Bath and a whole host of guides who'd abandoned their charges. But not everyone fled. A few people stayed, pressed against the windows and staring at Lucy as if she were a monster. Out of the corner of my eye, I saw Scarwood lounging against a wall, arms crossed. He gazed through a window onto the Bath, looking as bored as if he were only watching a rather tedious play.

Lucy's mouth opened again, and I braced myself. *"LUCK AT THE GAMING TABLES,"* she said.

A burst of wild magic shot out towards the Pump Room next door.

"What—?" I clamped my mouth shut as I realised: it was what Charles had asked for last night when he'd made his sacrifice.

Which meant... I squeezed my hands into fists, trying desperately to remember what Papa had told me about Sulis Minerva's shrine. People had left her sacrifices in exchange for favours granted. But not just pleasant, helpful favours for themselves – sometimes what they asked for was...

"A CURSE ON MY TUTOR," said the enormous, buzzing voice through Lucy's mouth. *"MAY HE—"*

"NO!" I gathered up everything inside me, aimed it all at the wild magic as it focused on the curse, and let my powers explode.

I woke up a minute later, lying flat on the damp stone

tiles of the corridor. Pain banged through my skull. Wild
magic still filled the air and that terrible voice still chanted.
I felt as if I'd been hollowed out and left scalded and
empty. I reached for my power...

But I had nothing left.

I stared numbly at the tunnel of wild magic around
Lucy's body. It was growing even stronger, more and more
clouded with sparks as she – or something – kept forcing
it out through her.

If I felt scalded just from trying to break that magic with
my Guardian powers, how did Lucy feel now? The real Lucy?

How much of her was even left inside?

I pushed myself up off the tiles, panting with effort. It
hurt to move. I had to do something, but I had no idea
what. I looked around for anyone left who could help.

The corridor was nearly empty now. Only Viscount
Scarwood remained, and he had plastered himself against
his wall, all amusement gone. As I looked, he met my eyes.

I swallowed my pride and reached out my arm.
"Please—"

His face convulsed with horror. He took a quick, shuffling
sidestep against the wall, gave one last look at Lucy in the
Bath... then turned and fled.

I was alone.

At some point, one of the other Guardians in the city
would sense the magic here and come to investigate. For
once, I would be grateful to see horrible Lord Ravenscroft.
But how long it would take for any of them to get here?
And how much damage would that thing inside Lucy do in
the meantime?

I felt a moment of pure despair. Without any Guardian
training, I didn't know what to do. I had nothing on my
side.

Except...

I pushed myself up onto my feet. My legs wobbled under me. The thing controlling Lucy didn't even see me go; her face was still turned up to the sky, chanting curses and favours in an endless, rolling list.

I shuffled back across the tiles like an old woman, leaning against the stone walls for support. The changing room we'd used earlier was empty; Angeline must have stalked out as soon as she had changed her clothing and all the cloth-women had fled.

I went straight to my pelisse where it hung on the wall. I reached inside to the inner pocket I'd sewn secretly, weeks before.

There.

Mama's mirror. My fingers closed around it and I felt a moment of sheer relief. It was cool and unresponsive, at first. Then the sulphurous dampness lingering on my hand soaked into it, and tingling warmth began to emanate from the golden case.

I held it cupped between both hands as I shuffled back to the King's Bath.

There was no one left in the corridor outside the Bath. But the windows of the Pump Room were sure to be absolutely crammed with colour now: all of Bath's most fashionable elite, taking in the show. I gritted my teeth.

Stepmama really would murder me for this.

Every step pushed against the pressure of the wild magic, like a giant hand forcing me back. My legs wobbled and shook. But I didn't drop the mirror.

I was still a Guardian, whether Lord Ravenscroft wanted to admit it or not. It was my job to protect Society from malicious magic, no matter how intimidating. I was Lucy's only hope.

I stumbled and slipped on the damp tiles, forcing my way against the magic. My breath came in short pants of effort. Inside the closest narrow doorway, on the step just above the madly bubbling water, I came to a stop.

In the centre of the Bath, the magical sparks formed a tight, whirling cloud around Lucy's body. Her head was still tipped back, her unfamiliar gaze still focused on the sky above. The great voice rolled through her, as powerful as ever, without so much as a hint of hoarseness.

I tightened my grip on Mama's mirror.

I couldn't break the cloud of wild magic around Lucy. I couldn't break the curses being carried through her mouth. But there was one thing I could do.

I took a deep breath and jumped.

CHAPTER EIGHTEEN

HEAT SURROUNDED ME ON ALL SIDES. HOT, PRICKLING steam surged through my throat and nose, suffocating me. Sparks battered at my face. The Bath didn't feel intoxicating any longer. It felt murderous.

I wanted to scream with pain. I ground my teeth together instead. Blindly, I struck out through the cloud of sparks, gripping Mama's mirror in my left hand. It trailed through the water of the Bath and I felt it wake to full strength.

The rolling voice surrounded me. I couldn't see, but I could hear, and I followed the sound.

"MY GREAT-UNCLE'S WILL TO BE REWRITTEN IN MY FAVOUR." Magic shot out in a burst, singeing my hair.

It was the opening I needed. For just one moment, there was a break in the tight cloud of wild magic. I threw myself through.

My vision cleared. Lucy's face was exalted, her blue eyes dilated. Her mouth opened again.

"HAIL—"

I grabbed her arm. Her skin burned my hand.

"SULIS MINERVA!" she bellowed.

I opened Mama's mirror, and the world turned inside out.

I landed hard on the floor of the Golden Hall. My whole body felt raw and scalded by the boiling Bath. *And* I'd hit my head again. Curses.

Or rather... I swallowed down a sick feeling in my stomach. I didn't want to ever use, or even think, the word 'curses' again. Not after today.

Lucy. I opened my eyes, feeling only emptiness in my hand where her arm should have been.

She was lying four feet away from me, limp and, thankfully, unconscious. Her bare arms looked perfectly unmarked, like my own, despite the heat of the water we'd both stood in.

But our troubles weren't over yet by a long way. Standing above Lucy...

"Interethting," Lord Ravenscroft lisped, and raised his quizzing glass to study me. He was wearing the same large, jewelled rings that he had worn the first time we met, but they glittered more intensely in the golden light this time, catching my eyes. For a moment, I almost forgot my panic. There was something about them, something different...

His eyes narrowed. I gulped, abandoning all distractions.

"Very interethting indeed," said Lord Ravenscroft.

There was no one else in the Golden Hall, but it was filled with power.

I wasn't fooled anymore by Lord Ravenscroft's dandified appearance or his fashionable lisp. As his right eye, hideously magnified by the quizzing glass, studied me from head to toe, I felt chills run through my whole body.

The Golden Hall was huge, but it had never made me feel small before.

Be polite, I told myself. *Remember you came here for help.*

"Please," I said. I pushed myself up, wincing as my palms pressed against the hard floor. The wild magic might not have physically burned my skin, but it still hurt. "I didn't know what else to do, so I brought her here. Mr Gregson knows—"

"Mr Gregthon knowth," Lord Ravenscroft repeated after me, in a deadly tone. "Doeth he indeed?" He turned his head slightly. *"Aloythiuth?"*

There was a feeling of pressure behind his voice, one I'd never felt before. Less than a second later, Mr Gregson appeared behind him looking startled.

"What—? Oh." My old tutor took in the sight before him, and his eyes flared wide behind his spectacles. Then his expression rearranged itself into careful neutrality. "My lord. Miss Katherine. And... Miss Lucy Wingate, I see."

"Lucy went mad," I said quickly. I started towards him, hoping for understanding. "It was at the King's Bath. When Lucy got into the water, she—"

"Enough!" Lord Ravenscroft's voice cut straight through my explanation. The lisp dropped away from his voice; he said sharply, "Aloysius, Miss Stephenson appeared here using her mother's portal, a portal which I had closed myself, and closed for good. She brought along this girl, a stranger to our Order, who has clearly been possessed by highly dangerous wild magic. And she informed me..." He turned the quizzing glass on Mr Gregson, and his voice froze into ice. "Apparently, you know all about it."

"She informed you of that, did she?" Mr Gregson gave

me a look of weary resignation. "Thank you, Katherine."

I groaned. "There's no time for this. We have to do something for Lucy! When she went into the Bath—"

"*Silence*," Lord Ravenscroft said, and shot me a look.

My voice dried up in my throat. I tried to speak. Nothing came out.

"Now," said Lord Ravenscroft, and his voice eased into cold civility. "Tell me, Aloysius. What exactly is going on, and why have you utterly neglected to tell me any of it?"

Mr Gregson sighed. "It was my intention to tell you, my lord, the next time we met. The incident Miss Katherine is referring to took place last night. She—"

I couldn't speak, but I shook my head vigorously. *Today*, I mouthed.

He frowned at me. "Ah, and something new has occurred today? Perhaps—"

"Later," Lord Ravenscroft snapped. "Continue."

"Yes. Ah." Mr Gregson coughed. "As it happened, I spent last night in the building that contains the King's and Queen's Baths, observing the primary outlet from the springs."

"Despite the fact I had clearly informed you that no such watch would be necessary."

"As you say, my lord. And in fact, you were correct that the Source itself revealed very little except an increasing surge in wild magic, beginning in the evening hours."

"We already knew the wild magic was becoming unpredictable in its rise and fall," Lord Ravenscroft said. "This tells us nothing."

"Not on its own, no. But when added to Miss Katherine's observations of the King's Bath..."

"Ah. Miss Katherine." Lord Ravenscroft turned his muddy eyes on me. "And what exactly was Miss Katherine doing in the Baths at night? Or in Bath itself, for that matter?"

I tried to speak, but nothing came out of my throat. I could have screamed with frustration. It was unbearable to see the look of contempt on his face and not be able to answer him.

"Miss Katherine's older sister is making her Society début in Bath this season," Mr Gregson said mildly.

"Ah. You mean the witch." Lord Ravenscroft sneered. "Yes, Lady Fotherington told me all about her."

I ground my teeth together.

"But what Miss Katherine witnessed last night," Mr Gregson continued smoothly, "may be just the clue we've needed to understand the magical anomalies Bath has been experiencing."

"Indeed?" Lord Ravenscroft's voice dripped with disdain.

"Indeed. Someone has been studying the ancient magic of Bath's hot springs – and its usage, of which even I was not aware until last night. A group of young Oxford students last night offered sacrifices in the King's Bath to the goddess Sulis Minerva."

"Oxford students? Invoking the rites of Minerva in modern Bath?" Lord Ravenscroft let his quizzing glass fall to the end of its ribbon. "Really, Aloysius. Is this a serious report, or some misguided attempt at a jest?"

Mr Gregson frowned. "Indeed, my lord, I am not speaking in jest. The chants they recited—"

"The chants Miss Katherine claimed they had recited." Lord Ravenscroft turned to me, twirling the quizzing glass by its velvet ribbon. His gaze rested on my face, but his words were addressed to Mr Gregson. "Remind me, Aloysius. Miss Katherine's father... before he married Olivia Amberson and took orders in the Church, was he not renowned at Oxford as a classical scholar? Even in my own year I recall hearing mention of his name."

Mr Gregson blinked. "Why... why, yes, I believe he was. He had a rather prestigious Fellowship, as I recall, and—"

"Quite. And you say that the entire story of last night's bizarrely classical rites came straight from the lips of his daughter?"

I was panting with effort, but no amount of magical pressure could force any sound from my mouth.

Mr Gregson's frown deepened. "Yes, it did. And yet we were both observers when the summoned and unleashed wild magic possessed the unfortunate Wingate girl, so—"

"Summoned and unleashed indeed," said Lord Ravenscroft. "And by whom, exactly?"

"My lord, I told you—"

"I can tell you that myself, without even having been there," said Lord Ravenscroft. "Evidence, logic, and history all point straight to the only possible culprit." He raised his quizzing glass on its ribbon and pointed it like an arrow. "Miss Katherine Stephenson," he said.

✧ ✧ ✧

My mouth dropped open. I shook my head wildly.

Mr Gregson said, "My lord—"

"No, Aloysius. Lady Fotherington was quite right about this girl's danger... and about your own gullibility to her schemes. If you could swallow such a farrago of nonsense as she fed you about last night's escapade, you would believe any of her mad deceptions. She is quite as wild and uncontrollable as her mother, and just as irresponsible in her magical usage."

My fingernails dug into my palms.

"My lord," said Mr Gregson, "as much as I dislike to contradict you, the magical instability has been ongoing in Bath for almost three weeks. Miss Katherine only arrived a few days ago. She can hardly be held responsible for the surges of wild magic that brought us here for our investigation."

"Responsible? No, of course not. These unpredictable surges are undoubtedly a natural phenomenon, as I have pointed out all along. Who can say what might cause flux and flow of wild magic, in the ordinary course of affairs? But when Miss Katherine arrived in Bath and sensed the magical disturbance here, she was quick to make use of it for her own purposes."

No! I mouthed. But neither man was looking at me.

Mr Gregson said, "What purposes would those be?"

"Is it not obvious?" Lord Ravenscroft shrugged. "Having been expelled from our Order, she required another magical outlet. More than that, she undoubtedly wished revenge. We have proof enough of that in the fact that she has illicitly reactivated her portal to our Hall. That can only have been intended for a nefarious purpose."

I was shaking my aching head so hard it almost blinded me. At the word 'revenge', though, my heart sank. Wasn't that exactly what Mr Gregson himself had accused me of the night before? Wanting revenge on Lord Ravenscroft?

"I have no doubt," Lord Ravenscroft continued, "she was surprised and horrified to see you last night in the midst of her magical misdemeanours. So, what did she create as an excuse? Why, exactly the sort of tale she must have grown up hearing from her own father. That was where Miss Katherine made her error. No one but a classicist – or a classicist's daughter – would even guess at the true ancient uses of the spring below the Baths.

Certainly the average Oxford student would not. The very speed with which she came up with her story is proof enough of her deception."

"Well..." Mr Gregson's eyebrows were pinched together; he didn't spare a glance for my shaking head, or for the words I was frantically mouthing at him. Finally he said, heavily, "I cannot believe she would have intentionally harmed her friend. Her distress at Miss Wingate's predicament was very real and could not have been feigned."

"Perhaps not." Lord Ravenscroft glanced down at Lucy's limp body without interest. "I wouldn't be at all surprised if that had been an accident. Wild magic is nothing to trifle with. That is exactly why we must be so stern in our punishment of any magic-worker so rash and misguided as to manipulate the natural sources of wild magic. Her malicious and selfish recklessness can only endanger everyone around her."

I didn't, I mouthed. *It wasn't me!*

Mr Gregson said, "Last night... Miss Katherine said she'd heard the students in the Bath talking of another man, someone who had persuaded them into performing the ritual."

"Really, Aloysius. Haven't we heard enough already of these mythical students?"

"There were other people in the Bath last night, though," said Mr Gregson, and I breathed a sigh of relief at the firmness in his tone. "I heard stealthy footsteps earlier in the evening – someone approaching the room where I waited. I believe that that person turned back only when they realised the room was occupied."

Lord Ravenscroft tapped his fingers on the silver rim of his quizzing glass. "The stealthiness of the footsteps was probably a figment of your imagination. No doubt it was only the manager performing a last check of the building, or one of the cleaning staff."

"Perhaps," said Mr Gregson. "But the two girls were definitely being chased when they came upon me."

"No doubt they had angered the nightwatchmen." Lord Ravenscroft shrugged. "Miss Stephenson has a talent for such things."

Mr Gregson sighed. "Yes," he said, and turned to look gravely at me through his spectacles. "That, she most certainly does."

I didn't do it! I mouthed at him. I prayed he could read the truth in my gaze.

He was my tutor, the one who'd told me about my powers and invited me into the Order in the first place, despite opposition from Lady Fotherington and everyone else who had hated my mama after her expulsion. He had been Mama's tutor, too, and the only one not to despise her for turning to witchcraft when she fell in love with Papa. Surely he had to have some faith in me, no matter how angry he'd been the night before. Surely...

"I did think at the time there was something odd about her story of the students," Mr Gregson said, and I closed my eyes in a moment of pure despair.

"Well, then. We are in agreement," Lord Ravenscroft purred. "In that case, there is only one thing to be done. As an inveterate and irredeemable misuser of magic to the danger of all Society, and as someone who can no longer be trusted with the possession of her own powers, Katherine Stephenson must be... pacified."

CHAPTER NINETEEN

PACIFIED. I FROZE.

"It could destroy her mind," Mr Gregson said.

Pacification was the worst punishment the Order could bestow. It took away a magic-worker's access to her own powers – and to those parts of her mind that had been used to control them.

"Better that her mind be destroyed than that she should cause havoc to all the innocent members of Society around her." Lord Ravenscroft raised his quizzing glass to study me. "Yes. It only takes one look at her face to see that her wilfulness is quite irredeemable. If her expulsion from the Order could not teach her humility, nothing can. Should you like to do the procedure yourself, Aloysius, or shall I?"

I looked around the Golden Hall wildly, searching for an escape route. But there were no windows or doors in the smooth, arching walls. I could catapult myself and Lucy out of the Hall with magic, if I were quick enough –

but that would take us straight back to where Mama's mirror waited for us, deep in the steaming King's Bath.

For a moment, that sounded almost tempting.

But I couldn't abandon Lucy here. And if I dived back into the Bath with Lucy in tow, Sulis Minerva would come back in full force, cursing with abandon. How many innocent people would sicken or die, just to save my mind and powers?

If I risked that for my own safety, Lord Ravenscroft would be right about me. And that would be the worst thing of all.

So I lifted my chin and set my jaw to keep it from trembling. I looked straight into Lord Ravenscroft's magnified eye through his fashionable, expensive quizzing glass and I hoped that it would happen fast. I prayed I wouldn't disgrace myself by screaming or crying if it hurt.

Mr Gregson said, "I should like to do it myself, my lord. And if I might beg one favour? I would appreciate the opportunity to do it alone. You know that she, as well as her mother, was my student. I would like to give her one final gift of privacy while the procedure takes place."

"Very well." Lord Ravenscroft shrugged. "But don't let her soften you with one of her stories. And remember – the kindest way to do it is with speed. I'll want to see evidence of the procedure, afterwards."

"Of course, my lord."

I was breathing quickly now, in short, shallow gasps. I could have hugged Mr Gregson for his request – now, even if I did scream, at least Lord Ravenscroft wouldn't hear it and Lady Fotherington would never know. But every passing moment made the truth of what was about to happen more and more real.

I would never do magic again. No, worse: I might never even recognise Angeline again – or Elissa, or Papa, or foolish, feckless Charles, who could be talked into anything, or even Stepmama...

Lord Ravenscroft gave Mr Gregson one last stern look through his quizzing glass, and vanished.

The constriction around my throat disappeared with him. I took a deep, ragged breath that held a shameful hint of tears.

"Katherine," Mr Gregson began.

My buried words came tumbling out, the most important first. "You have to help Lucy! I won't be able to tell you this afterwards, so you have to listen to me now. When she went into the King's Bath, she became Sulis Minerva – or Sulis Minerva became her."

He sighed. "First of all, there is no such thing as the goddess Sulis Minerva—"

"There was in the Bath today! She was cursing all the people she'd been asked to curse last night, and sending out magical favours – you can ask anyone, there were plenty of witnesses. Half the city must have been watching from the Pump Room windows, as well as all the people in the Baths, like horrible Viscount Scarwood, and..." *Dash it*. I felt tears building up in my throat again. I forced them back in a deeper breath. "I won't be able to help her myself after this, so you have to—"

"Katherine." Mr Gregson put one hand on my shoulder. "There is something you must do, which is to listen to me before you say any more."

All I'd done for the last ten minutes was listen, while they'd decided my whole future for me. But if I'd tried to say that, I really would have begun to cry with rage and frustration. So I only nodded, slammed my jaw together to hold back anything else and met his worried gaze as fiercely as I could.

"Katherine, I am not going to pacify you."

My jaw dropped open. "You're not?" It was such a shock, I felt dizzy. I had to reach out my hands to my sides for balance. "But—"

"I believe Lord Ravenscroft is mistaken in you."

"But you— but you said—"

"When his lordship makes up his mind, it is not easy to change," said Mr Gregson. "And he does not take well to insolence from anyone, as you have learned to your peril. Had I openly disagreed with him, he would have performed the procedure himself and the matter would have been finished. However, if I can present him with proof of the real malefactor's identity, I am certain he will be open to reason."

"Oh. Oh!" I let out my breath in a rush. "You did believe me, after all."

"I believe that the rites of Minerva were conducted by Oxford students, and I believe the conversation you overheard." Mr Gregson gave me a stern look. "But I also believe there is more to it than you have yet told me. You recognised at least one of those students last night, didn't you?"

I swallowed, trapped in his gaze. "I..." No. I couldn't do it. "I can't tell you who it was," I said, "but I *can* tell you that he didn't mean any harm. He was only talked into it – he thought it was only a game, I could tell."

"I see." Mr Gregson gazed at me. "And you would rather stay silent at such a dangerous moment – even under the very real threat of pacification – than reveal to me who this misguided young man might have been?"

I winced, but held firm. "Yes."

"Excellent," Mr Gregson said. "Then I may safely assume that it was your brother."

"No!" I lurched backwards. "I didn't say that! I mean, it wasn't! I mean—"

"Enough, Katherine." Mr Gregson waved his hand in a gesture of appeasement. "I am not about to blame young Charles for being tricked into participation, but this does provide us with an excellent set of clues. For one thing, you can ask him for the details of how he came to be there, and exactly who persuaded him into it."

"Ah... yes, I could do that." I looked at him nervously. "But the thing is, I don't think Charles tends to ask too many questions when his friends suggest schemes. And he has this stupid idea about gentlemanly honour, so even if he did know—"

"I'm sure you'll persuade him somehow," said Mr Gregson. "And even if not, this tells us something else quite important. At least one of the young men last night was a witch."

"I beg your pardon?" I snorted, finally beginning to relax. "Charles is hardly—"

"I didn't say he was a practising witch. But he is your mother's child, just as you and your sisters are, and he certainly will have inherited at least as much natural talent for witchcraft."

"Well, yes," I said, "but you don't know Charles. He's never cast a spell in his life!"

"That is probably just as well for the rest of Society. If one thinks of how much chaos the various witches and Guardians in your family have caused already..."

I scowled at him, but he wasn't paying attention. His face was drawn into a frown. "It would certainly be interesting," he said, "to know how many of the other young men last night came from witch-bearing families. It would be even more interesting to know whether that was why they were chosen... but at any rate." He shook himself, and looked back at me. "We cannot waste any more time in empty speculation. You must leave the Golden Hall, and I must devise a strategy to prove your innocence before Lord Ravescroft can discover our deception."

I glanced nervously around the empty Hall. If Lord Ravenscroft or Lady Fotherington appeared now... "There's only one problem," I said. "If Lucy and I go back to where my portal is, we'll land in the middle of the King's Bath."

"I see. Fortunately, I should be able to look after that part." Mr Gregson knelt down beside Lucy and took hold of one limp arm. "Katherine?"

Following his nod, I knelt down on Lucy's other side and took her other arm. "But I told you—"

The world turned inside out around us. "And I told you," Mr Gregson said, brushing himself off, "that I would take care of it."

We were in a room I'd never seen before – but of a type I recognised immediately: a gentleman scholar's study. It wasn't as messy or as crowded as Papa's study at home, but leather-bound books filled all the shelves and lay piled in neat stacks upon the desk along with assorted papers covered with neatly lined-up equations. Through the window, I could see the familiar spire of Bath Abbey rising above golden-stone buildings and the forested hills beyond.

"I didn't realise you lived in Bath," I said, as I knelt down to shift Lucy into a more comfortable position.

He looked surprised. "Indeed, I do not. I only arrived here a week ago, as part of our investigation."

I looked up at the abundance of books and papers, which looked like at least a year's accumulation, and thought: *Just* like Papa. At least it was a comfortingly familiar sight.

"So this is where you were when Lord Ravenscroft summoned you?"

"No, it is not." Mr Gregson walked to the window and drew the thin curtains against the sunlight, shielding us from public view. "In fact, I had only just entered the Pump Room, but I thought it would be far too remarkable an occurrence for the three of us to appear there now, with so many people present to witness our arrival, particularly as so many of the Society gossips will have seen your magical activities in the King's Bath. Here, we should remain safely unobserved if we are careful about your departure from my rooms."

Seeing my confused look, he tapped his spectacles – his own portal to the Golden Hall, just as Mama's mirror was mine. They glinted even in the darkness of the shrouded room. "A fully trained Guardian can use his or her portal for transportation across great distances as well as simple back-and-forth movements, and they can take their portal with them. You would have learned this skill in time, Katherine, along with greater control of all your powers."

"Yes." I sighed as I rose. No time for regrets. "But now we have to get Lucy safely home, and then I have to go back to the Baths."

"On the contrary!" He drew himself up. "My dear Katherine, if you have any sense left in you, you will stay well away from the Baths. After today's incident, every Guardian in Bath will be keeping a close eye on them."

"Yes, I know, but I told you – Mama's mirror is at the bottom of the King's Bath! Since Lord Ravenscroft closed the portal, it won't come back to me on its own. I'll have to get it back myself."

"Ah. Yes." He coughed. "I was afraid we might come

to this. I'm sorry to say you won't be taking back your mother's mirror today."

"I beg your pardon?" I was too surprised to be outraged. "Don't be absurd. I can't just leave it there."

"You heard Lord Ravenscroft," Mr Gregson said. "He expects me to provide evidence of your pacification. There is no evidence I could give him that could be so persuasive as your own portal, inherited from your mother."

"You must be joking," I said. "I would never let you—"

"Exactly." He nodded. "Can't you see? Lady Fotherington knows that as well as I do. She can verify to Lord Ravenscroft that you would never give up the mirror of your own accord."

"Well, Lady Fotherington can go—"

I cut myself off by biting my lip hard. But I could just see them, Lord Ravenscroft and Lady Fotherington, turning over Mama's mirror in their hands and laughing. Lady Fotherington had wanted Mama to be pacified for her illicit witchcraft; now she would think she had got her way at last. *Like mother, like daughter,* she would say, yet again, and she would smile...

I tasted blood where my teeth had bitten into my lip. I swung away from Mr Gregson.

"Fine," I said, and focused on the rows of books on their shelves, all neatly lined and ordered. "Fine. But I'm having it back when this is over."

"Well—"

"I am," I said, and turned to look him in the eyes.

He sighed, and drew his handkerchief from his pocket. "I will do my best to get it back for you," he said. "But in the meantime, I must urge you to exercise the strongest caution. Not only is Lord Ravenscroft himself in Bath, but Lady Fotherington is due to arrive today as well. Both of them will be alert to any sign that the pacification has not been completed. Even the merest hint of magic with your signature scent, whether Guardian or witchcraft..."

I closed my eyes against the pity in his face. "I understand," I said.

And I did. Despite all the powers that Mama had left me, there was nothing I could do with them now, even to prove my own innocence.

CHAPTER TWENTY

LUCY STILL HADN'T STIRRED BY THE TIME WE LEFT MR GREGSON'S rooms, but he was maddeningly unconcerned.

"She has undergone a series of considerable physical shocks," he explained, as we each draped one of her arms over our shoulders. "Between the wild magic's possession of her body, and the intense shock of transplantation away from the source of that magic, it wouldn't be surprising if she sleeps for a full day now, or even longer."

"Mm," I said, and thought of Mrs Wingate waiting for us at home. "That might be for the best, actually." Surely with a day or two to prepare, I could come up with some credible story to excuse Lucy's public magical display... couldn't I?

"I would keep Miss Wingate well away from the Baths for the foreseeable future," Mr Gregson added, puffing slightly, as we manoeuvred her down the narrow, winding staircase.

"That" – I was panting, too, as we came to a halt before the front door and peered through the window – "I had already guessed."

A stream of chattering passers-by filled the street outside – not as many as roamed the fashionable Circus area, but more than enough to be scandalised by the sight of two girls emerging from a private residence with only a gentleman for escort.

I looked at Mr Gregson across Lucy's lolling head. "Are you certain we can't just transport ourselves across town using your portal?"

"Unfortunately, that would be far too dangerous," he said. "For all we know, Miss Wingate's mother or sister may be waiting for her in her bedroom. And if anyone saw us arrive by such blatantly magical means..."

He sighed, looking out of the window at the busy crowd. "No," he said, "these circumstances, like last night's, are neither discreet nor urgent enough to warrant magical transportation. But I'm afraid the safer method may not be quite so easy this morning as it was last night."

He was right. But even as we negotiated the busy streets – both Lucy and I remaining invisible while Mr Gregson tipped his hat to various acquaintances – my mind was already worrying at the larger task ahead. The ladies and gentlemen promenading past us on the pavements as we neared Lucy's house in the Circus were overflowing with gossip... and all of it came straight from the Baths.

"Flashing lights everywhere, the entire Bath was glowing, and the wicked girl herself..."

"Casting spells in broad daylight. The shamelessness of it! The whole family will be ruined, of course..."

"Witchcraft in Bath, of all places! And a well-respected family, too – until now, of course..."

"Ruined, my dear, positively ruined, all of them, and quite rightly, too..."

I wasn't surprised to see all the curtains at the Wingates' house as tightly drawn as if there had been a death in the family. It was a clear message to anyone who cared to observe it: the Wingates were not at home to visitors. That hadn't stopped a crowd of gossips from congregating round their front gate, all quivering with excitement over the scandal and darting hopeful looks up at the curtained windows.

Mr Gregson's pointed cough cleared a space for the three of us to pass. He rapped sharply on the door.

"This," he whispered, "will be the tricky bit. But if we take some care..."

The butler opened the door, looking even more forbidding than usual.

"Aloysius Gregson," Mr Gregson said before the butler could speak. "Mrs Wingate sent for me to attend her."

"I beg your pardon?" The butler stepped back, frowning. "I'm sorry, sir, but I wasn't informed of any such request. The family is not at home to visitors."

"Perhaps you would care to send up my card? There may have been some mistake. Of course, I shouldn't like to intrude, but her message was quite specific. I really wouldn't like to disappoint her, today of all days..."

The butler looked positively ill at the thought. "No, sir. No, indeed. If you would please wait here?" He stepped back and gestured to the foyer.

Mr Gregson sidestepped in through the doorway, still holding Lucy. The butler's eyebrows rose as he watched Mr Gregson's rather bizarre motion, but he was too polite to make any comment. At the end of the chain of connection, I nipped inside just before the butler closed the door. He almost stepped into me as he turned back, but I hopped backwards to avoid him, still hanging on to Lucy's waist, and hit the wall with an audible thud.

He blinked, shook his head, and accepted the calling card Mr Gregson was holding out to him. "If you'll excuse me, sir..."

He moved up the marble stairs at a stately pace. When he opened the sitting room door, I winced; I could hear Mrs Wingate at full steam.

"If I have ever once regretted a generous nature – yes, Palmer, what is it this time? I said we were not to be disturbed!"

"I beg your pardon, Mrs Wingate..."

The door to the sitting room closed, shutting off the sound of their voices. I let out a sigh of relief and massaged my aching head. It really hadn't needed that extra bump.

"Now," said Mr Gregson, and the invisibility magic-working around us vanished. "If I were you, Katherine, I would move at some speed. But in the meantime, please remember..." He bent a stern gaze upon me. "Stay well away from the Baths, no matter what the temptation, and do not under any circumstances—"

"Work any magic. I know, I know! I promise." I rolled my eyes as I staggered towards the staircase, hauling Lucy with me and breathing hard with effort. "I'm not entirely a fool," I muttered.

Then I remembered everything he'd done for me that morning, and I turned back. "Thank you," I added. "For trusting me."

He nodded, his expression grave. "I do," he said. "Don't make me regret it. Now, hurry!"

But I was only on the third step of the staircase when the sitting room door opened. The butler emerged, looking flushed and uncomfortable under his powdered wig. Mrs Wingate must not have been pleased by his message.

"I beg your pardon, sir," he said as the door closed behind him, "but there seems to have been some— Oh!" He paused, one foot still hovering above the top step of the staircase. "Miss Katherine Stephenson. And Miss Lucy!" His gaze flicked straight to the sitting room door. He started to turn back.

It was time to change my strategy. "Oh, help!" I said, and stumbled artistically, as if I couldn't support Lucy's weight any longer. "She's so ill, and I can't— Oh!" I clutched the banister for support.

"Oh, dear. Yes. Yes, I see." He hurried down the steps to take Lucy's other arm. "Mr Gregson, I am afraid—"

"Never mind," said Mr Gregson. "I clearly misunderstood the message. Please convey my deepest apologies to Mrs Wingate for having disturbed her. I'll see myself out." He tipped his hat. "Miss Stephenson, Miss Wingate..." He stepped outside, closing the door quietly behind him.

Left alone with the butler, I let him scoop Lucy up into his arms, but I kept a firm hold on her shoulder as we mounted the stairs, for my own reassurance. Her face was still worryingly pale. "She needs rest," I said, "and—"

"Aha!" The sitting room door burst open. Maria Wingate grinned at me with pure, venomous satisfaction. "I told you I heard voices, Mama," she said over her shoulder. "They're home – and they were trying to sneak upstairs without notice."

I sneered at her. "We were hardly—"

Mrs Wingate's bellow cut me off before I could even get started. "Bring them inside. Now!"

Maria gestured me into the sitting room with a smirk. I gritted my teeth and stalked straight past her, leaving the butler to carry Lucy after me.

"Lucy is ill and unconscious," I announced, before anyone else in the room could say anything. "She needs to be put to bed."

She looked like the heroine of a proper romance now, held limp in the butler's arms with her blonde hair loose and trailing below her. It should have been an affecting sight.

Mrs Wingate's face had already been flushed with temper. Now she looked like a kettle brought to boiling point. "And she has been carried like this all through the streets of Bath, for anyone to see her?"

"Not... exactly," I said. It was probably best not to expand on that point.

I looked past Mrs Wingate. Stepmama sat on the neighbouring couch, her own colour high and her face pinched. Papa sat beside her, shoulders bowed, while Charles sprawled at the end of the couch, eyes glazed. For once, I actually hoped he was hungover. It was the least that he deserved, after what his foolishness had brought about.

Angeline, though, was nowhere to be seen. It wasn't likely that she would have been allowed to hide quietly in our room while the temper storms raged, nor was it like her to even try – which meant she still hadn't come home after the fiasco with Mr Carlyle. A thread of worry tugged at me. Angeline on her own for hours, distraught... if it had been anyone else, I might have found the idea piteous. Instead, it was terrifying.

I shoved it aside to deal with later. I had quite enough to cope with already.

"Katherine," Stepmama began, in her most ominous tone, "the very moment you have seen Miss Lucy safely settled in her bed—"

But before she could continue, Mrs Wingate said, "'Not exactly'? What, pray, is that meant to signify? And what *exactly* have the two of you wicked, shameless girls been doing for the past two hours since you disappeared in broad daylight in front of the entire Pump Room?"

"*And* in front of the other bathers," Maria added. She sat down, straight-backed, on the couch beside her mother, her eyes alight with malice. "Not to mention everyone who's heard about it since then. The gossip has been positively—"

"Yes, thank you, Miss Wingate," Stepmama said crisply. "I am certain we all know what the gossip has been like. You needn't—"

"Maria is quite correct," said Mrs Wingate. "Indeed, I can only wish I had taken her advice when we first read your letter, Cousin Margaret. But I had no expectation of just how much trouble your stepdaughters might cause..."

"Now, Cousin Caroline—"

"Nor, indeed, that *any* young ladies could have been brought up so improperly, so indecently—!"

"I beg your pardon!" Stepmama stiffened.

"And so you should beg my pardon. Mine and particularly my daughters'! When I think what a corrupting influence was allowed into my own house – into the very bosom of my family..."

Papa closed his eyes. Stepmama said, "*Corrupting?*"

I wondered whether, if I backed out very slowly and quietly, anyone would notice me leave.

Unfortunately, the butler, with Lucy draped across his arms, was filling the entire doorway.

"'Corrupting' is what I said, and 'corrupting' is what I meant. From the very moment your stepdaughters entered this house—"

"And which of my stepdaughters was the one to ruin the breakfast room this morning in a magical tantrum?" Stepmama shot the words out like bullets. "Which of my stepdaughters was the one to throw the entire King's Bath into scandalous magical uproar in full view of the Pump Room?"

"That has happened only since your stepdaughters arrived! My Lucy would never have dreamed of behaving in such a way before she came under their degrading influence."

"And don't forget, Mama," Maria inserted, "what Miss Stephenson was doing in the Baths with Viscount Scarwood, quite shamelessly, in front of any observers who cared to watch her!"

Stepmama said, "I should infinitely prefer to have a daughter with easily moved feelings – even when they do lay her open to the wiles of a hardened rake – than a daughter with so little proper affection for her own sister that she would take malicious delight in her public ruin!"

Maria's gasp sounded like a scream.

Mrs Wingate puffed herself up like a frog and said, "I beg your pardon!"

"And indeed you should," said Stepmama. "But far more than that, you should beg my stepdaughters' pardon for trying to blame your own daughter's misbehaviour on them. They have shown her nothing but kindness and friendship ever since their arrival – in shocking contrast, I may say, to her own sister's attitude!"

"How dare you!" Maria put one hand to her thin chest. It was too late, I thought, for her to pretend to have a heart there, but she certainly had a temper, which was making her expression look nearly demonic.

"Can you deny what we both saw in the Bath this

morning?" said Mrs Wingate. "Miss Katherine approached Lucy, and they disappeared together!"

Stepmama's voice steeled. "I saw exactly what happened. My Katherine was brave enough, unlike any of the nattering gossips around her, to approach Lucy even in the midst of Lucy's disgraceful magical display. She paid for that bravery by being swept away with Lucy by that magic – but she has now managed to return your daughter safely to the bosom of her remarkably unloving family, despite all the dangers she must have gone through on the way. And is this your thanks to her?"

I blinked. Was that truly how Stepmama had seen it? Perhaps I'd been lucky after all. If she truly believed—

Oh. Stepmama shot me a look I recognised all too well. *Later*, was the message it promised me.

Well, it was a good story she was telling Mrs Wingate, anyway.

Mrs Wingate said, "I don't know about that. All I can say is, none of this ever happened before your stepdaughters arrived."

"Perhaps no one ever paid Miss Lucy any attention before," Stepmama said, and gave a poisonously sweet smile. "It certainly says interesting things about her own upbringing that all this would come out now, does it not?"

"Well— well— well—!" Mrs Wingate huffed for breath, her head shaking from side to side.

"Mama, you mustn't listen!" said Maria. "Mama—!"

The sitting room door opened behind the butler. "Pardon me, Madam," a footman said. He held a silver salver in his hand, with a creamy calling card delicately balanced atop it. From the expression of pale fear on his face, he might as well have been stepping onto a battlefield.

"James!" Mrs Wingate swung around to aim the full

force of her cannons at him. "How many times must you be told? Miss Wingate and I are not at home!"

"I know, Madam," the footman said, looking pained. "Indeed, I have turned away several callers for you both already. But this caller came for Mrs Stephenson – and for her daughters, as well."

"For–?" Mrs Wingate shook away the message like gibberish. "What are you talking about? Which caller? Who?"

"Lady Fotherington, Madam," the footman said.

CHAPTER TWENTY-ONE

"LADY FOTHERINGTON?" MRS WINGATE REPEATED. SHE BLINKED rapidly. "Why— Lady Fotherington? Here? At my house?"

I didn't know why she was having such a hard time believing it. Everything else had gone wrong lately – why not this, too? I believed it absolutely and it petrified me. At least Stepmama's expression revealed every ounce of the real horror of the situation. She moistened her lips, her gaze darting wildly around the room, as if searching for escape routes.

"I— but— we could hardly— that is—"

"Not at home!" I supplied. My own voice came out as a squeak. I wanted to see Lady Fotherington even less than Stepmama did. This soon after my supposed pacification, there was only one reason why Lady Fotherington would pay a call: to satisfy herself that the procedure had been successful... and to gloat over it intolerably.

Stepmama seized on my suggestion, her face brightening.

"But of course, we must ask dear Lady Fotherington to return another time," she said. "We are none of us at home to visitors today, after such trials and tribulations this morning. Cousin Caroline, I would never ask you to suffer through—"

"Don't be absurd!" Mrs Wingate's own face was suffused with a glow I'd never seen there before. "Lady Fotherington herself! How could we turn her away? Especially..." She bestowed a smile of warm approval on me as I stood frozen by the door. "As dear Katherine's godmama, she is practically family herself, is she not?"

"Well..." Stepmama's voice strained to cracking-point. "That is— in a manner of speaking..."

"Nonsense." Mrs Wingate nodded briskly, all of her fury apparently vanquished by the miracle of Lady Fotherington's appearance. "Your scruples do you credit, Cousin Margaret, but they are far too fine in this case. James, see Lady Fotherington up immediately, and order our best refreshments. And Palmer" – for the first time, she seemed to notice the butler still standing with Lucy in his arms, looking rather more worn than he had ten minutes earlier. "For heaven's sake, don't just stand there! Carry Miss Lucy up to bed. Quickly! We don't want Lady Fotherington tripping over her."

"Yes, Madam."

Palmer carried Lucy out, followed by Papa, who moved across the room and out of the door with the silent speed and determination of a hunted animal. He was gone before Stepmama could utter the faintest sound of protest. Charles looked after him with open admiration.

There was nothing in the world I would have liked more than to follow Papa's example, but I squared my shoulders and stayed where I was. Lady Fotherington had come to see me, after all, and I wouldn't give her the satisfaction of thinking me too afraid to meet her.

"Come, Miss Katherine," Mrs Wingate said, in a warmer tone than I'd ever heard her use before. She patted the seat on the couch beside her, forcing Maria to move aside. "We wouldn't like your godmama to think you weren't being offered the best in our house, would we?"

I smiled weakly and obeyed. Maria's face pursed up like a prune as I sat down between her and her mother. She sniffed pointedly and looked away.

Stepmama leaned over and said in an urgent whisper, "Cousin Caroline, I think perhaps it would be best if we make no reference to Lady Fotherington's godmotherly relation to Katherine during her visit. We have never liked to presume upon the relationship, or— "

"Lady Fotherington!" the footman announced as he opened the door.

Mrs Wingate had made no answer to Stepmama's plea... but Maria stiffened like a hunting dog who'd just caught the trail of a fascinating new scent. Her eyes gleamed with interest and speculation.

I gritted my teeth and prepared to endure whatever came of it.

"My dear Lady Fotherington!" As Lady Fotherington swept into the room, resplendent in a deep green walking dress that positively reeked of high fashion, Mrs Wingate rose to her feet, beaming. "How delighted I am to welcome you to my home. I do apologise for your long wait—"

"No need for apologies, Mrs— ah, Mrs Wingate, yes, of course." Lady Fotherington's smile was all condescension, but her gaze had gone straight to me, piercingly eager. "I understand perfectly."

I stiffened my spine and sat as straight as Stepmama

had ever ordered, chin held high. I refused to drop my gaze.

Her green eyes narrowed. Cutting straight across a stream of welcoming speech from Mrs Wingate, she said, "But is Miss Katherine truly well enough for company? The stories I've heard about this morning..."

Curses. I ought to be limp and fainting, I supposed... or even babbling inanely if the procedure had damaged my mind, as I was sure she'd hoped it would. Well, the devil take all that. I wasn't about to give her such satisfaction. Not everyone's mind was damaged by pacification, and I was dashed if I would pretend to be helpless just to make her happy.

I said, as clearly and coldly as I could, "I have lost nothing that mattered to me."

"Hmm." Lady Fotherington swept up her skirts and took a seat in the winged armchair across from our couch without taking her eyes off me for an instant.

"Mattered?" Mrs Wingate let out a nervous titter as she sank back down onto our couch. "Why, I don't know what Miss Katherine could be referring to. She did not lose anything this morning that I know of. But Lady Fotherington, you need not fear for her. I do not know what you may have heard – you know how gossips are, and how far their stories stretch any semblance of truth or even reasonable probability. You mustn't trust to any mad stories of – of nonsense such as... well..."

She trailed to a stop as another footman entered the room, bearing a tray of refreshments. Perhaps she couldn't think of any polite euphemisms for scandalous acts of magic in broad daylight – especially when they'd been carried out by her own daughter. Instead, she busied herself in making and pouring the tea, a strained smile on her face.

Lady Fotherington only flicked her a quick, baffled glance

as she accepted a cup of tea. "I rarely trust to gossip, Mrs Wingate." Her gaze flicked back to me, her frown deepening. "But can you truly tell me that Miss Katherine has suffered no illness as a result? No weakness whatsoever, or—"

Stepmama's face brightened with sudden inspiration. "Katherine has indeed been very weak since she arrived home from her ordeal," she said, and rose from the couch, abandoning her own full teacup. "Indeed, for all her bravery in offering to stay, I know she truly ought to be in bed. Perhaps we should all—"

"Nonsense," said Mrs Wingate. "Cousin Margaret is too sensitive. You are perfectly well, are you not, Katherine?" She patted my arm and flashed me an artificial smile.

I hesitated, torn. "Well..." I knew the answer that would be sensible – but it fought against every instinct I had in Lady Fotherington's presence. And yet... "I'm not *that* weak," I muttered.

Lady Fotherington relaxed visibly. "I see," she said. "How brave of Miss Katherine to pretend to better health than she truly has, merely to set me at my ease." Her lips curved into the smile I hated most. "But truly, there is no need for pretence between us."

"Indeed," said Maria, with a bright, tinkling laugh, "how could there ever be pretence between Cousin Katherine and her own dear godmama?"

I froze. Stepmama fell back onto the couch with a stifled moan. Charles put one hand over his eyes and began to whistle softly under his breath.

For once, Lady Fotherington looked completely stunned. "I beg your pardon?"

"I think Katherine is looking very ill," Stepmama announced. Even she knew it was a losing battle, though. Strained to breaking point, her voice sounded cracked and fragile. "We do appreciate your visit, Lady Fotherington, but perhaps..."

"Her godmama," Maria repeated. "That is why you came to enquire after Cousin Katherine, is it not? As part of your godmotherly duties to her?"

"Now, Maria." Mrs Wingate directed a chastising look at her older daughter as she took a pink teacake from the tray. "We have already discussed this. I do apologise, Lady Fotherington. I know Cousin Margaret does not like to presume..."

"Does she not?" murmured Lady Fotherington. Her green eyes narrowed to jewelled slits as she looked from one face to another. "How utterly fascinating. And how is it, then, that you knew about this intimate relation between Miss Katherine and myself?"

"Well, of course, within the family..." Mrs Wingate began.

"Now *I* feel faint," Stepmama moaned. She put one hand to her head. "Oh, please—"

But Maria was faster than either of them. "Why, Katherine announced it herself," she said, and glowed with malicious pleasure. "The first day they arrived. She told us all about how important it was to you that she be treated with the highest status, as your own goddaughter. Because everyone knows Lady Fotherington's goddaughter deserves only the best."

"Maria!" Mrs Wingate put one hand to her chest. "Never did I expect to hear you speak in such a vulgar manner – and in front of company, too! Lady Fotherington, I do apologise—"

"There is no need," said Lady Fotherington. Her voice sounded like crystals chiming beautifully together. "No need for you or your daughter to apologise at all. Indeed, I am very sorry for both of you."

"For us?" Mrs Wingate ruffled like a hen, while Maria quivered happily beside me. "I'm afraid I don't understand."

"Hadn't you realised yet?" Lady Fotherington shook her head slowly, a smile playing about her mouth. "Many, many people have been taken in before by Katherine and her family – but never before by the use of my name. I feel I may owe you some apologies for that, myself."

"You," I said, "owe us an apology first." I met her jewelled green gaze and let all of my own contempt show in my stare. "You know exactly why I used your name – only a week after Elissa's wedding. After what you did."

"What? What?!" Mrs Wingate was visibly trembling. "I don't understand! I don't—"

"It's quite simple, Mama," Maria said. "Cousin Katherine is not Lady Fotherington's goddaughter at all. I always suspected that anyone so obviously countrified and ill-bred could not have been raised under the influence of a leader of fashion – and I was right!"

"Indeed," Lady Fotherington said. She didn't look away from me, but her smile deepened. "Miss Wingate has exactly mastered the realities of our little melodrama. Miss Katherine's own mother was a liar and a social climber, and—"

"She was not!" I said, and started up from the couch.

Or, rather, that was what I meant to do. But without so much as a pause in her speech, Lady Fotherington flared her eyes and power snapped into place around me, pressing down against my shoulders, stifling my tongue before I could utter a single word.

"I say," said Charles. Out of the corner of my eye, I glimpsed unexpected movement, as he dropped his hand from his eyes and sat up almost straight. "You are speaking of our mother, you know."

"Indeed I am," Lady Fotherington murmured. But she didn't take her eyes from mine.

It was too much, too absurd. I would have screamed with frustration if I could have. Yes, Lord Ravenscroft had forced me into silence and stillness, but his power had been insurmountable, impossible to challenge. Lady Fotherington's power was nothing compared to mine, this magic-working was nothing I couldn't break with a thought, a single explosion of righteous outrage—

Oh. I met her gaze and saw the calculating speculation there, mixed with pleasure.

This was the *real* test, now, and she'd been preparing for it the entire visit. Now was the moment when Mr. Gregson's scheme would either succeed or fail forever... and the only way to save my magic was to let her do whatever she wanted to me, without fighting back.

I stared at her with all the loathing I felt, and all the helplessness I felt, too. For once in my life, I was completely unable to give in to my temper.

Lady Fotherington nodded gently to me. "Katherine has inherited all her mother's worst tendencies. This is not the first time she has lied to advance her family in Society. It is" – she slipped me another, testing glance – "the only reason her oldest sister managed to entrap such an eligible husband. Were it not for my own assistance, her other sister would have entrapped Mrs Edmund Carlyle's only son this very year."

Power coursed through my skin, burning to be let out, to explode. I pushed it ruthlessly down, so not a trickle could escape and disrupt even a breath of Lady Fotherington's working. I kept my chin held high and saw every nuance of satisfaction that passed across Lady Fotherington's face as she savoured my defeat.

Someday, I promised myself. *Someday, she will regret this. Someday...*

Then someone moved between us, breaking our mutual glare. It was Charles, of all people. He stepped in front of me like a living shield. For the first time in ages, I realised how broad his shoulders really were, when he wasn't slumping or trying to disappear from the room.

"Those," he said, "are my sisters you're speaking of, and I don't appreciate it."

I wanted to cheer. Yet my eyes burned as though they wanted to weep. I hadn't seen my older brother show so much spirit since Stepmama first sent him away to boarding school, years ago.

Lady Fotherington only said lightly, "What a pity. You rather remind me of someone I used to know. He never measured up in the end, though, either."

"Cousin Margaret?" Mrs Wingate snapped. "Do you have nothing to say to me?"

Stepmama took a deep breath and stiffened her spine. "I cannot deny that Katherine misled you about her godmother's identity, but as to the rest—"

"I have heard enough!" Mrs Wingate rose to her feet, trembling with outrage and gathering up her colourful shawls like a peacock extending full plumage. "I took you all into my home! I offered you friendship and patronage despite my own daughter's best advice! I introduced you to my friends! I—"

"Perhaps it is time for me to take my leave," Lady Fotherington murmured.

"Yes," Charles said. For the first time in my memory, his voice actually sounded menacing. "I think you *should* leave, Lady Fotherington. Now."

"Really!" said Mrs Wingate. "Of all the rude and un-gracious behaviour—"

"Oh, you need not trouble yourself to defend me from any of the Stephensons, ma'am," said Lady Fotherington. She put her cup down and brushed off her slim hands. "Indeed, I should not like to intrude at all on such a private family discussion. Mrs Wingate, Miss Wingate... Mrs Stephenson... Mr Stephenson..." She sighed as her gaze brushed across Charles. "Yes, far too familiar. Goodbye." She walked out of the room at an unhurried pace, stopping only at the door to look back at all of us.

The power that held me disappeared as she released her working. I fell forward and nearly landed on the carpet. Charles grabbed my arm to steady me.

I drew a deep breath, my eyes on Lady Fotherington's elegant figure. There had to be something I could say – some perfect, sardonic line I could toss off that would cut her to the quick and show Mrs Wingate exactly where the blame truly lay...

"Oh, and Mrs Wingate?" Lady Fotherington said. The footman was already holding the door open for her; one dainty foot was poised to step into the corridor outside. "I just thought perhaps you ought to know... after all the confusing stories of this morning's catastrophes..."

"Yes, Lady Fotherington?" Weaving slightly, Mrs Wingate grasped hold of the couch arm beside her for support.

"Miss Angeline Stephenson is a quite unrepentant witch," said Lady Fotherington. "She and Miss Katherine were indubitably to blame."

The door closed gently behind her.

CHAPTER TWENTY-TWO

☆☆

AFTER THAT, OF COURSE, THERE WASN'T ANY QUESTION ABOUT what would happen next.

I had to pack for Angeline as well as myself, as she still hadn't come back. Lucky Angeline. If there was one small grain of relief left to me, it was that at least Stepmama and Papa were lodged on a different floor of the Wingates' town house. That meant I had at least half an hour's respite before I had to face Stepmama in private.

The crash of my door slamming open made me jump and drop the pile of gowns I'd been cramming willy-nilly into a crowded valise. I swung round, prepared for almost anything: Maria, come to gloat; Stepmama, too furious to pack before her rant; Lord Ravenscroft, knowing the truth about my 'pacification' and come to complete the job himself...

What I saw, instead, was Lucy, her face pale, and her hair floating around her in wild disorder.

"You're awake!" I said. "How are you feeling?"

Lucy's voice came out as a muffled shriek. "Tell me what is going on!" She pushed the door shut behind her and flattened herself against it, staring at me. "I woke up in my own bed, and I could hear everyone screaming at each other downstairs, and you" – she waved at the mass of clothing piled on my bed – "you're *packing*—!" She sounded on the verge of hysteria. "I don't even know how I got here or *what's happening to me!*" She ended with a wail as she sank down to the floor and covered her eyes with her hands. The cabinets in the room all rattled ominously in reaction.

I abandoned the packing and hurried over to her. Lucy might be a devotee of melodrama, but this time she was fully justified. It was too much to cope with on her own – and like it or not, I was going to have to leave her alone with it all too soon.

"Do you remember anything that happened in the Baths?"

Sniffling softly, she let me help her to her feet and draw her over to sit on the edge of the bed. "I remember feeling strange, as if I was floating outside myself, above the water. But then – then, something else filled me up. Something that wasn't me. It was terrible and wonderful and horrifying and – and I could see you, but I couldn't call to you, or—"

As she spoke, the pictures on the walls knocked so wildly against the flowered wallpaper that two of them wrenched themselves free of their mounts and crashed face down onto the floor in front of us. With a sob, Lucy broke off and buried her face in her hands. "I'm a monster!"

"No, you are not," I said. "Don't be absurd."

The drawers in the chest of drawers jerked themselves

in and out as she sobbed, and I stifled a groan. No doubt Mrs Wingate would assume I'd thrown a temper tantrum and wrecked the room intentionally on my way out.

Still, there was nothing to be solved by worrying about that now. "You are not a monster," I said firmly. "You've been possessed by wild magic, which is not your fault."

"Possessed by – what?" She lowered her hands and blinked out at me tearfully.

"Wild magic," I said. "Those fools we saw in the King's Bath last night raised the magic without realising it, and it came speeding up out of the Source looking for a host. You were the most helpless one there, so it chose you. It could have happened to anyone."

"To anyone?!" She stared at me, her cheeks flushing pink. "But—"

"Anyone without magic of their own," I corrected myself. "Mr Gregson and I could both defend ourselves, so..."

She swallowed visibly. "Are you trying to tell me that despite everything that's happened today – even despite *that*" – she pointed to the wildly rocking drawers and the rattling pictures on the wall – "I am not a witch?"

"No!" I said. "Of course you're not." I blew out a sigh of sheer relief. "Is that what you were worried about this whole time? That you'd turned into one of the villainesses from those novels you read? I'm so sorry – I should have explained before. No witch would ever have let that happen to herself."

"Well, of all the unfair things in the world!" Lucy stamped her foot, the last of her tears drying up completely. "You would think that at least there'd be some benefit to all this!"

"Um..." I blinked. She still looked like herself, and yet... "I don't understand. You do know witches are scandalous and completely banned from good Society and—"

"Well, of course I know all that." She waved her hand impatiently. "But that's going to happen to me anyway, now that everyone's seen me in the Baths. I thought at least I'd have some interesting new powers to make up for it."

"Oh." I did my best to digest that. "Well..." I glanced from her furiously impatient expression to the rattling pictures on the wall. "Not even your mother can ignore how you feel anymore... at least, not until this is fixed," I offered.

She growled deep in her throat. One of the drawers in the chest of drawers wrenched itself free and shot across the room, slamming into the far wall.

I added hastily, "When Sulis Minerva took over your body today, you did amazing things. You – you even gave Charles good luck at the gaming tables. I didn't think that was possible!"

The pictures slowed in their rattling, but Lucy only shook her head. "Sulis who?"

Before I could answer, an all-too-familiar knock sounded on the door. *Dash it.* "I'll explain it later," I promised. "Somehow. But in the meantime, stay away from the Baths! I'm hoping this will all wear off eventually, but—"

"Katherine!" The door opened, and Stepmama stalked in. "The amount of noise that has been coming from this room – oh, I see. Miss Lucy." She looked from Lucy's flushed and tear-stained face to the expensive pictures lying face down on the floor and the drawer lying askew against the far wall.

Lucy's shoulders hunched even tighter together in reaction, and the tall cabinet in the corner of the room gave a tentative jiggle. Stepmama sighed.

"I am pleased to see you awake," she said. "But shouldn't you be resting?"

"I—"

"She came to say goodbye," I said.

"How kind of her." Stepmama gave Lucy a polite smile and me a narrow-eyed look. "However, as you are still less than half-packed, and our hired carriage is already waiting at the door—"

"What about Angeline?" I said. "We can't leave without her."

"Angeline..." Stepmama began.

But my mind had already leaped ahead. "We can't!" I said. "And I won't." I stood up to glare at her. "I will not leave Bath without her, no matter what she's done or what stupid threats you made to her before we came. She's still my sister, and I will not let you—"

"Katherine!" Stepmama's voice rapped out with all the authority of a hundred Guardians. "*If* you will stop gibbering for a moment—!" She glared back at me. "What I was going to say, before you interrupted me, was that Angeline will find our address waiting for her with the butler whenever she finally deigns to return. We, meanwhile, shall retire to a respectable coaching inn for the rest of the day and spend the night there before we leave Bath."

"So we're not leaving her behind?"

"Not yet." Stepmama bit off the words like bullets. "Not until I have spoken to Angeline myself and had the opportunity to weigh all sides of this morning's story."

Oh Lord, I thought. I said, "About this morning..."

"You and I will be discussing that matter at great length, and in detail. *Later.*" Stepmama opened the bedroom door. "Come, Miss Lucy. You should be resting, and Kat" – she gave me a Look – "should be packing."

"Oh." Lucy stood up obediently, twisting her hands together. "Yes, of course. I— Kat..."

I met her desperate gaze and winced. There was nothing I could safely say in front of Stepmama. "Goodbye," I said.

Her lips quivered. A third painting flung itself off the wall and crashed to the floor. Stepmama winced.

"Goodbye," Lucy whispered, and fled.

༠ ༠ ༠

We arrived at the Pelican Inn a half hour later. It hadn't been pleasant to make our way out to the hired carriage through the whispering, tittering crowd of promenaders outside Mrs Wingate's house, but the knowledge that Maria Wingate was watching our progress from an upper window kept my spine as rigid and my head as high as any grand lady.

This hired carriage could never have passed for fashionable; the paint was peeling and the driver looked sullen. I imagined I was Angeline and stepped into it like a princess on her way to the opera.

Once we were at the inn, though, and I'd sat through the expected hour of ranting from Stepmama, there was nothing left for me to do but pace and worry.

Stepmama had ordered me not to leave the tiny fifth-floor bedroom I was meant to be sharing with Angeline, on threat of dire punishment. It was barely ten feet in length and six in width, and it felt as if it teetered as high as the clouds above the street below – and above everything that was happening in Bath without me. I paced the little rectangle until I thought I would go mad, while the busy inn yard below bustled with real action and movement.

The day advanced, inexorably. Somewhere outside, Mr Gregson was handing Mama's mirror to Lord Ravenscroft, and Lady Fotherington was smirking over it. Lucy was alone, battered by wild magic and her family's outrage.

And Angeline... who knew where she was, now? Still walking off her rage on the streets of Bath, even as the sky darkened? Or – even worse – coming up with a new and even more disastrous scheme? Either way, she should have arrived by now.

I moved back to the window, pushing my nose against the dirty glass and searching for her in the gathering darkness. The inn yard was still crowded with men yelling back and forth, and carriages rattling in and out of the yard. Boys shouted out advertisements for nearby boxing matches; colourfully dressed women pressed up against the new arrivals; and...

Oh. My breath stopped for a moment as I glimpsed a familiar figure weaving through the crowd at the inn's front entrance.

I flew out of the room, ignoring all of Stepmama's strictures. A minute later, as I hurtled down the very last flight of stairs, I met the inn's maid just about to start up the stairway.

Her eyes widened, and she dropped a quick curtsey as she recognised me. "Pardon me, Miss, but there's a gentleman come—"

"I know," I said. "You needn't bother to tell my parents. They've sent me down to talk to him myself."

Her eyebrows rose.

I added hastily, "He's my cousin, here to – ah – escort me to my school tomorrow."

She shrugged, a gesture that would have sent Stepmama into a frenzy of irritation. "As you say, Miss. He's taken a private parlour. It's just this way..."

I followed her through the inn, sighing with relief. The last thing I could afford, if I was ever to sort this tangle out, was an audience.

She ushered me into the dimly lit private parlour a moment later. It was lined in dark brown wallpaper and full of ancient-looking, fraying couches and chairs. She curtseyed and left the two of us alone, leaving the door open the three inches that propriety demanded.

This was no time for propriety. I pushed the door firmly shut and strode across the room to join my visitor by the minuscule fire. He stood with one hand braced against the stone mantelpiece. Shadows flickered across his strained face.

"Thank goodness," I said. "You didn't bring your mother."

Frederick Carlyle's lips twisted. "If my mother knew I was here..." He looked pale and grim, with none of the wit and easy humour I was used to seeing on his handsome face. "Never mind," he said. "I don't care anymore. Kat, I have to see Angeline."

"I know," I said, "but she isn't here."

"Not here?" He frowned. "The Wingates' butler said you'd all removed here. Surely—"

"She's on her way," I said, and hoped that I was telling the truth. "But we should talk first."

"Talk," Mr Carlyle repeated. He let out a laugh that held no humour. "Yes. Indeed. There certainly is plenty for us to talk about, isn't there?" His right hand tightened around the rough stone of the mantelpiece until I cringed in sympathetic pain. "You were there, Kat. You saw..."

He raked his free hand through his thick blonde hair and let out a huff of breath. "I thought once I resolved matters with my mother, everything would be fine. I never imagined... I knew your stepmother would exert pressure upon her, but I never dreamed Angeline would actually give in to it!"

"I wouldn't say she's given in, exactly—"

"The worst of it is, I didn't recognise him at the time. But later, when I realised..." He swung away from the mantel, dropping his hands to his sides and clenching them into fists. "That was Scarwood, wasn't it? Viscount Scarwood, of all the scoundrels in England, kissing Angeline in the King's Bath?"

"Well... yes," I said. "But—"

"Scarwood." He snarled the name like a curse. "If it were any other man in the world, I could understand. I could even stand aside, if that were what Angeline truly desired. But if you knew what I know about that man..."

"Angeline does," I said. "I think that was the point."

"The point?" He stared at me. "One of the worst rakes in England, notorious for ruining women's reputations, destroying innocent lives—"

"Exactly," I said. "Stepmama told Angeline she would be expelled from the family if she didn't attract an eligible new suitor while we were in Bath. So the one suitor Angeline chose to publicly encourage and entice was the only one Stepmama would never, ever approve, the only one whose offer Angeline would never be allowed to accept..." I watched enlightenment spread across his face, and relaxed. "You see?"

He shook his head. And then he laughed. This time, it sounded painful. "Oh Lord. Oh, Angeline. Oh, what a fool!"

"You are not a fool," I said. "It's not your fault you didn't grasp it immediately. What happened in the Baths did look terrible. That's why she arranged it there – so that everyone in the Pump Room would see them together, and push Stepmama into—"

"I wasn't talking about myself," he said. "Angeline's the fool. She thought she could manipulate Scarwood as easily as a girl playing with her toys." His face turned grim again. "She has no idea how dangerous Scarwood really is."

I moved closer to the fire, for warmth against the sudden chill. "Why, how dangerous do you think he is?"

He looked away for a moment, compressing his lips into a hard line. Then he said, "I know he can be utterly ruthless when it comes to taking what he wants. Now that he's chosen Angeline as his latest diversion, he won't give her up easily."

"But..." My breathing was coming quickly now. "Angeline has her witchcraft. She can protect herself with magic—"

"Can she use her witchcraft to protect herself if she's drugged and carried away in his carriage while unconscious? Or use it to save her reputation after an 'elopement' that never ended in marriage?" He shook his head, his blue eyes looking fiercer than I'd ever seen them before. "Angeline is the strongest woman I've ever met, and I'd gamble everything on her wits against Scarwood's, but he is no gentleman. He won't rely on his wits alone, and she cannot afford to risk herself – especially not for the sake of a mere stratagem against your stepmother."

"No," I said. "No, of course not. But we're leaving Bath tomorrow. He doesn't even know where we live."

"Then she needs to be kept safe tonight." He leaned down to stare straight into my eyes. "Tell me the truth, Kat. I trust you. Where is she right now?"

"Now?" I moistened my lips, fighting down nervousness. I knew what Angeline would want me to do. I had to think of a good story to explain her absence – one that she would approve of, one that wouldn't make him worry.

I couldn't think of a single idea. "Well," I said, "the truth... the truth is..."

The scent of lilacs suddenly filled the room – Angeline's magic, unmistakable. *Thank goodness.* I spun around to face the door.

It was still firmly closed. Angeline was nowhere in sight, and the scent was already fading away. I groaned with frustration. Behind me, Mr Carlyle said in a strangled voice,

"Kat? Have you seen this?"

A folded letter sat on the battered old couch behind me. The inscription read: *Addressed to Miss Katherine Stephenson, Only.*

It was written in Angeline's handwriting.

CHAPTER TWENTY-THREE

☆ BEFORE I EVEN OPENED THE LETTER, I KNEW I WOULDN'T LIKE IT.

Dear Kat,

Angeline's handwriting swirled across the page, confident and sweeping as ever.

> *I am telling you this only so that you won't go racing into trouble trying to find me. In case you're even mildly tempted, I should also inform you that I've enspelled this letter not to find you until at least four hours after I've left Bath.*

I choked.

"What?" said Mr Carlyle. "What is it? What's the matter?"

I shook my head at him, breathing hard, and kept on reading.

We both know I've ruined my chances with Frederick Carlyle, as well as enraging Stepmama. I very much doubt she would take me back into the family fold now, and I know (there was an ink splotch here, the first sign of discomposure) *Frederick will never understand or forgive me for this morning's misadventure, not when his mother is there to remind him that all her warnings against me have been proven true. Please don't waste your time thinking 'I told you so', Kat. It was not a bad plan, but it was hideously ill-timed, and there is nothing to be done about it now.*

I ground my teeth together. If Angeline would ever talk to anyone else about her stupid schemes instead of sailing ahead without taking anybody's advice, not even her own sister's...

Mr Carlyle was leaning towards me, trying to see over my shoulder. I stepped away, twitching the letter out of his sight. Until I knew the worst, I wouldn't know how to deal with him.

But I still wasn't prepared for the next paragraph.

I have taken the only reasonable step in these circumstances.

My stomach sank even before I read the next words.

The fact is, I have lost my chance to marry the only man I will ever love, and I see no point in begging Stepmama to be allowed home, only to listen to her recriminations for the next ten years. Therefore, I have eloped with Viscount Scarwood.

For the first time in my life, I felt like swooning. It wasn't shock that made my head swim, though. It was blazing fury. My fingers loosened on the letter as I fought to stay upright.

Frederick Carlyle seized the opportunity and snatched the letter from my hands.

"Wait!" I said. I reached for it – but his face had already turned the colour of chalk as he read.

Too late to save him from the worst, then, or save Angeline from his full knowledge of the situation. I stood on tiptoe to read the last lines of the letter over his shoulder.

> *Before you even begin to criticise this decision, I know perfectly well that Scarwood has no intention of taking me all the way to Gretna Green for a true marriage. His plan is certainly to ruin me quite as thoroughly as he has numerous other unfortunate young ladies. However, he has never yet dealt with a witch, and he shall find this elopement to be quite unlike all his earlier adventures. My one consolation is the knowledge that, even if I have lost all chance of love for myself, I can at least save other innocent young ladies from damage at his hands. Once we are married, his future career shall be very different, and as for myself* (there was another telltale ink splotch) *at least Stepmama may be pleased that I married a wealthy suitor after all. Perhaps I shall even learn not to be too unhappy, in time.*

> *If you ever desire my forgiveness for your earlier interference, do not tell Stepmama what I have done until it is far too late to disguise matters. Nothing can be achieved by it except even more*

scandal and gossip – of which our family has experienced more than enough already.

Yrs., affec.^{tly},

Angeline

I clenched my fingers around the muslin skirts of my dress. I would have given a great deal, at that moment, to shake the life out of my beloved sister.

Mr Carlyle didn't look up to shaking anybody. He looked as if he had been turned into a statue.

"Well, you were right," I said. "Angeline has been a fool. But if we want to—"

"No," said Frederick Carlyle. His lips barely moved to form the word; he was still rigid with shock, staring sightlessly in the direction of the letter. "No, not Angeline, after all. It was I who was the fool. I should have known – should have understood immediately when I saw her that something was amiss, not what it seemed. I should have trusted her." His fingers clenched around the letter with sudden violence, crumpling it. "If I hadn't been such a fool – if I hadn't driven her away, refused to listen to her explanations, snubbed her in the worst possible manner, only because I was stupidly jealous and blind with it..."

"Well..."

"This is my fault," he said. "Entirely my fault. What else could she think, after I'd said such things to her? After I'd walked away from her when she begged me to listen? After – good God!" He stalked away to pound one clenched fist against the mantelpiece.

I said, "If you hurt your hand by pounding it like that, you won't be able to hit Viscount Scarwood."

He froze for a moment. Then he let out a short laugh and turned back to me. "A good point." His shoulders relaxed, but his expression was deathly grim. "There's no time for self-recriminations, is there? If it's been four hours since she left Bath—"

"At least four hours, according to her letter," I said. "So if he really is taking her north, towards Scotland and Gretna Green..."

"Then they'll be over halfway to Gloucester by now. But if he's actually intending to take her somewhere quite different..." His blue eyes looked unnaturally bright as he refolded the letter and slipped it into an inner pocket of his coat. "You have to help me, Kat."

"Of course I will. If we set out now and question all the coaching inns we pass, to see if Scarwood stopped at any of them—"

"No," he said. "I mean with magic."

"Oh." I stared at him. *Oh.* My chest suddenly felt far too large and echoingly empty. I said, "The problem is—"

"I've never asked for the details of what you do," Mr Carlyle said, "and Angeline never told me. But I know you have powers – you broke Angeline's spell over me, didn't you? And you've done other magic, I know, although I never asked to understand it."

"Yes, but—"

He dropped to his knees in front of me. It was the most disconcerting thing that had happened yet. "Please, Kat," he said. He took my hands in a strong grip as he gazed pleadingly up at me. His fingers were warm around mine and felt very strange. It was the first time any man outside our family had ever held my hands.

"I know all the dangers of practising magic in Society," he said. "Please believe that I would never ask you to do it if there was any other choice. But Scarwood may have taken her anywhere. I might race my horses all night long and only find that I'd gone in the wrong direction. Angeline might be a hundred miles to the south of me by then, and I would be far too late to save her."

"I know," I said, and felt my stomach clench. "But the problem is—"

"All we need is a location spell," he said. "Anything to find her, the way her letter found you."

"I don't know any spells like that," I said. "Angeline kept Mama's magic books. And even apart from that—"

"Something else, then. Anything!"

"I can't!" I said. "You don't understand. I can't do magic anymore!"

"What?" He leaned back, blinking. "What do you mean?"

"I—" I tried to wave one hand in a vague gesture, but his grip was too strong. "It's too complicated to explain, but if I do any magic, we'll all end up in even more trouble, and it'll take away any chance of my helping Angeline at all. It's too dangerous right now to even try." I imagined Lord Ravenscroft and Lady Fotherington swooping down onto the inn together to perform the pacification ritual and I fought back a shiver. I'd be no good to anyone after that. And what would happen to Mr Gregson, if they discovered that he had lied to them for me on such an important matter?

"You won't risk a bit of danger to help Angeline?" Mr Carlyle dropped my hands and rose to his feet, frowning down at me. "You don't sound like yourself. The Kat I know wouldn't let any danger stop her from saving her sister."

"I can't!" I said wretchedly. "I'm sorry. But I will come

with you to find her, and I'll do everything I can to—"

The door swung open behind me. "Why—!" Stepmama's voice broke off in a gasp.

It was nearly drowned out by a shriek of outrage from beside her. "Frederick! What in Heaven's name can be the meaning of this?"

Frederick Carlyle closed his eyes briefly, with a pained expression. "Good evening, Mama," he said.

"What— what—?" Mrs Carlyle looked like an agitated partridge, from the spray of dyed-blue feathers that burst from the top of her round bonnet, to the way her arms wiggled helplessly at her sides as she looked back and forth between me and her son.

Stepmama's own cheeks were flushed with temper, but her voice remained even. "Mr Carlyle," she said. "What a pleasant surprise. I'm sorry we weren't all here to greet you, but for some reason, I wasn't told of your arrival."

"Ha!" Mrs Carlyle said. "So you claim. A likely story! I can see the truth for myself. You've been encouraging them to meet secretly, my son and that— that—" She waved one plump arm in a gesture of contempt.

Stepmama sounded as if she were speaking through gritted teeth. "My elder stepdaughter is not even here at this inn at the moment, Madam."

Frederick Carlyle gave me a meaningful look. I winced. *I really can't*, I mouthed at him.

"You see? You see? She's giving him messages from her sister, even now, as we watch!" Mrs Carlyle collapsed onto the closest couch, her monumental bosom heaving. "Such ingratitude – such wanton disrespect – my poor head... Frederick, you have made your own mother feel faint. My smelling-salts – in my reticule – hurry!"

"I wish I could, Mama, but I must be on my way.

Immediately." He gave me another pointed look. "There is no time to be lost."

"On your way? No time— What? What?" Mrs Carlyle batted blue feathers out of her eyes as she gaped up at him from the couch. "What on earth are you babbling about?"

"I fear there is no time to explain. Mrs Stephenson..." He bowed to Stepmama. "Miss Katherine..." His eyes met mine in a look of sizzling reproach. "I must take my leave of you, as you will not help me. Goodbye, Mama."

"Don't be absurd. You are not going anywhere until you have explained exactly what— Frederick? Frederick! Come back here at once!"

The parlour door closed behind him.

I clenched my hands into fists so tight that pain shot up my arms. I couldn't have done what he'd asked. I *couldn't*.

I wanted to hit something. Or, even worse, to cry.

Mrs Carlyle glowered at Stepmama. "From the moment your family came into corrupting contact with my good, obedient son—"

"Really, Madam," Stepmama began. I recognised the sound of her voice. Her temper was about to snap.

"May I be excused?" I said.

Stepmama waved one irritable hand. "Go to your room, Kat. Wait for me there – I want to talk to you as soon as I'm finished here." Her voice hardened. "But as far as *corrupting influences...*"

I ducked out of the room as quickly as I could. The sound of Mrs Carlyle's shriek of fury followed me up the dark, narrow stairs. I was breathing hard. Jumbled phrases from Angeline's letter and Frederick Carlyle's reproach mingled in my head.

"You won't go racing into trouble..."

"You won't risk a little danger...?"

"I can't," I whispered. "I can't, I can't."

I'd promised Mr Gregson. More than that, every Guardian in the city would be on the lookout for my magical signature – especially the two I feared most.

I knew I was making the sensible decision, the only decision I could make. So why did it feel so wrong?

Halfway down the dingy corridor that led back to my bedroom, I came to a halt.

I couldn't do any magic – not until the mystery of the Baths was sorted out and I was proven innocent. But there was something I could do to speed that part up, at least. And I had to do something right now, or I would burst.

I knocked on Charles's door. There was no answer. I rolled my eyes at the closed door. He was sound asleep, no doubt – Charles could sleep at any time of day, if he was bored enough. I banged on the door as loudly as I could. There was still no answer.

If he'd sneaked down to play cards in the inn's taproom... I hit the door as hard as I could, just in case.

The door swung open with the force of my knock. Clothes lay scattered across the room. His valises stood open, with half their contents spilling out, as if Charles had torn through them all, searching for something in particular. But my brother was nowhere to be seen.

Why would he need to hunt through his luggage only to play cards?

I stepped into the room, closing the door behind me. Something felt wrong. Something was missing...

Aha. Clothes lay scattered across the room – but I couldn't see his hat or his greatcoat. Charles hadn't only left his room; he'd left the inn itself.

A sheet of writing paper lay on top of his bed, half-hidden by a pile of socks. A letter. I snatched it up, feeling my heartbeat speed up uncomfortably.

I was starting to dread reading letters.

Stephenson,

this letter read, in handwriting I'd never seen before.

> *Ready for one last night of fun? Same place as before, as soon as you can. He's ready to go for something really big tonight – I know you'll be up for it, there's a good fellow. Bring along something special to toss into the water for your part, and for God's sake, old chap, don't dawdle! You don't want to miss the best night of your life, do you?*

I let out a strangled groan and ran out of the door.

CHAPTER TWENTY-FOUR

I COULDN'T USE MAMA'S SPELL To DISGUISE MYSELF THIS time, or use my own Guardian powers for invisibility. My pelisse was striped blue and white, and it would stand out with horrible clarity in the lights of the city at night. I cursed Charles, Angeline and Lord Ravenscroft with indiscriminate fervor as I hurried down the inn's narrow stairway.

My bad luck wasn't yet over for the evening.

"Kat?" Papa spoke from above me in a puzzled tone. "Where are you going?"

I took a deep breath and turned, holding onto the banister. He was standing ten steps above me, one finger tucked into a book, frowning in confusion. I knew I should feel lucky that it was he, rather than Stepmama, who had caught me, but impatience sizzled through me. If the rites of Minerva had already begun...

"Don't worry, Papa," I said. "I'm fine."

"But..." He took a few more steps towards me, frowning harder. "You're dressed to go outside. Your pelisse—"

"I know," I said through gritted teeth. He blinked, and I softened my tone. "Don't worry. I'll be fine. I'm just going on an evening walk. I'll be perfectly careful, and you can just—"

"This is a large city, my dear." Papa took the last few steps faster than I'd expected. "It would not be wise for you to venture out alone. Even with your sister as company, it still wouldn't be safe at this time of night. And on your own..."

"Charles will be my escort," I said. "I'm to meet him in the taproom, and then—"

"But Charles is not in the taproom," Papa said. "He left the inn some time ago. He was going to meet some friends of his from Oxford. He borrowed a book from me on his way out, nearly half an hour ago."

Blast. Why did Papa have to choose tonight of all nights to suddenly become observant?

It took a moment for the second part of his statement to hit me. Then I said, "Charles? Borrowed a book?"

"Indeed." Papa's lips curved into a pleased smile. "I believe it was some sort of classical study group he was going to attend. I belonged to a few such groups in my own time, but I hadn't realised that Charles was taking an interest in such matters."

"I wish he weren't," I muttered.

"I beg your pardon?"

"Never mind," I said. "The thing is..."

I searched for inspiration, a convincing story to spin. But my skin was crackling with impatience, and my mind was swirling with the beginnings of true panic. Charles had left the inn nearly half an hour ago. Who knew how much could have happened in that time? At least Angeline had her witchcraft to protect her from violence, and she had Mr Carlyle galloping after her to try to rescue her from her own stupidity. Charles had no defence but me.

If the Guardians caught him with the rest of his group of Minerva-worshippers, none of Mr Gregson's arguments would be enough to persuade Lord Ravenscroft that Charles wasn't involved in whatever monstrous scheme he thought I had developed for the wild magic of the Baths. Charles was my brother and he had witch blood, just like I did. That meant he could be pacified.

The thought of Charles with even less brain than he currently had was the stuff of nightmares.

"I have to go," I said. "I'm sorry. Please don't tell Stepmama."

"But—"

"Goodbye!" I said, and flung myself down the steps.

I pushed my way through the inn's crowded front hallway, out into the night. The inn yard was even more crowded now than it had been in broad daylight. The people were different, though. Some of the women were even more brightly dressed than I was, in garish oranges and pinks that would have given Stepmama a Spasm. They didn't pay any attention to me, though, and the men were mostly watching them, so I managed to slip past more easily than I'd expected. I was out on the open street in moments, slipping and sliding through groups of gentlemen, heading towards the Baths by the flickering lights of the passing carriages. I estimated that it would take approximately twenty minutes to walk there if I were very, very fast. Once I was there...

I was trying so hard to come up with a plan, I didn't even realise that I was being followed – until a hand closed around my shoulder from behind.

"Aah!" I clenched my other hand into a fist and began to swing even as I spun round. I caught myself only an instant before my fist could land on my own father's chin. "Papa!"

"Kat," he said, and released me. "I called out to you, but you didn't hear me."

I stared up at him through the darkness. Other people walked past us, casting more shadows across his worried face. "What are you doing here?" I said.

He stared back, his wavy grey hair disordered by the breeze. He wasn't even wearing a hat for propriety's sake, or a greatcoat against the chill in the evening air. "My dear girl. You went running out of the inn in the middle of our discussion. I could hardly let you go alone, could I? I told you, it is quite unsafe for a girl of your age to be out in the city at night. If you only understood the dangers—"

"I do," I said. "Trust me, I do. But it's important." I could hardly believe I was even having this conversation with Papa, of all people. I cast a longing look back over my shoulder. "I told you there was nothing to worry about, so—"

"Katherine." Papa's voice was as mild as ever, but it held a note of reproach that stopped me more effectively than Stepmama's most irate shriek could ever have done. "I may not always be as observant as I should be, but do you really think you ought to treat me like a simpleton?"

Something twisted painfully in my chest as I met his eyes. "I don't think you're a simpleton," I said. "Of course I don't."

"I am glad. Then perhaps..." He studied me gravely. "Would you care to amend your story?"

The truth came out in a half-whisper. "I didn't think you would even notice."

"Not notice?" He shook his head. "Angeline has still not arrived at the inn, and it is now well after dark. Your stepmother and I are both deeply concerned. And now you wish to go rushing out, too, without any word of explanation?"

"I..." I looked into his kindly, concerned face – Papa, for once giving me his full attention – and I felt my voice dry up in my throat.

I couldn't talk to Papa about magic. Not after the ruination of his career by Mama's blatant witchcraft. Not after the public revelation of Angeline's own witchcraft, less than two weeks ago. He knew – he must know – that I could do magic, because Stepmama had seen me do it in the past. But I'd never had to see him acknowledge that truth, or seen his reaction to it.

"I have to do this," I said. "Please trust me."

He studied me as closely as he might have studied one of his old books. Then he sighed, and his shoulders slumped. "Ah," he said. "I see."

"You do?"

"Indeed," he said. "I had better come with you."

"What?" I stepped back instinctively.

A carriage rattled past, casting a flare of light across his resigned expression. "What else could I possibly do?" he said. "I could hardly let you go off on your own into danger, could I?"

"But..." I fidgeted, feeling time slip away from me. I couldn't let him come. But if I wasted any more time arguing, I might be too late for Charles.

"Well, Kat?"

If it had been Stepmama, I would have turned and run, sliding and ducking through the passers-by until she could never find me, and accepting that I would be punished for it later. Somehow, though, I couldn't do that with Papa.

Papa never raised his voice to any of us. I couldn't even remember the last time he had ordered any punishment. But the knowledge of his disappointment always felt far worse than any of Stepmama's rages.

"I don't think you'll be happy about what you'll see," I said at last.

"Probably not," Papa agreed. "But if you cannot be persuaded to come back safely to the inn..." He held out his arm courteously. "Shall we?"

My head spun as I accepted his arm like any proper young lady accepting gentlemanly escort. This wasn't the way I'd imagined charging in to save Charles.

"Where exactly are we going, may I ask?"

"The Baths," I said, and started forward. Papa's long legs moved quickly enough that I had to hurry to keep up. "That's where Charles will be," I added, "but he's made a terrible mistake."

"Oh, dear." Papa sounded pained. "Not more gambling? Your stepmother will—"

"No," I said. "Nothing like that. But those friends of his from Oxford..." I paused as we made way for a group of men to pass. They looked half-intoxicated already, but their gazes went from me to Papa and slid right past us. There were some advantages to having a proper escort, after all.

"His friends?" Papa prompted, as we reached an open section of pavement.

"They've talked him into something that" – I hesitated, searching for the right explanation – "well, it isn't a good idea. He thinks it's just a game, but..."

"Ah." Papa sighed. "Poor Charles is rather susceptible to persuasion, I fear."

"Yes," I said grimly.

"And is Angeline a part of this?"

I blinked. "No. No! Don't worry about that."

Worry about something else, I added silently. If there was ever someone who could have used a bit more susceptibility to persuasion, it was Angeline. But I couldn't betray her trust by telling him that. All I could do was pray that Mr Carlyle was riding in the right direction, and that he would be fast enough to save her.

Even thinking about Angeline, and about the stupid, terrible risk she was running, made me want to break down into sheer panic. So I wrenched my thoughts away from her.

Two streets from the Baths, every thought in my head cut off abruptly. Wild magic slapped against my skin like a cloud of stinging insects.

"Kat?" Papa stopped walking as I stumbled back. "What's amiss?"

"It's nothing," I said. Fighting for breath, I moved forward. The air was charged with painful, prickling sparks.

Last night, I'd sensed the magic just outside the Baths, but it hadn't felt anything like this. It hadn't been nearly this powerful, or this far-reaching.

The courtyard that held the Pump Room was dark and empty, like the Baths beyond it. I couldn't see any flickering lights this time, or any last incoming groups of students. If it hadn't been for the sizzling wild magic all around me, I would never have known that they were there.

Papa said, "Are you quite certain that Charles is here? I don't see anything..."

"Perhaps he isn't after all," I said. I let go of Papa's arm and filled my voice with as much innocence and sincerity as I could. "Why don't you wait here for me? I'll just take a quick look inside the Baths, and if he isn't there, I'll come directly back. It'll only take me a few minutes to look around."

I couldn't see his face in the darkness, but I heard his sigh. "You needn't try to protect me, Kat. Whatever Charles may be up to, I dare say I shall face the sight of it without too much shock. I was a young man once, too, you know."

Not like this, you weren't, I thought.

But I knew I'd failed. "All right," I said. "Follow me."

CHAPTER TWENTY-FIVE

THE SIDE DOOR WAS UNLOCKED, AS IT HAD BEEN BEFORE. We felt our way down the steps in total darkness. I could hear Papa's breathing behind me, but unlike my last companion, he didn't try to chat.

At the bottom of the steps, I paused, listening. The air was warm and damp, filled with the sulphurous smell of the Baths. There were no lights illuminating the corridor this time, but I didn't need them. The wild magic was so strong here, I could feel it pushing against every inch of my skin. I took Papa's arm to guide him, and started down the darkened corridor.

Halfway down, the voices reached us. But they sounded very different from last time.

Last time, I'd heard shouts of laughter and singing and splashing water, all the noises you'd expect from a group of young fools having a really raucous night of play, even in the very middle of the rites of Minerva themselves. This time, I heard no laughter or splashing coming from the King's Bath, only low-voiced chanting. All the male voices spoke as one, rumbling words I couldn't quite make out.

I didn't like it at all.

"Hurry," I whispered to Papa, and sped up. By the time we reached the door that led to the fork in the corridors, I was nearly running.

Flickering torchlight lit the turning where the first wooden doors led onto the Baths. I could see Papa frowning beside me, his head cocked as he listened to the rumbling chant through the closed doors.

"Latin," he murmured. *"Dea divina..."*

"Papa, please!" I hissed. "Don't you join in, too. It's dangerous."

"Dangerous?" He shook his head. "My dear, if this is meant to be a classical study group, someone really ought to speak to them about their sources. The form they're using—"

"You can explain it to them later." I pulled him past the lit torches to nudge open the closest door. I pressed myself against the wall, only daring to peek around the corner of the door frame. "Right now, all that matters is... oh Lord."

Under the star-specked night sky, the Bath was full of young men. They stood in a circle in the water, thick steam swirling around their bare shoulders. More torches were set in sconces around the Bath, sending flickers of light into the darkness above them. Wild magic hung so thick in the air, I could barely breathe against the pressure in my chest. The men's heads were all tipped back, their eyes closed.

One young man stood in the centre of the circle. Wild magic poured into him, illuminating him more brightly than any torch.

"Charles!" The name that escaped my lips felt more like a curse.

Of course it was Charles.

None of them heard me. I wondered if they could hear anything at all. Their lips moved in perfect synchronism.

"Dea divina, Sulis Minerva, tibi offerimus..."

"What are they saying?" I whispered to Papa.

"It is a very mangled form of the original chant," he said, "but I believe... no, no, that makes no sense at all. It cannot be right."

"What is it?"

"Well, if what they intend to say – not that their usage is exactly correct, but then—"

If he hadn't been my own father, I would have grabbed him by his cravat and shaken the meaning out of him. It was all I could do to keep from screaming. "Just tell me!"

"Well... they seem to be offering the goddess Sulis Minerva some sort of sacrifice," Papa said. A frown knit his eyebrows together. "But I can't see anything there for them to sacrifice, can you?"

I looked at the circle of men inside the Bath. He was right. None of them held any trinkets to be tossed into the water. None of the young men even looked in any state to move outside the Bath to find more sacrificial items. Inside the Bath and inside the circle, I could only see...

"Charles!" I yelped, and started through the doorway. "Oh, you fool!"

"Kat?" Papa's voice sounded strained. "Were you aware—"

A far-too-familiar voice spoke behind me, replete with satisfaction. "I might have known it."

I turned so quickly, my feet slipped on the damp tiles. I had to grab the wooden door frame for balance.

Lady Fotherington stepped out from the shadows further down the corridor. Her black hair was, as usual, perfectly coiffed; her muslin walking dress had been replaced by a shimmering, low-cut evening gown of emerald-green silk that swished softly around her as she moved towards us.

Reluctantly, I turned my back on Charles to face the more imminent danger. The low-voiced chanting continued unbroken from the Bath, the wild magic growing stronger and stronger with every passing moment.

"You've been watching this?" I said. I shifted so that I stood between her and Papa. "You knew what was happening, but you stood by and—"

"Fine words," said Lady Fotherington, "from the girl who engineered all of this."

"I beg your pardon?"

"You needn't attempt one of your deceptions on me." She shook her head, not sparing a single glance for Papa. "Even I am astonished at your audacity. That you would come yourself to observe your work, when you must have known the Baths were being monitored? Lord Ravenscroft told us all of your perfidy, but even I had not expected you to be so reckless with it. And yet..." Her lips curved unpleasantly. "I must confess, I am rather pleased by the discovery." She was only six feet away now, and I could see her green eyes gleaming in the torchlight. "It gives me such an unexceptionable excuse."

Oh Lord. I knew what was coming next.

Papa cleared his throat. "Lady Fotherington—"

"This is none of your concern," she snapped. "You should not even be here, in the middle of a magical crisis." Her eyes focused on me, and narrowed.

I braced myself. If I was very, very fast and strong...

"Lydia, please," said Papa, and I jerked around to stare at him, open-mouthed.

He was gazing at her, his expression weary. "Lydia," he repeated. "I am certain there has been some misunderstanding. If you would simply take the time to listen to my daughter—"

"A misunderstanding?" Lady Fotherington laughed harshly. It was an odd, broken sound, with a note in it like pain, and it made me turn to look at her. "You said that once before, didn't you? When I tried to tell you the truth about her mother. I still remember every word you said: *'There must be some misunderstanding'; 'Everyone makes mistakes'* – but I was the one proven correct in the end, was I not? I would think, by now, you would have learned to listen to me when I gave you warnings against the women in *her* family."

I froze, completely forgetting my strategy. Lady Fotherington had tried to warn Papa against Mama? I hadn't realised they even knew each other. How could they have a whole history I didn't know about?

Papa sighed. "Everyone does make mistakes," he said, "and any mistakes Olivia may have made, she certainly paid for in her life. I have never been able to understand what you found so unforgivably hateful in her."

I looked into Lady Fotherington's face as she gazed back at Papa, her expression twisted between rage and shocking pain, and I had a flash of the most profoundly uncomfortable revelation I had ever experienced in my life.

I understand, I thought. But now that I did, I wished I didn't.

Papa must have been very, very different when he was a young man.

There was no time to think about any of that now. The

wild magic was pressing around me like fire, and the chanting around Charles grew stronger and louder until it reverberated in my bones. It was time to make my move, now, while Lady Fotherington was distracted.

And the only option left was...

"Kat!"

The cry came in Lucy Wingate's voice.

Papa, Lady Fotherington and I all spun round.

Lucy stepped out of the darkness into the torchlight looking positively spectral. Her blonde hair trailed about her white nightgown; her pale feet were bare against the tiled floor. She held her arms stretched out as if to keep her balance and there was something strange about her face, something I couldn't make out from this distance.

"Lucy?" I kept a wary eye on Lady Fotherington as I stepped forward, but she looked just as baffled as I felt. "What are you doing here? I told you to stay away from the Baths."

"You warned your friend away, did you?" Lady Fotherington's voice had lost its vulnerability and returned to its usual tone of smug confidence. "Even more evidence, if I'd needed it."

"I couldn't help it," Lucy said. She was walking towards us with the oddest gait I'd ever seen, her toes pointing forward and her body leaning perilously backwards. Her loose hair fluttered in the open air.

I couldn't run to meet her, not without leaving Charles hopelessly far behind me with no one to look out for him. I hesitated, torn between the two of them. "What do you mean?"

"I'm not walking!" she said.

I looked at her moving feet. "Um..."

"It's not me doing it!"

Papa said, "Kat, what is going on?"

"I don't know," I said.

Lucy was only seven feet away, now, and I could see the panic in her face. The heavy torches jiggled in their sconces against the stone pillars, responding to her fear. Flames shot higher as she passed.

"I don't know," I repeated softly.

Lady Fotherington smirked. "What, hadn't you realised all the implications of playing with wild magic? It's a good thing Lord Ravenscroft left me here to guard the Baths tonight. He knew something like this would happen. Even after your pacification—"

"Her *what*?" Papa said.

"Kat, *do something*!" Lucy shrieked. "It wants to walk me straight into that water!"

"Papa, grab her. Quickly!"

"I beg your pardon?" Papa stepped back, looking horrified. "I'm not sure—"

"Just do it!"

"Do you normally allow your daughters to order you about in such a forward manner?" Lady Fotherington said.

I clenched my fists at my side. "Papa, please! It's important. Trust me!"

He swallowed visibly and drew himself up. "Er, if you wouldn't mind, Miss Lucy..."

"Oh, please!" Lucy said, and clutched at his coat sleeves like a drowning woman. Her feet kept moving, though, unbalancing them both. Papa staggered. She ended up draped across his left arm, her toes still moving in mid-air and pointing towards the open doorway to the steam-covered Bath. Her long hair fell over his arm, the ends of it brushing against the tiled floor. A whimper escaped her mouth. "Kat, make it stop!"

"Indeed, Miss Katherine." Lady Fotherington crossed her arms. "Perhaps you are finally regretting your actions now? Or are you too hardened to even care?"

"I didn't do it!" The words erupted from me in a bellow, and I saw Papa wince. But the chanting behind me continued unbroken. I could have screamed or ripped all my hair out – nothing would have disturbed the young men in their circle. I took a long, steadying breath through clenched teeth.

Think of Lucy, I thought. *Think of Charles. Don't think about breaking* her *nose again.*

"Would you please tell me," I said to Lady Fotherington, "if you observed any of the ritual that put these men into their trance? And how long ago that happened?"

There. I hadn't snarled or cursed. Elissa would have been proud of me.

Her eyebrows drew into a frown. She said, "Is this a joke?"

"A joke?" My hard-won poise slipped. "That's my brother in that circle, about to be sacrificed! That's my friend, possessed by wild magic! Do you really think I would joke about any of that?"

She said, "If you've lost control of your own schemes—"

Papa said, "Sacrificed?"

Lucy began, in an ominous tone, "Kat, I really, truly think—"

A new voice spoke over all the rest, coming from the same side entrance Papa and I had used earlier. Mr Gregson said, "What on earth is going on here?"

Papa jerked round to the source of the noise. His foot slipped on the damp tiles.

Fury flashed across Lady Fotherington's face. She looked from Mr Gregson's advancing figure back to me, and her green eyes hardened. She drew herself up, her whole body stiffening.

A TANGLE OF MAGICKS

As Papa slipped, Lucy fell out of his arms. "No-o-o!" she wailed. But her toes marched her forward inexorably towards the Bath.

Mr Gregson said, "Lydia— Katherine— Miss Wingate— what—?"

That was when Lady Fotherington attacked.

CHAPTER TWENTY-SIX

GUARDIAN MAGIC SHOT TOWARDS ME THROUGH THE CLOUD of wild sparks that filled the air. It wasn't just a harmless paralysing spell this time. I could feel the fury that powered it, and the strength. This was going to hurt, and hurt badly.

My own power came roaring up to meet it, drawn by pure instinct before I even had time to think. Pressure streamed up through all my limbs and exploded into the air.

Her magic-working shattered into a million pieces and disappeared.

Lady Fotherington's mouth dropped open. Behind her, Mr Gregson winced and put one hand to his head.

I swallowed hard and met Lady Fotherington's eyes. I'd done it now.

"You," she said. "You. You!" She swivelled around to glare at my former tutor. "I might have known it! There was no pacification."

"Lydia," Mr Gregson began.

How long did I have left? Goosebumps raced up my skin as I strained all my senses. It wouldn't take long for Lord Ravenscroft to arrive. And when he did...

"She twisted you around her finger," Lady Fotherington said. "And you let her. You lied! You lied to the Head of our Order and to every single one of your colleagues." She was breathing hard, now, almost panting. "You know what the punishment for that will be."

"Lydia," Mr Gregson repeated, "I had excellent reason to believe—"

"You would believe whatever lies she told you," Lady Fotherington said. "Exactly like her mother!" Her voice rose to a shriek. "Why won't anybody ever listen to me?"

The volume of her shriek was almost, but not quite, enough to cover the sound of a splash behind me.

I spun round.

Lucy was in the water.

"Oh, *damnation*," I said.

"Katherine," Papa said reproachfully.

There was no time for explanations. I could already see the sparks in the Bath dividing, half of them abandoning the circle of young men to swarm about Lucy's shoulders and head like a cluster of buzzing bees.

"When Lord Ravenscroft realises what's happened—" Lady Fotherington began.

"Where exactly is Lord Ravenscroft?" asked Mr Gregson.

There was a momentary silence behind me. I gritted my teeth against the sudden chill of fear that wanted to envelop me. I didn't have time to waste being afraid of Lord Ravenscroft or anybody else.

I ran down the stone steps into the Bath.

The shock of contact with the gathered wild magic was so

strong, it drove every thought out of my head. When I came back to myself, I was shoulder-deep in the King's Bath and the clustered sparks were already abandoning me to race back towards Lucy, swirling with the steam around her head. Her eyes were closed, sparks dancing around her eyelids.

"Lu—" My voice cracked. My throat felt sore, my head scalded from sparks. I coughed and tried again. "Lucy, can you hear me? Are you still yourself?"

She opened her eyes. In the torchlight, beneath the stars, they looked dark and enormous.

"Oh, Kat," she breathed. "I'm still me. But not – I don't think – not for very much longer."

"Right," I said. "You have to get out, now!" I splashed clumsily towards her through the hot, steaming water. The long skirts of my gown and pelisse wrapped themselves around my legs and tried to trip me with every step. I was only a few feet from the closest of the young men in the circle, but not a single head turned to watch me. "Take my hand and—"

"I can't." Lucy shook her head with dreamy slowness. "My arms won't move, you see. But, oh, the way it *feels*—!" Her head tipped back in the steam until she was gazing straight up at the star-studded night sky.

Oh Lord. I didn't have any time left at all. I lunged towards her – and fell victim to my clinging, irritating skirts. My foot slipped, and I fell head-down under the surface of the Bath.

Hot, sulphurous water flooded my nose and mouth. The chanting from above the water echoed through my bones. My feet kicked out, searching for the tiled bottom of the Bath, but they tangled in my own skirts, which were twisted around the bottom of my shoes. I struck out desperately with my arms, struggling to pull myself back up. The water felt thick and resistant. Every inch of my skin sparked painfully with the contact of wild magic. I cursed myself for never learning how to swim. Elissa had said it wasn't ladylike, but...

No. I would not let myself drown in a pool that wasn't even as deep as I was tall. With a burst of fury-fuelled energy, I kicked and scrambled upright. I shot up above the water, gasping and spluttering.

Thick steam surrounded my head and shoulders. I gasped for breath, spitting out disgusting Bath water. My legs and arms were shaking too hard for me to move. Only Mr Gregson's voice broke through my haze, and only then because I'd never before heard him sound so angry.

"I asked you a simple question, Lydia. Where is Lord Ravenscroft?"

"You have no right to put any questions to me in such a manner! You weren't even supposed to be here tonight. You were specifically instructed—"

"When I felt the mass of wild magic gathering here, I came to investigate and assist whichever Guardian had been assigned to monitor the Baths tonight. Lord Ravenscroft will understand—"

"Lord Ravenscroft will certainly not understand! Once I tell him how you betrayed our entire Order for the sake of this dreadful girl, how you shamelessly deceived him and all the rest of us..."

I gritted my teeth and started towards Lucy again, moving slowly and carefully this time, keeping the tiles underfoot with every step.

"You still haven't answered my question," Mr Gregson said, "and I am beginning to suspect that I know why. Lord Ravenscroft does not even know that you are here tonight, does he, Lydia?"

I froze halfway through a step. *Wait...*

"Don't be absurd." Lady Fotherington's voice fluttered with strain. "Why should I be here without his knowledge?"

"That, I cannot say. Then again, why should you have tried to attack Katherine in such a violent manner just as I arrived?"

"Because I knew you would believe whatever wild story she spun you!" She nearly screamed the words. "I caught her coming back here to the scene of her crime even as her wicked schemes were bearing fruit – just as Lord Ravenscroft suspected she would! I proved her guilt beyond all doubt, just as I proved Olivia's. But I knew, the moment you arrived, she would wriggle her way out of it somehow, just as Olivia always did."

My thoughts were circling as madly as the clouds of sparks that swirled around Lucy, but I forced myself to stop listening.

"Lucy," I said, and I took my last step towards her. "Look at me!"

Three things happened all at once: my hand touched Lucy's arm; her head jerked down to face me; and a scream of pain ripped itself out of my throat.

The palm of my hand was red and raw, as if it had touched an open flame. And Lucy's eyes were full of stars.

The angry voices behind me cut off.

"Kat!"

Papa's voice seemed to come from a long way off. I cradled my burning hand and stared into Lucy's goddess-eyes.

"Kat!" Papa repeated. "Child! Are you all right?"

Was I all right? I could have laughed at the absurdity of the question. But the laughter would have ripped me open.

Lucy had been possessed. *Again.* I hadn't managed to

keep her safe, even after she'd begged me for help. Charles was trapped in a magic circle. And as soon as Lord Ravenscroft found out what had happened, I would be pacified for good.

Was I all right? Did Papa even have to ask?

Papa said, "I am coming in to help you—"

"No!" I spun round, still cradling my injured hand. Papa stood in the open doorway at the edge of the Bath. "You mustn't come in," I said. "Don't even touch the water. It's too dangerous!"

"Then why are you standing in it?"

I was already moving away from Lucy, towards the chanting circle of young men. I reached out one hand.

A wave of wild magic slapped me back from the edge of the circle and knocked me three feet through the water. I kicked myself upright, panting.

The circle was unbroken. The chanting continued. This time, when I focused hard, I could see the glint of a wall of sparks surrounding the young men. No wonder they hadn't heard us. Nothing could go into that circle – and no one could come out.

In the centre of the circle, Charles's head was tipped back, his eyes closed. A foolish smile rested on his lips.

I wanted to murder him and weep, all at once.

"I'm coming in," Papa said.

I shook my head. "No," I whispered. "I'm coming out."

The blast of wild magic had already pushed me most of the way back to the edge of the Bath. I trudged the last few steps, feeling all the weight of my soaking skirts as I forged through the hot, steaming water. The stars glinted imperturbably in the sky overhead. I wondered how long it would be before the water began to bubble, this time. How long before the magical sacrifice took place.

Before...

I stopped, blinking through the steam.

"Kat!" Papa's voice was unnaturally sharp. "What's amiss?"

"The magic," I said. "It's divided."

"Divided?" Mr Gregson spoke behind Papa. "What do you mean?"

"Are you still listening to her?" Lady Fotherington said. "After all this—"

"Get out of that Bath, now!" Papa said, sounding more like a conventional father than I had ever heard him in my life. "I don't care about any magic. I want you out of that water!"

I was too absorbed to feel more than a flicker of surprise at his tone. "I'm coming," I said. "But the point is, the magic..."

His hands fastened on my upper arms, pulling me up the steps. I tried to help him, but the skirts got in my way, weighing me down. My right hand hurt too much to grab hold of the tiles, and my brain was too busy to worry about it. If the magic had divided, then that meant...

Two sets of hands hauled me up out of the water: Papa's and Mr Gregson's.

"I thank you, sir," Papa said. He was breathing heavily, and no wonder; this had probably been more physical exertion than he'd taken in years.

"No need for thanks." Mr Gregson regarded me grimly as he wiped his hands with a neat white handkerchief. "Now, Katherine. Explain exactly what you were saying before."

Chill night air blew in through the open doorway, horribly cold against my sopping clothes and dripping hair, but I was too intent to care. "The wild magic in the

Baths," I said. "It was called up tonight by the young men's rites, just like last time, but it hasn't come into full effect yet because of Lucy."

"Lucy?" Papa blinked at me. "What—"

"She was possessed by the wild magic last night," I explained. "And she was possessed by Sulis Minerva this morning."

"I have told you," Mr Gregson said, "there is no such real goddess as—"

"The Romans believed there was," I said. "Didn't they, Papa?"

He blinked. I could see the relief bloom in his eyes as we finally arrived at a topic he could understand. "Indeed they did, my dear, just as the Celts before them had their own goddess associated with these springs. There has always been a *genius loci*, or guardian spirit, of this place – Sulis Minerva for the Romans, and before her—"

"So maybe what truly matters is belief," I said, cutting ruthlessly across him. "It's how the wild magic is focused. Because it was called up by the rites of Minerva last night, it created a Sulis Minerva in response. Lucy is its Sulis Minerva, now. That's why it called her back here tonight."

"Yes," Mr Gregson said slowly. "Yes... I can see that the magic has an affinity for her. But that still doesn't quite explain—"

"When she stepped into the water, I saw half the sparks come flying over to her," I said. As all the pieces fitted themselves into place, my words came out faster and faster, tumbling over each other. "The magic was supposed to all stay within the circle tonight. That's what he'd planned."

"'He'?" Lady Fotherington said sharply. "What do you mean, 'he'?"

I waved my hand at her impatiently. "Whoever planned all this. I heard the men talking about him last night. Whoever he is, he meant the magic to build through the chants and explode with Charles's sacrifice."

"Must you keep nattering on about a sacrifice?" There was a desperate tone to Lady Fotherington's voice now. "This is all utter nonsense. If any of you are foolish enough to actually believe her—"

"Continue, Kat," Mr Gregson said. "I think I am beginning to see. So the magic that was supposed to have exploded by now has instead been divided—"

"Exactly. That's why the sacrifice hasn't been completed yet, and why the Bath hasn't started boiling for Sulis Minerva yet, either. They're both only halfway there."

"Ah – forgive me, my dear, but that chanting is still going on," Papa said. "Do you think, perhaps..."

"Exactly," I said. "It's gaining power, even though it's been divided. And as soon as the power's strong enough for both the circle and Lucy – Minerva—"

Breath hissed through Mr Gregson's teeth. "I see," he said. "Yes. So, we have very little time."

"Charles," Papa said. He was staring at the circle. "So that's what you meant earlier: Charles will *actually* be—"

"Sacrificed," I said. "Yes."

"But why?"

I looked at Mr Gregson. "Last night all the power came roaring up from the Source," I said. "Remember? Because we were there, it tried all of us, but settled on Lucy as the easiest."

"Yes..." He frowned. "Good God. So whoever is managing this final, most drastic ritual—"

"Will be waiting in the same place you waited last night," I said. "The primary outlet for the Source. And he'll be waiting alone, to make sure that no one else takes the magic this time."

"Good God," he repeated. "Good God. Yes. Indeed. We must hurry."

"Where are we going?" Papa said.

"To the Source," I said. "And then—"

I stopped. Lady Fotherington had moved to block us. Her chin was raised, her eyes wild.

"No one is going anywhere," she said.

CHAPTER TWENTY-SEVEN

☆ ✧

"LYDIA," MR GREGSON BREATHED. "WHAT—?"

"You must all stay exactly where you are until Lord Ravenscroft arrives to deal with you himself," Lady Fotherington said. Her figure was so rigid, it looked as if it could snap at any moment. "I am the only loyal Guardian here, and I cannot allow—"

"This is nonsense!" Mr Gregson said. "Of course we shall all meet with Lord Ravenscoft later, but in the meantime, we must work quickly if we are to prevent a truly monstrous magical rite and the death of an innocent young man."

"She doesn't want to prevent it," I said. I looked at Lady Fotherington's beautiful face and shook my head. "Haven't you realised yet? She's helping him."

"'Him'?" Papa said.

Lady Fotherington only pressed her lips together. But her glare could have scorched skin.

"Why do you think she was here in the first place?" I said. "She was left here as a guard to keep all the rest of us away from the Source. She knows who's in there, and she's working as his assistant."

"I am not anyone's 'assistant'," Lady Fotherington snapped. "Of all the impudent—"

"Dear God," Mr Gregson said. He took a step backwards, as if the news had been an actual, physical blow. "After all these years of loyalty and service – Lydia, how could you?"

"I am loyal!" she said. "I am the only one here who is still truly loyal. That is exactly why—" She stopped, her face tightening as she cut herself off.

But I knew how her sentence should have ended. "Of course," I said. "I should have seen it before." I turned away from her, to Mr Gregson. "She really does think she is loyal," I said. "You see, she's following orders."

"Orders? But—"

"You were wrong when you said Lord Ravenscroft didn't know she was here tonight."

He shook his head. "I don't know what you mean."

"Don't you?"

His eyes widened behind his spectacles. "No," he said. "No. That simply isn't possible. Lord Ravenscroft—"

"Lord Ravenscroft told you he was in Clifton yesterday morning, although I actually saw him coming out of the Baths," I said. "He was angry that you had gone to the Baths yourself to investigate the wild magic. He was the one whose footsteps you heard when you were waiting by the outlet from the Source last night – it was because you were waiting there, against his orders, that he couldn't be there himself to see the results of his experiment. Lord Ravenscroft wanted me pacified and my mind broken the moment I discovered the very first hints of what he had been planning."

"But..." Mr. Gregson's pale eyes looked suddenly lost and vulnerable. "That isn't... that simply couldn't be..."

"Don't listen to her!" Lady Fotherington said. "She's warping the truth, the way she always does. She's the one who's done all this. She set up these rites – she did everything! Lord Ravenscroft is only trying to make things right, to fix the magical imbalance she caused. He can't do it with anyone else fussing around him. That's why he came tonight – why he trusted me to keep everyone away from the primary outlet for the Source—"

"Oh, Lydia," Mr Gregson said softly. He sighed and took off his spectacles to wipe them with his handkerchief. His face, for once, showed all of his age, reminding me that he was even older than Papa. "Do you truly believe any of this, I wonder? Or have you been working with him all along?"

"That doesn't matter," I said. "We'll figure all of that out later, but right now we have to hurry. She can't hold both of us back, so..." I stopped. Mr Gregson was shaking his head. "What is it?"

"We cannot," he said.

I stared at him. "You said yourself—"

"You and I alone cannot stand against Lord Ravenscroft. Even if Lydia were to change her mind and aid us, his lordship's power would still be too great for us to fight." My former tutor's face was grave. "You've felt it before. You know that what I say is true."

"So you want to just let him get away with it?" I was breathing hard. "You think we should just stand here and let him... let Charles be sacrificed?"

"We need reinforcements before we can act," Mr Gregson said. "I will be back as soon as I possibly can. I must gather more Guardians together – enough to stand against him, once they are presented with the evidence of his wrongdoing. If we all work together, we just might be able—"

"Charles will be dead by then!" I said. "And Lucy..."

"I must go now, before any more time can be wasted," he said. "I wish there was another way, but there is not. Be patient, Kat."

"Patient?" My voice rose to a bellow as he put his spectacles back on. "Patient?! Of all the—"

He disappeared before I could finish. I let out a wordless shout of rage.

Lady Fotherington was glaring at me as if it were all my fault, her eyes narrowed into snakelike slits. "I knew you would bring only trouble to our Order," she hissed, "from the moment I first saw you. Creating havoc, disruption, disloyalty..."

The insults continued, but I ignored them. The chanting was growing louder behind me. No matter what Mr Gregson said, there was no way I was going to stand here and wait while the ritual was completed.

"Goodbye," I said, and started forward.

"Kat!" Papa grabbed the sopping left sleeve of my pelisse and dragged me to a halt. "Where are you going? That gentleman just said it was too dangerous—"

"Too dangerous?" I looked up at his worried face and spoke as slowly and carefully as if I were translating into one of his beloved classical languages. "Papa, if I don't go now, Charles will die."

His lanky body sagged. But his eyes remained steady on my face. "If you go, though, you—"

"I have to go," I said. "I'm a Guardian. It's my job to protect society. Even when society is made up of a bunch of silly Oxford students." My voice broke on the last words.

"You're only twelve years old," he said. "You can't be expected—"

"I am a Guardian," I said, and gently pushed his hand off my arm.

He leaned over and pressed a kiss on my damp forehead. "I have already lost your mother," he whispered. "I cannot lose you, too."

Tears pricked at my eyes as he straightened. I tried to speak, but something was choking my throat.

Papa said, his voice steady, "I will not have either of my children die tonight, Katherine."

"I told you—"

"I understand," he said. "That is why I am coming with you."

"That is quite enough out of both of you!" Lady Fotherington drew herself up to her full height, nearly as tall as Papa. "You cannot imagine that I will allow either of you to pass. Lord Ravenscroft gave me strict instructions. I shall not betray my duty, no matter what wild falsehoods you choose to invent."

I looked up at her measuringly.

I hadn't yet had my proper training as a Guardian. I didn't know how to attack someone with magic, the way she had, or how to transport myself to different places, the way Mr Gregson had. I could defuse every one of her magical attacks, but that would get me nowhere. So there was only one option left.

I lunged forward and grabbed her around the waist in the wrestling hold that Charles had taught me just before Elissa's wedding.

"What – in Heaven's name – ohh!"

Her words turned into a scream of outrage as I twisted with my hips. She lost her balance and fell straight through the open doorway. The massive splash almost drowned out her scream as she landed in the steaming water. Sparks of wild magic descended around her.

Papa's mouth hung open. I grabbed his arm.

"Hurry!" I said. "She'll be out again any moment!"

We ran together down the corridor and through the rooms full of dripping pumps. I didn't slow until I found the right doorway. Even if I hadn't remembered it from last time, I would have known it now. Power gathered behind it, a power that felt like an inescapable magnet to all the sparks of wild magic in the air, drawing them inside.

Behind that door, waiting to use all that power...

My feet stopped moving.

I whispered to Papa, "Won't you please wait out here? It would be so much safer for you."

He didn't bother to answer. He just looked at me. I sagged.

I had no strategy, no plan of attack. Compared to Lord Ravenscroft, I had no powers at all.

But Charles's life was at stake.

I put my hand on the door and opened it.

CHAPTER TWENTY-EIGHT

THE FIRST THING I SAW AS I WALKED DOWN THE STEPS into the big, shadowy room was the outlet from the Source. It drew my eyes despite everything else: pure wild magic, to the core. Illuminated only by the light of a small lantern, the dark green water bubbled up from the ground in a steaming rush. There were no beautiful pillars surrounding this pool, no statues or magnificent surroundings. Yet it throbbed with power as it flowed down the plain stone culvert, under the ancient, crumbling Roman wall and past the broken tiles.

"Good God," Papa breathed, from the step above me. "An original temple wall. Why did you not tell me, Kat? No wonder..."

He kept talking, but I didn't hear a word he said. All my attention was fixed on the man who stood gazing down into the dark, green water. Flanked by piles of rubble and carved Roman stone, Lord Ravenscroft was an incongruous figure in his skintight burgundy coat, golden waistcoat and elaborately tied cravat. But cold shivers raced across my skin, despite the steaming warmth of the room, as he turned to face us. His greatcoat lay neatly folded on the floor beside him.

"Ah," Lord Ravenscroft said. "Miss Katherine." He lifted his quizzing glass to his left eye. His voice was calm – even amused – but all traces of his fashionable lisp had disappeared. "I thought I felt your powers nearby. Still unpacified, I see. Gregson will pay for that."

"No, he won't," I said. I couldn't force my voice not to wobble, but I lifted my chin up and looked straight into his hideously magnified gaze. "He knows what you've done and he's gone to fetch more Guardians, to stop you. They'll be here any minute."

"Will they?" He smiled and lowered the quizzing glass. "And what do you imagine they will be able to do to me when they arrive?"

"You're not stronger than the entire Order," I said.

"Not yet," he said. "But I will be soon. And I won't be staying in England to bother with them, anyway."

"You won't?" I stared at him, caught off balance. I didn't know why he hadn't attacked me yet, or silenced me. "Why would you leave England? Where would you go? We *are* at war with France, you know. No one travels to the Continent anymore. It isn't safe."

The door flew open behind me.

"Aha!" Lady Fotherington cried. I heard her panting as she ran down the stairs behind me. I couldn't see her, but I *felt* her power fly at me, arrowing down in a tight, fast attack.

I pulled up my own power and threw it back at her. Her magic-working exploded in mid-air. We both staggered with effort.

It was Papa who answered me. "I believe I understand," he said. "This gentleman – Lord Ravenscroft, I presume?"

Lord Ravenscroft bowed mockingly.

"I believe, my dear, he must be a spy for the French."

"A *what*?" said Lady Fotherington.

"I am nothing so common as a mere spy," said Lord Ravenscroft. "I have never been so vulgar as to read other people's private letters, nor have I yet given privileged information to Napoleon Bonaparte."

"Well, of course not," Lady Fotherington said. "Of all the outrageous—"

"Not yet," I said. I was watching Lord Ravenscroft. "But you are going to, soon, aren't you?"

He didn't answer, but a smile played about his thin lips.

Lady Fotherington said, "Sebastian, tell her she is speaking nonsense. Of course she is speaking nonsense!"

"You needn't worry, my dear Lydia," Lord Ravenscroft said. He smiled indulgently at her. "I shall not leave you here to face the wrath of the Order on your own. I will be very glad of your companionship on the journey. Indeed, I believe you will find much to your liking in the change of scene. After all, secondhand Parisian fashions are nothing in comparison to the real thing, are they?"

"But— but—" I could hear her quick breathing behind me. "But why?"

"Do you truly need to ask?" Ruby and emerald rings flashed in the lantern-light as he waved one hand, and lace fluttered against his wrist. "Look at us! The most powerful and best-bred people in our kingdom, and yet we're expected to do society's dirty work. Do we even receive any payment for it from our government? Hardly. They expect us to fritter away our time and energy protecting the rest of society with no reward, as if we were common peasants in their eyes."

"We are Guardians," I said. "That is our reward."

Lord Ravenscroft snorted. "You're old enough not to be so naïve. I saw you staring at my rings earlier today. Are you going to pretend you didn't notice that the stones had been replaced by glass?" His face drew into a snarl. "My father may have been kind enough to pass on his title – and what he called 'our magical responsibility' – but he didn't bother leaving enough money to live up to a gentleman's standards or to pay for even half my wardrobe. Do you really expect someone like me to settle for a life spent pawning real gems for false, all the while smiling and pretending not to care?"

He looked past me to Lady Fotherington. "You know the welcome Bonaparte will give us. All the French Guardians were slaughtered in their Revolution and the commoners with talent have no training. When *we* arrive – the cream of British Guardian magic – bearing the wild magic of England itself, ripe for use in an invasion..."

"You, my lord, are a traitor," said Papa. "I am ashamed of Oxford for having produced you."

"And you," said Lord Ravenscroft, "must be George Stephenson. I have read your work. We shared the same tutor at Oxford, you see, although I studied Classics with him some time after you had shocked all your colleagues by abandoning your Fellowship for your scandalous marriage. In fact, you may be pleased to know that I used one of your own treatises as the basis of the rites I devised."

"You drew my own son into it," Papa said. "How dare you even speak to me?"

I was too confused to say a word. Lord Ravenscroft still hadn't attacked us. Why had he not attacked?

Then I saw his gaze slip to the bubbling pool beside

him and I understood. He was distracting us. All he had to do was wait for the rites to be complete and the power to come flowing up from the Source. But to ensure that the wild magic came only to him, he needed to use his full Guardian powers. He couldn't afford to waste them on us when the magic might explode at any moment.

All he was waiting for was Charles's death.

I set my jaw. There was only one sensible thing I could do, no matter how much I hated it.

I turned to face my mother's nemesis, the woman I hated more than anyone else in the world.

Lady Fotherington was dripping onto the stone floor. Cold steam rose off her wet skin. Her beautifully arranged black hair was a wet, slimy mess, and her elegant gown hung, ruined, about her limbs. I doubted the silk would ever recover. She was staring at Lord Ravenscroft and, for once, completely ignoring me.

I said, "You have to help us."

She didn't even turn her head to look at me. "I beg your pardon?"

"I know you're loyal to the Order," I said. "Please – you can't let him betray it now. And not just the Order, but all of Britain! You have to help me stop him. You're a Guardian. It's your duty."

Lord Ravenscroft smiled, serenely unbothered by my words. "This is exactly what you'll be escaping when you come with me, Lydia. Bonaparte will let us establish our own, new Order, with entrance requirements set by you and me. There will be no more old-fashioned rules dragging us down. No more nitpicking Aloysius Gregsons to enforce them. No more wild Olivia Ambersons or insolent Katherine Stephensons. You shall be in charge of choosing our first members, and we shall accept none that you dislike."

"Well..." Lady Fotherington trailed off, nibbling her lip. Her hands were tightly clasped.

"What about all your colleagues back in England?" I asked her. "What about all your Society friends? What will they think of you if you go with him? Your country invaded because of your betrayal—"

"That is enough," Lord Ravenscroft said. "Lydia, silence her. It's long past time."

"I'm not the enemy," I said. "Help me against him!"

Lady Fotherington looked from Lord Ravenscroft to me and back, her eyes wide.

Papa said, "Lydia, surely you will not turn traitor now."

"Lydia!" said Lord Ravenscroft. "Will you let Miss Katherine have all her own way? Again?"

Lady Fotherington let out an audible moan of pain. Then she did something I would never have imagined.

Elegant, fashionable Lady Fotherington, leader of High Society, flopped down onto the hard stone floor and buried her face in her hands.

"I can't!" she moaned. I didn't know if she was talking to me or Lord Ravenscroft or the whole world. "I can't."

Oh, *bother*. I looked down at her limp figure and my heart sank.

There was only one thing left to try. I would have to make a sacrifice.

I could only pray that it would be strong enough to save my brother's life.

I looked up. Lord Ravenscroft was watching me through his quizzing glass again.

"My goodness," he said. "Lydia was right from the very beginning. You truly are a troublemaker, aren't you?"

Papa stepped up beside me. "You shall not use such terms to my daughter, my lord."

"Shall I not?" Lord Ravenscroft's gaze darted from the pool beside him to Lady Fotherington's prone figure and back to me. "Surely you must be used to hearing scathing words spoken about the women of your family, sir."

Why, oh why, did I not have any pockets in my gown? And why hadn't I thought to put anything in the secret pocket of my pelisse to replace Mama's mirror?

Papa drew himself up to his full, lanky height. He stood an inch taller than Lord Ravenscroft and looked surprisingly dignified despite his wildly disordered grey hair. "I have never been anything but proud of the *ladies* in my family, sir. And I shall not allow you to speak against them, especially as you prepare to murder my only son."

I stepped back, casting my gaze desperately around the room. I knew what would be in Papa's pockets – one of the Greek or Latin texts he always carried with him. *Useless.* Whatever I sacrificed had to mean something to me, to give the ritual true power. That meant the lamp on the floor would do no good, either. Nor would Lord Ravenscroft's greatcoat, lying folded on the ground nearby...

Wait.

There was a bulge at the top of Lord Ravenscroft's multi-caped greatcoat. It was a small, round bulge, pressing out from one of the greatcoat's pockets. I knew that shape. I would have recognised it anywhere.

I stared at it, only two footsteps away, and I felt my throat grow dry.

No. There had to be another way.

But there was nothing in the world that meant more to me, and Charles's life was at stake.

Slowly, I edged towards the coat. Lord Ravenscroft turned, keeping me within his line of sight, but his focus was still on Papa.

"You shall not allow me?" He raised his quizzing glass and studied Papa like a scientific specimen, even as my right foot brushed against the greatcoat on the floor.

Through the thin soles of my shoes, I felt it. There it was, that small, rounded bump.

All I had to do was reach down and scoop it up.

I couldn't move. I couldn't breathe.

Lord Ravenscroft laughed in Papa's face. "And how exactly do you plan to stop me, pray tell? As violent as your daughter's tendencies may be, I never heard that you were a man of action."

That did it.

"He doesn't need to be," I said. "He's something better. He's a scholar." I looked at Papa, standing proud and tall despite his disordered hair and lack of weapons, and I felt a burst of love so strong, it made my voice strong, too. "Just watch this," I said to the Head of the Order of the Guardians. "Papa, tell me: who was the guardian spirit of these hot springs before Sulis Minerva?"

"What?" Lord Ravenscroft said. "Of all the moments—"

"That would be the goddess Sul, my dear," said Papa. "The Celts worshipped her before the Romans ever arrived, and dedicated this place to her."

"Thank you!" I said.

I scooped up Lord Ravenscroft's massive greatcoat and grabbed the small, gold-encased travel mirror out of its pocket. My fingers closed around its smooth, curving sides as if they were coming home.

Mama's magic mirror. My portal to the Golden Hall. My only link to her.

"The destruction of Lord Ravenscroft's powers and the breaking of all his rites," I said. "All hail, Sulis Minerva and Sul herself!"

I threw Mama's mirror into the bubbling green water that came straight from the Source, the core of all the wild magic in the Baths and Bath itself.

"NO!" Lord Ravenscroft screamed. He lunged forward, hands outstretched.

Papa grabbed my arm and pulled me out of his way. But Lord Ravenscroft wasn't aiming for me.

He grabbed for the mirror in the pool. The moment his smooth white hands touched the water, he let out a howl of sheer agony.

Buzzing sparks of wild magic filled the water, multiplying into a heaving mass that swept up around the mirror – and devoured it. The whole mass disappeared into a sudden vortex in the water.

I choked back a sob. The air around us shivered with mounting pressure. Something was coming. Something huge.

Lord Ravenscroft turned on me, his eyes wild. "You think you've been clever?" he snarled. "You stupid little upstart. I'll show you what a real Guardian can do."

His power swept up, thickening the air with rage and strength. I felt it gather above me, preparing to crash down like the crest of a killing wave.

"Get Lady Fotherington out!" I yelled to Papa. "Run!"

Lord Ravenscroft's power fell towards me. I closed my eyes and braced myself for the impact.

I had saved England, saved the Order and, most importantly of all, saved Charles's life. If I had to die for it, that was the risk a Guardian ran.

A great, booming voice spoke through the open door. "HAIL SULIS MINERVA AND SUL HERSELF!"

Lord Ravenscroft's power froze in mid-air, just before it could touch my skin.

Lucy stood at the top of the staircase, her arms spread out, her eyes wild.

"THE DESTRUCTION OF LORD RAVENSCROFT'S POWERS AND THE BREAKING OF ALL HIS RITES!"

Wild magic exploded around her in a great, billowing cloud. It swept toward Lord Ravenscroft's mass of gathered power and enveloped it completely. Then the magic shattered.

Lord Ravenscroft's eyes rolled up in his head. With a groan, he fell backwards into the bubbling, green water.

CHAPTER TWENTY-NINE

LUCY FELL AT THE SAME TIME AS LORD RAVENSCROFT, collapsing across the top three steps. I ran for her even as I called out to Papa.

"Don't let him drown!"

I could hear Papa dragging Lord Ravenscroft back from the water, but all my attention was on Lucy. I dropped to my knees on the step below her. Her head lolled against her shoulder, her fair hair streaming across the front of her wet nightgown. I grabbed her hand. The contact didn't burn me. Her skin felt damp and warm. The sparks were gone.

"Lucy," I said. "Lucy! Wake up!"

Her eyelids drifted partly open. I could only see a hint of her blue eyes, but what I saw was clear and familiar.

"Kat?" she murmured. "Kat." A smile curved her lips. "It's gone. She's gone. Both of them."

"Well, thank goodness for that." I looked back over my shoulder. Lord Ravenscroft was lying on the ground below us, still unconscious but breathing, while Papa hovered over him uncertainly. "Now, if we can only get rid of him as easily..."

"They did leave something behind, though."

I swung back to Lucy. "What did you say?"

She was grinning at me. "I said, they left me a gift." She dropped a wink that would have scandalised her mother and sister. "Watch."

Sparks of wild magic raced past me. I turned just in time to see Lord Ravenscroft's quizzing glass leap straight into mid-air and fall back to the ground, performing a dainty pirouette as it landed. Papa lurched back, throwing one hand before him.

I stared at Lucy. A giggle burst out of her mouth, the same kind that had irritated me so much only twenty-four hours ago.

I said, "You actually meant that to happen, didn't you? It wasn't accidental, or just because you were upset or scared or—"

"Well, of course not. You are slow tonight, Kat." Lucy pushed herself up, wincing with effort.

"And you don't have Sulis Minerva or Sul or— "

"Only me," she said. "With a little extra power of my own, now. Won't Mama and Maria be surprised?"

I blinked. Then I started to laugh, and her giggles burst out in full force. Below us, Papa sighed and took a guarding stance above Lord Ravenscroft's prone figure.

"You'll have to be careful, you know," I said, when I finally managed to stop laughing. "Society has already seen you work magic. Your family won't let you out in public again for—"

"Oh, not for years," Lucy said cheerfully, "if they ever do again. They'll probably send me away to stay with my spinster aunts in Scotland, where there are only sheep and goats and no eligible young men at all, much less any as handsome as your brother. But at least I finally have something more interesting to think about, now. *And* something to practise!"

Lucy held out her hand to me. My scalded right hand still hurt too much to use, but I reached out with my left hand, and together, we helped each other up. In the distance, as we walked down the stairs to join the others, I heard a commotion begin – cries of confusion coming from the King's Bath. I felt something else, too: a ripple in the air that signalled Guardian magic.

Mr Gregson and his colleagues had arrived.

I took a deep breath. "Will you see to Charles?" I asked Papa. "He was so entranced, he'll be terribly confused."

"Of course," my father said. "I'll make certain he knows exactly what happened – and what could have happened, if not for you."

Papa and I traded a long look and I felt a spark of sudden optimism light inside me. My brother's life had been saved. If I was very lucky, he might not be quite the same ever again.

Of course, one never knew with Charles. But surely this brush with death would finally make him begin to question his Oxford friends' idiotic games. At least, I could hope so.

Papa gave one last worried glance at Lord Ravenscroft's prone figure. "You're quite certain he cannot harm you?"

"He can't harm anyone anymore," I said. "Don't worry! I'm perfectly safe."

"Well, if you're sure..." He hurried up the stairs and out of the door, looking more purposeful – and more capable – than I'd ever imagined him before tonight.

Charles was definitely due for a surprise.

Lucy said, "Do you think they're all still naked in there? I wonder—"

"Let's talk about it later," I said.

I didn't have much time. I could already hear approaching footsteps and voices above us.

I hurried across the stone floor to where Lady Fotherington sat slumped, her face in her hands. She knew, and I knew, what was about to happen.

Mr Gregson knew she had aided and abetted Lord Ravenscroft. For once, my word was going to mean more than hers. It was a moment I could have savoured, after everything she'd done to me and my family. All I had to do was tell the other Guardians the truth – that she had refused to aid me against Lord Ravenscroft even after hearing his confession of treason – and she would be expelled from the Order, just as Mama and I had been. For all I knew, she might even be pacified, too.

It was exactly what she had wanted for me.

I dropped down to the tiled floor to face her and took a deep breath. "I have a bargain to offer you," I said.

✧ ✧

There were ten Guardians accompanying Mr Gregson, none of whom I'd ever met before. I couldn't tell whether they were more relieved or appalled to find that their powers weren't required after all. When they looked from Lord Ravenscroft's limp body, resting by the pool, to me, standing alone and unsupported, I saw outright horror on some of their faces.

Mr Gregson took me aside as Lord Ravenscroft was carried away. The others were standing in a far corner, whispering together and darting uneasy glances at me, but there was no fear in my former tutor's face – only a grave pride.

"You are sure that you are uninjured, Katherine?"

"Don't worry," I said. "The only thing I hurt was my hand. Well, that and..." I swallowed, looking down at the bubbling, dark green water. *Mama's mirror*, I thought. But I couldn't bring myself to say the words out loud, not again. I'd had to tell the whole story to the gathered Guardians once already. It had been painful enough to say it that first time.

There was no sign left in the pool of the magical vortex that had swallowed Mama's mirror and swept it away from me forever. But I would never forget.

Mr Gregson followed my gaze and nodded as if I had spoken out loud. "Guardian powers come with a heavy price," he said. "Perhaps Lord Ravenscroft inherited his too easily to ever comprehend that... but I believe you have proven yourself to understand it perfectly."

He looked across at the whispering group of fellow Guardians. As they grew aware of his mild gaze resting upon them, they gradually stopped whispering and turned to face us. He raised his eyebrows pointedly.

Some of them looked unhappy, some of them looked reluctant – but every one of them lowered their head in a bow.

They were bowing to me.

I took a deep breath and thought of Mama. Carefully, gracefully, and with all the dignity I possessed, I picked up my sopping wet skirts and curtseyed back to them.

But I looked each and every one of them in the eye as I did it.

Mr Gregson coughed and turned away from the others as they dispersed. "You need have no more fears about your admittance to the Order, Katherine. I am only sorry that we may not be able to find you a replacement portal for some time. With the hereditary Head of our Order deprived of all his powers and guilty of treason to the throne... well, it will be quite a while before anything can be properly sorted out. The line of inheritance has been broken for the first time in over a century, and magical warfare was very nearly reintroduced to the modern world. The government will be deeply concerned. As to what any of us will do next..." He shook his head, looking grimmer than ever. "Such a thing has never happened before, not since the time of the Civil War. It is an absolute disaster."

"Oh, well," I said, and shrugged.

As far as I was concerned, the Order could do with a good shaking-up, and this was none too soon for it. But I had something far more important to take care of right now than any political crisis. And I would need his help for it.

"I do promise that you will be properly initiated into the Order as soon as possible," Mr Gregson said. "And of course, as soon as everything else is settled down, the Order will want to express its gratitude for your—"

"Gratitude," I said. From somewhere deep inside, beneath all the exhaustion and the grief for what I'd lost, I managed to summon up a wicked grin. "So you agree that you all owe me a favour?"

"Ah..." My old tutor looked alarmed. "What sort of favour were you thinking of, exactly?"

"I want another magic lesson," I said. "And this time, I want you to show me how to travel across great distances."

☆ ☆

We landed in a small, dimly lit room with a thud. The impact knocked me sprawling onto my hands and knees, sneezing dust from the ancient floorboards. Mr Gregson, of course, was still on his feet. He watched with a resigned expression as I pushed myself back up with more speed than dignity.

Well, never mind. I'd learn the trick of it soon enough. In the meantime...

"Ah, Kat," Angeline said, before I could even turn to look for her. "I thought you might turn up somehow, despite all my warnings."

She was standing behind me, in front of a closed door. It was a bedroom – an inn bedroom, I guessed, as I took in the narrow window and the noise of male voices rising from downstairs. She was fully dressed in the same sprig-muslin gown she'd worn that morning. Her hair was perfectly arranged, as always, and her voice positively dripped with cynicism.

Even in the dim candlelight, though, I could see the redness around her swollen eyelids. My arrogant older sister had been crying before we came.

I started forward, fury taking over. "We didn't come too late, did we? If he's hurt you—"

"Him?" She snorted. "Of course not. I wouldn't let him."

Something heavy struck the thin, wooden door with a crash. I jumped. The door shuddered but stood firm.

"Let me in, damn you!" bellowed an all-too-familiar voice. *Viscount Scarwood.*

For the first time, I noticed the lingering scent of flowers in the air. I looked at Angeline with respect. "You barricaded the door against him with witchcraft."

She nodded. "I didn't trust the lock."

"Very wise of you," said Mr Gregson. He was looking

around the room with distaste. "If we are where I believe we are... I fear this inn does not have the most savoury of reputations."

"I'm not surprised," Angeline said. "The food is terrible, too. I've never eaten such a tasteless supper." She sat down on the edge of the bed, heaving a sigh. I thought she meant it to sound world-weary, but it only sounded miserable. "Never mind. You've come, you've seen that I'm perfectly safe—"

"And you think we're going to leave you here?" I stared at her. "Of all the cork-brained notions!"

"What else do you expect me to do?" Angeline said. "You know what happened earlier. Even if Stepmama would agree to take me back—"

"She will," I said. "If you'll just listen—"

She waved one hand dismissively as another heavy crash hit the door. "It doesn't matter. There's no point in going back to Yorkshire only to be lectured and treated as an object of charity." She looked down, her lips twisting. "Being an old maid forever, under Stepmama's roof—"

"You won't be," I said. "Frederick Carlyle still wants to marry you."

Her head jerked up. "He does not," she said. But I saw the sudden vulnerability in her dark eyes.

"He certainly does," I said. "When I saw him last, he was racing off in his carriage, desperate to catch up with you and Viscount Scarwood. He didn't know which direction to take, though, so if you want to be kind to him, we should leave quickly and put him out of his misery."

"His—?" She cut herself off, breathing hard. "Don't you dare try any of your schemes or wild stories on me, Kat. If you're making this up just to bring me home—"

"I'm not," I said. "I swear it. I stood in the parlour of our inn not three hours ago and heard him say how much he regretted walking away from you this morning."

I decided not to add the part where he'd said that her mad elopement was all his fault. After all, Angeline could use a little humility, now and again... and anyway, he was sure to tell her all that gushing nonsense himself later on.

Angeline gave me a long, measuring look. Viscount Scarwood began to curse venomously at the door. I'd never even heard most of those words before.

Mr Gregson coughed. "Perhaps, for ease of thought..." A ripple of Guardian power shot through the room. The sound of Lord Ravenscroft's curses disappeared. A moment later, I saw the door shudder with another blow, but I couldn't hear the crash.

"Much better," I said. "Thank you."

He sighed. "Well, if you will continue to drag me into situations like this..."

Angeline stood up and walked rapidly to the far wall, only six steps away. When she swung around, her eyes looked wild. "Even if Frederick has forgiven me, that still won't change his mother's attitude. Without her permission..."

"You have it," I said, and grinned at the shock on her face. "Or you will have it, anyway," I amended, for the sake of honesty, "as of nine o'clock tomorrow morning, when Lady Fotherington finds her and Mrs Wingate in the Pump Room and tells them both how terribly wrong she was about you and about our entire family."

Mr Gregson let out a strangled sound behind me. I ignored him. Angeline tried to speak, but nothing came out. She stopped, swallowing visibly. Then she said, enunciating each word clearly, "Why on earth would Lady Fotherington do that?"

My smile widened until it hurt my cheeks. I didn't care. "Because I helped her to realise how very wrong she had been," I said. "That is why she is going to apologise to Mrs Carlyle and Mrs Wingate for passing on such horrible false rumours about us both. Then she is going to personally recommend to Mrs Carlyle that she open her heart and home to you as her future daughter-in-law." I said that last line with particular satisfaction. I'd made Lady Fotherington repeat it after me twice, to make sure she would say it exactly. Each time she'd said the words, I'd enjoyed them even more.

Mr Gregson let out a heavy sigh behind me. "More wild schemes," he mumbled. "Heaven help us..."

I chose not to hear him.

Angeline was looking only at me, her expression a blur of emotions I couldn't interpret. Finally, her lips curved into a smile.

"Oh, Kat," she said. "I give in. Come here."

I ran straight into her arms. They were warm and strong around me, and every bit of her scent was familiar.

My maddening, aggravating, beloved older sister would be coming home after all.

"Thank you," she whispered, too softly for anyone but me to hear her. "Thank you so much."

Out loud, as we moved apart, she said briskly, "So how shall we find Frederick? I liked the way you both landed here. Can we use the same technique again now? Somehow, I don't think my escort deserves a proper goodbye before we leave."

"He certainly does not," Mr Gregson said. "Now, all that the three of us need do is join hands, and then..."

"Just a moment," I said. I looked at the door, which was shuddering under the onslaught of a new crash. I said to Angeline, "I do think Viscount Scarwood deserves some kind of farewell, though, don't you? After all the trouble he took to bring you here?"

"Ah... Kat?" Mr Gregson said. "I'm not certain..."

But Angeline's face was already mirroring the mischief in my mind. "A proper send-off, you mean? So that he really feels my gratitude for his kind care?"

"I really don't think—" Mr Gregson began.

But it was too late. With a single thought, I'd already broken Angeline's spell on the door.

It crashed open, sending Viscount Scarwood staggering in, off-balance. He caught himself with one large, strong hand on the door frame and looked straight at Angeline, his handsome face twisted in rage. "You think you can play games with me?" He slammed the door behind him. "You think—"

I didn't even need to tell Angeline my plan. She was already whispering under her breath, while the scent of flowers rose to fill the air.

For the first time, Scarwood noticed Mr Gregson and me standing near her. "I don't care if you've smuggled in your brat of a sister to help you," he snarled, "or some old man who can't protect you. You are not getting away from me this easily!"

"No?" Angeline smiled at him sweetly. "Perhaps you ought to try the door handle yourself, just in case."

"What?"

"Just try it," I said, as I took Angeline's hand in one hand and Mr Gregson's hand in the other. Even the pain of my scalded right palm was nothing compared to my satisfaction. "Please," I added, and I gave him my most innocent smile.

Mr Gregson shook his head beside me, but he didn't say a word. He knew better.

"What...?" Viscount Scarwood put one hand on the door handle behind him. It didn't move. He turned. He started to shake it. It wouldn't budge. "What—? Damnation, what—?"

"*Now* we're ready," I said to my tutor.

Guardian magic swept up around us.

Holding hands, my sister and I disappeared from the dingy inn bedroom, leaving only the sound of our laughter behind us.

AUTHOR'S NOTE

Everything that Kat learns about the history of the Roman Baths (except for the bits about the wild magic) is true. The springs on which they were built really were considered a sacred spot, not only by the Romans (who left offerings along with requests for favours or curses, just like Charles and his friends) but also by the Celts who lived there beforehand.

If you visit the Baths now, you'll see them laid out as the Romans enjoyed them, and you can find out more about the temple to Minerva that once was there. However, you won't see them laid out as described in this novel because the layout of the Baths and the buildings around them was quite different in 1803.

There was an enormous amount of building done in the last quarter of the eighteenth century and in the later nineteenth century. I have used eighteenth-century maps along with early nineteenth-century records and descriptions to try to establish as authentic a setting as possible for Kat's adventures. However, I also used my imagination to fill in the blanks and felt free to make small changes to accommodate my magical history.

If you're curious about the Baths and can't visit them yourself, you can visit their website: www. romanbaths.co.uk. I especially recommend checking out their photograph of the gorgeous bronze head of Sulis Minerva that was unearthed in 1727, almost eighty years before Kat would have arrived. It's eerie, beautiful... and very magical.

ACKNOWLEDGEMENTS

I owe huge thanks to all my friends who read and critiqued this novel: Tiffany Trent, Jenn Reese, Karen Healey, Ysabeau Wilce, Lisa Mantchev and Patrick Samphire. Thank you guys so much!

Special thanks to Jenn and Karen for providing lightning-fast responses to brand new chapters when I flung them at you in my last-minute rewriting madness. You guys kept me sane!

Thanks so much to my parents, brothers and grandmother for being so supportive of my books and of me. It means the world.

I owe an enormous debt of gratitude to my parents and my mother-in-law for babysitting so that I could get the second draft of this book written. I truly couldn't have finished it on time without your help.

I am so lucky to have Barry Goldblatt and Nancy Miles representing my work in the US and the UK, and Namrata Tripathi and Emma Goldhawk editing it in both countries. Thank you guys so much! And I owe big thanks to Philippa

Perry and Jayne Roscoe for all their generosity and hard work on my (and especially Kat's!) behalf.

Thank you to Gail Hammond for actually making me laugh and enjoy having my author photos taken (something I never would have imagined possible!), and to David Burgis for making brilliant book trailers and button designs, and helping out in a zillion other ways. This trilogy is all about family, and my family has rallied around me amazingly to help with it.

Thank you to Anne Yvonne Gilbert and www.the-parish.com for my gorgeous book covers and to Su Box for her sharp-eyed copy-editing.

Thank you to the wonderfully supportive community of commenters on my LiveJournal, and thank you so much to everybody who's written to tell me they love Kat. I cherish every email and reread them whenever I need motivation to write on a bad day.

Last but definitely not least, I owe an infinite number of thanks to Patrick Samphire, my husband and best friend. So here's a condensed version:

Thank you for hundreds of brainstorming sessions and insane amounts of childcare and housework, on top of designing and maintaining my website. Thank you for taking endless videos of the Baths as we walked through them – and then helping me with even more endless research after we realised, halfway through the building, that the Regency layout had actually been completely different from the layout we could see now. Aack! Thank you for drawing me countless maps and being patient with all my contradictory directions about them. (Thank goodness at least one of us is capable of spatial visualisation... but that one sure isn't me!)

Most of all, though, thank you so much for being mine.

ABOUT THE AUTHOR

LIKE HER HEROINE KAT, STEPHANIE BURGIS COMES FROM A BIG, noisy, loving family. She grew up in Michigan, USA, where as a little girl she became addicted to reading and writing stories. At the age of ten, Stephanie's favourite books were *The Lord of the Rings* and *Pride and Prejudice*, and, in her own words, 'Writing the Kat books was my chance to finally combine fantasy adventure and nineteenth-century romantic comedy – the two kinds of story I love best.'

Before Stephanie became a full-time writer, she was a student of music, playing the French horn. She won a prestigious Fulbright Scholarship to study in Vienna, Austria, and earned a Master's degree in music history. Stephanie has had lots of different jobs, including teaching English to teenagers in Vienna and editing the website of an opera company in northern England.

Stephanie now lives in Wales with her husband, toddler son and their sweet border collie dog, Maya.

Visit **www.stephanieburgis.com** to find out more about Stephanie, Regency England and The Unladylike Adventures of Kat Stephenson.

*If you haven't read Kat's first Unladylike Adventure,
why not catch up on what you've missed...*

At twelve years old, any proper young lady should
be sitting quietly at home, practising her embroidery
and keeping her opinions to herself.

But Kat Stephenson is no ordinary young lady.

Kat's father may be a respectable vicar, but her late
mother was a notorious witch, her brother has gambled
the whole family into debt, and Kat herself is the newest
target of an ancient and secretive order.

In the first thrilling instalment of The Unladylike
Adventures of Kat Stephenson, Kat sets out to win her older
sisters their true loves, battling highwaymen, practising
magic and breaking all of Society's rules along the way.

ISBN 978-1-84877-007-2 Paperback £6.99
ISBN 978-1-84877-019-5 (EPub)
ISBN 978-1-84877-020-1 (Mobi)

Other Templar books you might enjoy...

Forgive My Fins
by Tera Lynn Childs

'I simply adored
this book!'
Alyson Noël, author of
The Immortals series

Unrequited love is hard enough when you're a normal teenager,
but when you're half-human, half-mermaid, like Lily Sanderson,
there's no such thing as a simple crush. Especially when your
crush is gorgeous (and 100% human) Brody Bennett.

The problem is, mermaids aren't the casual dating type – the
instant they kiss someone, they 'bond' with them for life.
When Lily's attempt to win Brody's love leads to a ginormous
case of mistaken identity, she finds herself facing a tidal wave
of relationship drama.

ISBN 978-1-84877-134-5 Paperback £6.99
ISBN 978-1-84877-135-2 (ePub)
ISBN 978-1-84877-136-9 (Mobi)

The Crimson Shard

by Teresa Flavin

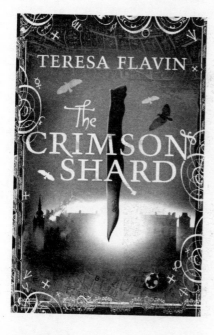

Captives in another time; custodians of a powerful secret...

A visit to a private London museum takes a sinister turn when fourteen-year-old Sunni Forrest and her friend Blaise are lured through a painted doorway into the past. As a clandestine, eighteenth-century world of art thieves, forgers and bodysnatchers closes in on them, they must take their chances on the treacherous streets of the city. Can they evade their captors and keep an ancient secret from falling into the wrong hands? And will they find the key to unlock the only way home – before it closes forever?

ISBN 978-1-84877-073-7 Paperback £6.99
ISBN 978-1-84877-087-4 (ePub)
ISBN 978-1-84877-088-1 (Mobi)